Wild Heart

Frontier Hearts Saga
Book 4

Colleen Hall

Anaiah Press

Copyright © 2023 by Colleen Hall

All rights reserved.

No part of this book may be reproduced in any form or by any electronic or mechanical means, including information storage and retrieval systems, without written permission from the author, except for the use of brief quotations in a book review.

I'd like to dedicate Wild Heart to the memory of my mother, Corinne Goodell, whose love of reading set an example for me. Mom's support for my writing efforts all through my growing-up years encouraged me to keep on writing.

And without the support of my loving husband, Warren, whose devotion and sacrifice enabled me to pursue my writing dream, this book wouldn't have been possible. Warren, I dedicate this book to you.

Denver, Colorado
Early Summer, 1911

Chapter 1

Cole Wild Wind. The name tantalized her as Garnet Morrison peered between the burgundy tasseled curtains of the steam train's window. To her Eastern ears, *Cole Wild Wind* sounded mysterious and dangerous. What would he look like? Would he be dark-haired or blond? Short or tall? Handsome? Garnet smiled to herself as she conjured up visions of a tall, dark-haired man wearing a cowboy hat, jeans, and a six-shooter. He'd be strong, strong enough to stand up to her banker father. Perhaps he'd play the hero and carry her away into the Colorado mountains. He'd take her far enough away to free her from her father's domination.

Here her imagination faltered. Cole Wild Wind owned a uranium mine. Did uranium mine owners wear cowboy hats and carry six shooters? He wasn't the cowboy hero of her fantasies, but he might be strong enough to rescue her from a threatened marriage to her father's young associate, Albert Davies, who, at this present moment, sat across the compartment from her and eyed her with an unblinking stare.

If her father, Asa Morrison, and Mr. Wild Wind decided on a business partnership, she could stay in Colorado. She and Cole Wild Wind might become friends, perhaps even more than friends.

The train ground to a crawl at the Denver station, then stopped with a final jerk and squeal. The engine belched black smoke. Cinders rained onto the platform and peppered with ash any unfortunate individuals who stood along the railway.

Garnet's father stirred and ground out the stub of his cigar in the ash tray on the small mahogany table at his side. "It seems we've arrived," he said. "I hope Cole Wild Wind won't keep us waiting."

"I'm sure he's already here. He wouldn't dare be so rude as to keep Asa Morrison waiting." Garnet lifted a sardonic gaze to her sire.

If her father noticed the irony in her voice, he ignored the jab. He rose and adjusted his top hat, then tugged at the cuffs of his white shirt sleeves so the proper inch of fabric showed beneath his sack coat's sleeves.

Garnet eyed her father. His burly shoulders and barrel chest strained the material of his loose, gray sack coat—shoulders she'd ridden as a toddler. Above a waistcoat of paler blue, his striped, gray silk tie hung loose from the high collar of his shirt. When his cold gray gaze rested on her, she turned her attention once more out the window.

Where had the beloved father she used to call Papa gone? The man who now inhabited her once-beloved father's body seemed almost a stranger.

Albert rose to his feet. "I hope Denver won't be too provincial. I wonder if there's an opera house here. I can't imagine the city has much to offer in the way of society. Too many cowboys." He shuddered.

Garnet returned his stare. "If you don't find Denver suitable, you can always take the next train back to New York." Before she could stop them, the words tripped off her tongue.

Albert's amber eyes flashed, and his mouth compressed in a tight line. "You know as well as I do why I'm here. It's not to see Denver."

"You should have stayed in New York. You're wasting your time." She studied her ambitious suitor. His pin-striped, brown sack suit flattered his tall, athletic form with careless style. One gloved hand clutched an ivory-topped walking stick. His natty appearance might appeal to some young ladies, but Garnet's heart remained unmoved.

Albert's mouth curled in a humorless smile. "That's not what your father tells me. He promised me that before summer's end, we'll announce our betrothal. He only allowed you to come along with us so you could spend more time with me. Spending time in my company will secure your affections." Albert preened.

Garnet threw him a disparaging look. "No amount of time spent with you will 'secure my affections.' A marriage between us would be nothing more than a business merger."

Albert narrowed his eyes. "We'll marry, with or without love. Our union will benefit both our families. Love is for the lower classes, anyway."

With a shrug, Garnet dismissed him and turned away.

At that moment, her father snapped his fingers in her direction. A large ruby in its ornate platinum setting on his pinky finger winked in the light. "Come, Garnet. What are you waiting for?"

Garnet stood. She gathered up her fringed and beaded reticule before she twitched the slim skirt of her traveling outfit into place. Feeling disheveled from the trip, she inspected her reflection in the long mirror on the cabin's opposite wall.

Masses of pale silk roses and an ostrich plume adorned her wide-brimmed hat, which tilted at a jaunty angle atop her red-gold pompadour. Her high-necked cream blouse and her slim, dark skirt embodied her Gibson Girl image. Kid leather ankle boots peeked from beneath her hem. The looking glass threw back the reflection of a demure, fashionable young lady.

Garnet turned her back on her reflection. Mirrors lied. She didn't feel the least bit demure. Eagerness to shed society's restraints and find freedom in the West trembled through her.

The trio moved into the narrow aisle along one side of the first-class passenger car and descended to the platform. Daisy, Garnet's maid, trailed behind and carried a small tapestry valise and a hatbox.

The engine huffed. Steam billowed from beneath the iron monster's belly. The suffocating scent of coal smoke stung Garnet's nose and coated the back of her throat.

She stepped away from the train into the din that echoed beneath the station's vaulted roof. Other trains on parallel tracks disgorged their passengers, men and women who tumbled into the press of humanity below.

Beyond the belching iron engines lay the street, where motor cars, horse-drawn buggies, and drays jockeyed for position.

Behind her, her father directed the unloading of their baggage. Daisy stood nearby to identify the pieces of her luggage. Conscious of Albert at her elbow, Garnet turned away and ambled to the far edge of the gray, wooden platform. She descended the steps to the walkway that fronted the street and stood a little way out of the crush. Her gaze traveled along the clusters of men, women, and children who bustled about the platform.

Nearby stood a dark-haired man who loomed taller than everyone about him. His height first caught her attention, but a closer look stirred an appreciative female interest. Beneath a brown felt cowboy hat, raven curls tumbled over his brow. Since his clean-shaven face sported no beard or mustache, Garnet could admire his features' strong, tanned planes. A bold blade of a nose gave his face an arresting appearance. His well-tailored sack coat fit with snug precision across impressive shoulders. Garnet guessed he had no need of padding in the shoulders of his suit jacket.

Though obviously a gentleman, the man exuded the aura of an untamed and dangerous wild creature. The cowboy hat set him apart from other well-dressed men, most of whom wore a derby hat. Wrapped in austere stillness, the gentleman appeared to be looking for someone. As if he felt her scrutiny, he turned toward her and leveled a forceful stare at her.

His black gaze pierced her with the force of a blow. Garnet sucked in her breath. Ensnared by the power of his regard, she froze. Their glances locked while the noisy world faded away. Nothing existed for Garnet except this man and herself, bound together by wordless communication. After a moment, the gentleman nodded and returned his attention to the crowd.

Garnet gulped in a trembling breath. What had just happened? She raised quivering fingers to her mouth. Dazed, she shook her head to free herself of the stranger's lingering essence. Not daring to look his way again, she turned her scrutiny to the activity along the walkway.

At first, quieting her heart's hammering concerned her more than the activity along the verge. As her composure returned, two ragged urchins engaged in a game of marbles on the curbside caught her attention. They seemed oblivious to the nearby traffic.

Garnet strolled closer. She'd been watching for several moments when one of the idling engines emitted a sudden shrieking whistle accompanied by hissing steam. The sound echoed in the confines of the station and rolled outward. People flinched. Ladies covered their ears. Above the whistle, the shrill neigh of a terrified horse added to the din. Garnet glanced toward the sound.

A wild-eyed sorrel harnessed to a curricle galloped toward her along the road's edge. The driver sawed on the reins in a vain attempt to bring the horse under control. The unresponsive beast continued his mad plunge in her direction. The equipage barreled toward them, the near wheels riding along the walkway's perimeter. People leaped to safety. As Garnet registered the danger of the out-of-control vehicle, she saw that the urchins playing marbles knelt in the path of the oncoming horse.

"No!" She lunged toward the boys in the vain hope of snatching them to safety.

Heedless of her own welfare, only the danger barreling toward the two youngsters filled her thoughts. The curricle approached in a blur of motion, yet to Garnet the scene slowed to a frame-by-frame sequence. Sound became suspended. She heard nothing except silence and blood through her ears. Neither the sharp clatter of hooves, the screams of the onlookers, nor the hissing of the engines penetrated the bubble that enveloped her. Like a marionette controlled by an invisible puppeteer, she turned her head in the direction of the oncoming equipage and realized her peril for the first time. The horse galloped so close she could see the white ring around its eyes. She stretched out her hand as if to hold disaster at bay.

Within the space of a heartbeat, a pair of strong arms scooped her off her feet and whirled her out of the death's path. She clutched her rescuer's shoulders while the world careened about her. A mere hand span from her gallant savior, the horse and curricle whipped past, shattering the spell that held her in thrall. Once more the engines' cloying smoke layered on her tongue. The crowd's babble beat against her ears, and the glaring sunshine on the street beyond the Denver Depot dazzled her. All these impressions faded as the man set her on her feet.

"Can you stand?" He gripped her waist.

Still clasping his shoulders as if her very existence depended upon the contact, Garnet tipped her head back to gaze into the face of the gentleman who'd caught her attention just minutes earlier. Tiny lines fanned out from the corners of his dark eyes. Creases bracketed his mouth. Concern etched his features.

Reaction set in, and tremors shook her. "I... I'm not sure. I think so." Her voice croaked.

The gentleman seemed disinclined to release her. His fingers tightened around her slender waist as if to buttress her trembling limbs. Her hands still rested on his shoulders while she dragged in great gulps of air. When her head cleared, she remembered the reason for her near accident and peered around her rescuer's shoulder.

"The boys?" The spot where the urchins had been engaged in their game of marbles was vacant. The ragamuffins had vanished, apparently endowed with a strong sense of self-preservation.

"They skedaddled about the time you tried to rescue them."

Garnet closed her eyes against the vision of their battered bodies being tumbled about beneath the hooves and wheels of the horse and curricle. She breathed a relieved sigh as she lifted her lashes to peer into her rescuer's face. "Thank God."

With intent gazes fixed upon each other, the two of them stood unspeaking for a moment, creating an island of silence amid the station's din. The man's essence surrounded her.

The bunched muscles she gripped represented strength and safety. She curled her fingers about the solid muscle beneath her palms. As she'd suspected, this man needed no padding in his jacket. The strong hands that spanned her waist induced a quivering that had nothing to do with her recent near brush with death. Garnet closed her eyes and savored the luxury of male solicitude the stranger focused upon her.

"Garnet! Whatever are you doing?" her father barked at her.

Garnet's eyes flashed open. Her father's disapproving tone recalled her to the moment. What a spectacle she must present, with her hands still on the man's shoulders and herself encircled within his embrace. She slid her palms down his arms and stepped back. He dropped his hands from her waist. "I can't thank you enough. I'm sorry I put you at risk."

The gentleman inclined his head. "Think nothing of it. I'm glad I reached you in time."

Albert stepped closer and touched her elbow. "Are you all right? You look a trifle pale."

Garnet took another deep breath. "I'm fine. Just a little shaken."

Asa Morrison's breath hissed between clenched teeth. His gray walrus mustache quivered. "What have you done now, Garnet? Must you always make a spectacle of yourself?"

Humiliation flooded her. Her face heated. "I—"

The stranger raised a hand to cut her off and interjected himself into the conversation. Addressing her father, he said, "Your—daughter?"

Asa Morrison swung his head in the stranger's direction. "My daughter, yes."

"Your daughter showed incredible courage attempting to rescue two young boys from the path of a bolting horse. She had no thought for her own safety. She should be commended."

Asa narrowed his gaze at the other gentleman as if taking his measure. At last, he gave an abrupt nod. "Garnet is impulsive, but I thank you for your timely rescue." He turned to his daughter. "Perhaps next time you'll think twice before you put yourself in danger and require a stranger to risk life and limb saving you from your own folly."

Mortified to be so addressed before her handsome rescuer, Garnet couldn't reply. Her tongue froze over the words she couldn't utter. She slid a glance at the stranger.

His face had darkened. A muscle jumped at the corner of his mouth. "Don't blame your daughter, sir. I would have done the same had I been closer to the boys."

Garnet held her breath and risked a quick glance at her father. Asa Morrison wasn't used to censure. She waited for the explosion.

Silence dropped about their group like a rock falling into a pool, while Asa studied the younger man. Apparently concluding that the gentleman wouldn't be bullied, he threw back his leonine head and guffawed. "I believe you would have." He thrust out a beefy paw for the stranger to shake. "We men have to take care of the weaker sex, eh? They sometimes let their soft female hearts lead them to do foolish things."

The stranger didn't smile. "I wouldn't consider what your daughter did to be foolish." He stood with his head tilted back, staring down his chiseled nose at the older man. Long moments passed while he made no move to take Asa Morrison's hand. When at last Garnet thought he'd decline her father's gesture, he accepted the older man's overture with a firm shake.

Asa winced at the pressure and pulled back his hand. "Forgive my manners. My name is Asa Morrison. And you are...?"

Her rescuer's expression didn't change, but strong emotion beneath his urbane façade rippled toward Garnet. Once again, silence hung about their little group, and the air developed a charged feel. Finally, the stranger spoke.

"Cole. My name is Cole Wild Wind."

Chapter 2

Cole Wild Wind. Garnet cut a sharp glance at her father and caught her breath.

Asa Morrison concealed whatever chagrin he must have felt and stared at his potential business partner with an expressionless face. His bulldog chin jutted. At last, he chuckled and spread his hands wide in a conciliatory gesture. "Mr. Wild Wind, my apologies. I do believe we've gotten off to a bad start. Shall we forget this little misunderstanding and begin again?"

A hearty *bonhomie* layered through his words.

Garnet studied her father through half-lowered lashes. She'd never seen him go to such lengths to curry favor with anyone. He must really want Cole Wild Wind's partnership. Normally, he made sure he held the upper hand in all of his financial dealings. She turned her perusal to Cole Wild Wind. His expression hadn't warmed, but the taut lines of his face had relaxed. Would he accept her father's olive branch? Doubtless, he'd been tempted to tell Asa Morrison to take the next train back to New York city.

Cole Wild Wind gave a stiff nod.

Her father thrust an arm toward Albert. "This is Albert Davies, a junior partner at the bank." He indicated Garnet, almost as an afterthought. "And you've already met my daughter, Miss Garnet Morrison."

Her rescuer dipped his head in Albert's direction, then turned his dark gaze on Garnet. He swept off his cowboy hat and held it down alongside his thigh. "Miss Morrison, I'm pleased to formally make your acquaintance." With his other hand, he grasped her fingers and gave them a gentle squeeze.

Garnet warmed at his western gallantry. "I don't think I've ever had such a memorable introduction. You literally swept me off my feet." She aimed an impish smile in his direction.

His eyes crinkled down at her while he scrutinized her.

His attention made her feel inclined to babble. "Truthfully, I can't thank you enough. I'm only now realizing how close I came to being badly injured or killed." Her insides quaked at the memory.

He continued to study her a moment longer before he replied, "Most young ladies of my acquaintance would be in hysterics now, so you have nothing to apologize for. I'm pleased I was able to render you a small service."

"What you did for me was more than a small service! You saved my life at risk of your own safety. I can never thank you enough."

Their glances locked. An invisible skein drew them together, a wordless communication that caused Garnet's stomach to quiver.

Her father's harrumph interrupted the moment.

Cole Wild Wind released her hand. "You all must be exhausted. Let me take you to the hotel. My motor car is right over there." He motioned to a dark green touring car with black trim parked beside the walkway.

At that moment a porter appeared, trundling a dolly piled high with their trunks and valises. Daisy trailed behind.

Cole appraised the mountain of luggage. "I can take a few pieces in the boot of my motor car, but the rest will have to be delivered later. Choose which pieces you need to go to the hotel with us, and I'll make arrangements for the rest."

After some juggling, three small trunks were stowed in the boot, and Cole had arranged for the rest to be delivered that evening. Her father settled himself in the front passenger seat. Albert moved toward Garnet as if to open the touring car's back door, but Cole Wild Wind forestalled him. Stepping forward, his expression froze Albert in midstride. Cole reached for the latch with one hand and drew Garnet toward him, a firm grasp on her elbow with the other. He opened the door but made no move to seat her.

He bent his head toward her ear. "What is your maid's name?"

"Daisy. Daisy Forrester."

He freed Garnet's elbow and beckoned Daisy. "Daisy, come with us. Miss Garnet will need your services this afternoon."

Daisy sidled closer, reluctant to accept Cole's invitation. Doubt clouded her features, and she glanced at Garnet.

Garnet smiled at her. "It's all right, Daisy. Mr. Wild Wind has invited you to ride with us."

Cole thumbed back his cowboy hat and stared at Albert over Garnet's head. "Mr. Davies won't mind sitting beside you, will you, Albert?"

Albert glared, resentment evident in the tight line of his mouth. "Certainly not." Spinning on the heel of his Italian leather shoe, he stalked around the back of the touring car and climbed in on the other side.

Daisy clambered into the vehicle, nearly stepping on Garnet's toes, and scooted to the middle.

Garnet glanced at Cole again to find him watching her.

"Miss Garnet." After he settled her in the back seat, he flashed her a smile and shut the door, then eased away. Halting by the driver's door, he leaned in to flip the starter switch before he skirted the front bumper and gave the crank a couple of turns.

The engine coughed twice and purred to life.

Wedged into the opposite corner of the back seat, Albert brooded in silence, arms crossed. His full lower lip turned down. The petulant expression on his face reminded Garnet of a sulky boy. She gave a mental shrug and let him stew. If he wanted to sulk, she wouldn't jolly him out of his foul humor.

Daisy huddled between them, her clenched hands gripped together between her knees.

During the drive to the hotel, Garnet watched the back of Cole Wild Wind's cowboy hat while he maneuvered the motor car through Denver's wide streets. He handled the automobile with careless skill, weaving around other vehicles, horse-drawn carriages, bicycles, and pedestrian traffic, all while carrying on a conversation with her father. His wide shoulders rose above the back of the front seat and filled the driver's space with the essence of strength.

Garnet hid a smile and marveled that Cole Wild Wind had outmaneuvered both her father and Albert. She wouldn't have believed the feat had she not seen it. She'd butted heads with her father often enough to know he possessed a will of iron, unbending and inflexible. From what she'd seen of Cole Wild Wind, she guessed he'd be a worthy opponent for her father. She expected nothing less than a figurative earthquake when the two of them sat down at the bargaining table.

When they reached their hotel, the Grande Palace, Garnet stared. She hadn't imagined Denver could boast anything so opulent. The triangular building soared nine stories and took up a whole city block. Its exterior of polished red granite made an imposing statement. *Denver can compete with anything the East can offer,* the hotel seemed to boast.

Even Albert brightened when Cole halted the vehicle before the Grande's wide arched doors.

Motor cars chugged along the thoroughfare, mingling with street cars and horse-drawn drays. The city throbbed with life.

"I booked your rooms here. The Grande Palace is Denver's finest hotel," Cole said, while his guests ogled. "Presidents Roosevelt and Taft have both stayed here." He glanced at Asa Morrison.

The banker seemed suitably impressed. "Well, I guess if it's good enough for Teddy Roosevelt and President Taft, it ought to be good enough for us."

Albert grunted, but he didn't disparage the hotel's appearance.

Garnet leaned forward and tilted sideways a bit to address Cole Wild Wind. "I'm sure we'll be most comfortable here. Thank you for your thoughtfulness."

Her rescuer twisted toward the back to better address her. "I wanted my guests to have a taste of western hospitality."

Garnet smiled at him.

Albert glowered.

Cole Wild Wind swung out of the motor car. He reached for the back door handle and opened Garnet's door wide. "I remain at your service, Miss Garnet. Let me help you." He gripped her hand and pulled her from the vehicle, then did the same for Daisy.

Daisy flushed crimson at the unaccustomed chivalry, but she took his proffered hand.

Garnet's feet had just touched the pavement when two men wearing the hotel's black uniforms faced with scarlet piping stepped from the arched doors to greet them and unload their luggage. The hotel's employees bore their baggage into the building's depths and vanished.

Before Garnet could appreciate the red sandstone griffin heads etched on either side of the Grande's entrance doors, their group was whisked inside. While Cole conversed with the desk clerk, Garnet surveyed the interior lobby.

Walls of polished brown stone encircled the octagonal atrium lobby. Wide arches in the Italian Renaissance style graced the second-floor mezzanine. Filigreed iron railings laced the upper floors' balconies and circled the lobby in lacy loops all the way to the ninth floor. Her gaze traveled up dizzying heights to a glass dome nine stories high, then dropped to the ground-floor lobby.

Tall ferns in huge pots marched along the lobby walls.

Even her father was impressed into silence, Garnet noted. His sharp gaze missed nothing, and Albert had stirred himself out of his habitual critical air into a measure of approval.

Cole Wild Wind's arrival with two hotel room keys dangling from his hand interrupted their inspection. He held out one key to Asa Morrison. "I've reserved a suite for you and Miss Garnet on the fourth floor. Daisy has a room in the staff wing." He extended the other key to Albert. "Your room is on the other side of the hotel."

Albert's expression darkened.

Before the younger man could protest his room assignment, Asa Morrison spoke. His gray eyes reflected approval. "Good, good. It's best to keep the two love birds apart. Young love is impulsive, wouldn't you agree, Mr. Wild Wind?"

Garnet cringed at her father's unsubtle comment. He had no right to pair her with Albert when she hadn't agreed to a marriage between them. She intended to set the matter straight with Cole Wild Wind once she could get away from her manipulating parent.

Cole's sharp glance sliced toward her, then back to her father. He shrugged. "I wouldn't know. I've never been in love, even in my younger days."

Asa Morrison's mouth turned up with expansive good humor. "My daughter and Albert will announce their betrothal when we return to New York. Their marriage will create a solid dynasty between our two families."

Garnet tried to avoid being steamrolled by her father. "Sir, I know that's what you want, but I haven't agreed to the marriage."

Asa Morrison waved a dismissive hand. "Women love to be coy and keep us men guessing, but in the end, Garnet will be an obedient daughter and make Albert a happy man."

"Garnet may be willful, but she'll be my wife." Warning laced the glance Albert sent to Cole Wild Wind.

Garnet grimaced at Albert's smug tone.

Cole didn't glance her way again, though tension rolled from him in waves. His big form loomed over her shorter father and the slighter Albert. "I should think the decision of whom she marries would be up to your daughter."

Asa narrowed his eyes at the taller man. "Perhaps that's how things work here in the wild West, but back East, daughters defer to their parents in such matters."

Garnet held her tongue, not wanting to risk her father's anger by protesting further. She balled her hands into fists. *I won't be bullied into marrying a man I despise. I won't!* She breathed through her nose to calm herself.

Tense silence fell. When Cole replied, his expressionless tone spoke volumes, though he didn't refer to the topic of her marriage to Albert. "I'm sure you'd appreciate an opportunity to refresh yourselves before we eat. I'll leave you now and will return in time for dinner. Will six o'clock be suitable?"

Asa nodded without consulting his companions. "Certainly."

"I'll meet you here in the Atrium Lobby, over there by the stairs. I've reserved a table for us in the dining room." He paused. "My brother will join us for dinner. As I've mentioned in our correspondence, Rafe is my partner in the mine."

"Fine, fine. I'm eager to meet your brother." Asa exuded bluff heartiness.

Cole nodded, then spun and strode across the lobby. His long strides carried him to the Grand Entrance and outside before Garnet could bid him goodbye.

Her father watched his departure through narrowed eyes. "Dealing with that young man will be a challenge, but I'm confident I can bring him to heel."

The lobby's double doors closed behind Cole Wild Wind, shutting him from their view. Garnet's thoughts followed him, imagining him cranking his touring car to life and driving away, his tanned hands strong and sure on the steering wheel. Though she didn't want to return to New York, she hoped Cole could best her father's manipulations, even if that meant the partnership never developed.

Albert's grip on her elbow brought her back to the moment. He hissed in her ear. "You see, you *will* marry me. You can't win this one, Garnet. Your father won't allow you to defy him."

She pulled her arm from his grasp and gave him a cold glare. "The days of fathers forcing their daughters into distasteful marriages is past. My father can't make me marry you."

Albert thrust his face close to hers. "If you think that,

then you don't know your father. And you don't know me. We'll have our way in this. If you know what's good for you, you'll put any romantic notions of Cole Wild Wind right out of your pretty head and start getting used to the idea of being Mrs. Albert Davies."

Chapter 3

"Daisy, I can't decide which dress to wear to dinner tonight." Garnet eyed both gowns spread out on the four-poster bed's cream silk counterpane.

Daisy knelt beside Garnet's camel-backed trunk, her arms elbow-deep in silk underthings. Rocking back on her heels, she frowned at the dresses draped across the bed, then nodded toward the gown on the left. "That rose pink would flatter you. If you want to gain Mr. Davies' attention, that is."

At Albert Davies' name, Garnet made a moue. She trailed her fingers across the silk and lace fabric of the gown. "The *eau de nil*?" She lifted the frock and held the garment against her front as she drifted across the room to the cheval glass in the corner. With her head tipped to one side, she studied her image in the glass. "You don't think the color would clash with my hair?"

Freed from the pins that had restrained it during her travels, her tresses floated about her face in a golden-red cloud and rippled in a curling mass down her slim back.

Her pale complexion made wearing the fashionable pastel evening colors taboo, so Garnet normally favored richer hues. However, the *eau de nil* silk had caught her attention, and she'd had her dressmaker fashion an evening gown from the fabric. Now she studied her image with a critical eye.

The silk had enough underlying hue so she wouldn't look too pale, she decided, and the overlaying lace gathered at one shoulder and draped across the skirt's front held the rich gleam of dew-kissed roses.

"Actually, I thought I might catch Cole Wild Wind's eye." With her head still tipped in concentration, Garnet studied her image.

Behind her, Daisy's head came up and whipped toward her. A loose hank of blonde hair swung with the motion. "That Mr. Wild Wind, he's sure a handsome gentleman," Daisy said after a pause. She tucked her hair behind her ear.

Her thoughts on her dramatic introduction to her rescuer, Garnet smiled. She still felt his hands about her waist. "He certainly is."

Daisy narrowed her blue eyes and pushed to her feet. "You're going to get yourself in a peck of trouble with your daddy if you get too friendly with Mr. Wild Wind, no matter that he has a face to make a lady swoon." She clutched Garnet's lingerie against her bosom.

Garnet spun from the cheval glass. "My father will have to realize that he can't force me to marry Albert. Besides, once Papa gets involved with the mine he'll forget I'm even here. You know he never remembers I'm alive unless he needs me for something."

Daisy shook her head. "For your sake, I hope you're right. But he sure seems to have his heart set on you marrying Mr. Davies."

"He has his heart set on the merger of our families. My marriage to Albert would make us one of the richest families in New York." Garnet's eyes flashed. "Albert told me the only reason my father allowed me to come to Colorado was so I could spend time in his company. My father thinks I'll be more amenable to marrying that sniveling weasel if I spend time with him."

"If your father thinks that, he doesn't know you." Daisy sighed. "I don't know how you'll get out of a marriage to Mr. Davies, and that's the truth." She cast a pitying glance at Garnet.

"I'm no pawn in his power games. I'll think of something." Garnet paced across the room and tossed the garment across the bed. "Help me get dressed, Daisy. We're meeting in the lobby for dinner in half an hour."

With Daisy's skillful ministrations, Garnet dressed for dinner in record time. A fashionable pompadour lent elegance to her coiffure. Diamond droplets dripped from her ears and swung about her jawline, flashing fire in the light.

"Which hat do you want to wear to dinner?" Daisy paused with a large hat in each hand.

With one hand on her hip, Garnet considered the headgear. "Tonight I'll wear just a bit of hair jewelry." She rummaged in her mother-of-pearl jewelry box atop the dresser's gleaming mahogany surface and plucked a diamond-studded clip from the clutter of jewels. Leaning toward the mirror, she nestled the jewelry in the tresses just above her left ear.

"There." She snatched her white silk gloves from the dresser and worked them over her fingers. With the gloves in place, she stole a final glance at herself in the mirror. Pale rose tinted her cheeks, and her blue eyes sparkled. Her oval face glowed with an inner flame. The Empire-style gown's low, square neckline and slim lines flattered her willowy figure.

Garnet whirled away from the mirror. She grasped Daisy's hands and squeezed. "I feel as though my life begins now, tonight. For some reason..." She shook her head. "Maybe it's the air out here, or the mountains. I feel I'm on the edge of a grand adventure, and my life will never be the same."

Daisy squeezed her hands in return. "I hope so, Miss Garnet. I do hope so."

Garnet freed Daisy's hands. "Now, I'm off to catch the eye of the handsome Cole Wild Wind." She paused with one hand on the doorknob. "Who knows? Perhaps he'll rescue me from Albert."

When the elevator had rumbled to the ground floor and the gilt-barred door had slid open, Garnet stepped into the Atrium Lobby. She paused. Off to her left, near the foot of the central staircase, stood her father, Albert, Cole, and another dark-haired man whom she presumed to be Rafe Wild Wind. The brothers seemed to have been fashioned from the same mold. The family resemblance was unmistakable.

As if he sensed her presence, Cole lifted his head and speared her with his gaze. Garnet halted. The silk gown whispered about her ankles, and her glance locked with his.

Cole excused himself from the group and strolled toward her with a long stride, easy yet purposeful. Garnet's breath hitched as he approached. When he halted before her, she tried to slow her breathing.

His warm gaze slid over her. "Miss Garnet, may I take you in to dinner?"

Unable to speak, she nodded.

He offered her his arm. When she placed her hand on his dinner jacket's dark sleeve, the muscled firmness of his forearm reminded her of his strength. Her stomach fluttered. They strolled toward their dinner companions with slow, matched steps.

He cocked his head at her. "I hope you had an opportunity to refresh yourself this afternoon."

His small talk relaxed her, and she found her voice. "Yes, I did. The hotel staff has been very attentive, and the room is most comfortable."

"Good. I would expect nothing less." He paused. "Would I be too bold if I told you that you look very fine tonight?"

Garnet peered into his eyes. His dark gaze, warm with admiration, met hers. Unspoken communication shimmered between them, rendering her mute once more. Their stroll slowed to a halt, and without conscious thought, Garnet half-turned toward him. She gathered her wits. "You wouldn't be too bold. Thank you for the compliment."

Another dark glance perused her ensemble. "The gown flatters you. The color makes me think of the prairie roses that bloom on our family's ranch in the spring."

"Prairie roses. They sound beautiful." She smiled at him. "The ranch? You live on a ranch? I thought you lived here in Denver when you aren't at the mine."

"I live in Denver when I'm not at the mine, but my family owns a ranch northeast of here. If I'd cared to stay, I could have had a job at the Slash L."

"What kind of job? Working cattle?"

"My parents run the horse-breeding side of the ranch. We raise Quarter Horses that are purchased by other ranchers from all over the West. My half-brother Jake works the breeding program with them, so my help isn't really needed."

Half-brother? Cole Wild Wind had a half-brother? The question tantalized. Garnet resolved to quiz him about that when they'd become better friends.

"My cousin, Aaron, ramrods the cattle side of the ranch. I could have helped him, but I'd rather work with horses. And my cousin Jesse heads up the oil side of the business."

"Horses, cattle, and oil. The ranch must be a prosperous enterprise."

Cole glanced away, then brought his attention back to her. "It is. Clint Logan, my great uncle who founded the Slash L, is a man of vision and business sense."

"You don't want to work with your family on the ranch, so that's why you went into mining?" Curiosity to learn more about him consumed her.

He shrugged. "You could say that. I blame my independent streak. I wanted to do something on my own instead of coasting along on the family's coattails. And I didn't want to go into politics, another family tradition." He nodded toward the tall man with her father and Albert, who was watching them. "Rafe is like me that way—wanting to be independent. We make a good team."

Garnet glanced at Rafe Wild Wind. She couldn't miss the family resemblance. Both men had lean, bold features, the same dark hair, and the same powerful frames.

She ignored her father, who frowned at her in familiar irritation, and Albert, whose countenance mingled both jealousy and boredom. "Rafe looks like you."

"We take after our father." A grin tilted up the corners of his mouth. "Except for our curly hair. We get that from our mother."

Garnet shared a smile with him.

"We'd best join the others. Your father doesn't seem happy to see us together."

She didn't have to look at her father again to know Cole spoke the truth. Even from this distance, her sire's displeasure enveloped her like a hot tide. "He's not. My father doesn't like to be thwarted."

"I've gathered as much." Cole's dry tone indicated he'd taken her father's measure.

Without further conversation, they resumed their stroll to their dinner companions. When they halted before the group, Cole turned her toward his brother.

"Rafe, may I present Miss Garnet Morrison? Miss Garnet, my brother and business partner, Rafe Wild Wind."

Rafe took one of Garnet's gloved hands and smiled down at her, all easy charm and male confidence. "Miss

Morrison, I'm pleased to make your acquaintance. You're a beautiful representative of Eastern womanhood."

With an instinct as old as Eve, Garnet sensed Rafe Wild Wind enjoyed the company of women and probably flattered all members of her sex. Despite that, his gallantry charmed her. "Thank you. And I've found Westerners to be very hospitable."

Rafe grinned down at her. "We have to be hospitable in order to lure Easterners out our way."

Asa Morrison harrumphed. "You've kept us waiting, Garnet. Come along. We men are hungry." He reached for her arm and towed her away from Cole, then slanted the other man a belligerent glance. "I'll accompany my daughter to the dining room."

Cole's expression shuttered at the older man's tactlessness, though he didn't argue. "Certainly, Mr. Morrison." He motioned toward the dining room's entrance on the other side of the staircase. "This way, if you please."

Garnet resented her father's tight grip on her elbow as they followed Cole and Rafe to the dining room. To be denied the right to choose her own dinner escort made her yearn to escape her father's autocratic rule. One day, she promised herself, she'd be free of his dominion. Except for the stretches of time when he seemed to forget her existence, her relationship with her father had been one of rocky turbulence and a struggle for freedom. Ever since her mother's death...

Her thoughts jerked back to her surroundings. She waited while Cole conferred with the maître d'hôtel, who led them to a table at one side of the room. When they'd been seated and given menus, he bowed himself away.

After her father had seated her between himself and Albert, Garnet raked the room with a swift glance. The Grande Palace Hotel's dining room boasted the same opulence as the Atrium Lobby and the suite allocated to her and her father. Crystal goblets and heavy silver cutlery sat atop white damask tablecloths. Chandeliers dripped with crystal prisms and cast rainbows on tables and diners alike.

"I recommend the antelope steak and baked potatoes." Cole leaned back in his chair and sent a glance toward his companions, whose heads bent over their menus. "Anything you order will be first-rate, but if you want to experience a truly Western meal, this is the place to get it."

"I'd advise starting your western cuisine here." A grin lurked about Rafe's mouth. "Once you get to the mining camp, the food won't be nearly as appetizing."

Asa Morrison grunted. "I can hire a cook if need be."

"Suit yourself." Cole shrugged. "Meals are hurried affairs, though. Sometimes we eat standing up, off a tin plate."

Albert looked aghast. "How positively barbaric!"

"The mining camps don't claim to boast the finer points of civilization." Cole pinned Albert with a stare. "If you want civilization, you'd best stay in Denver."

"And the hours are long." Rafe seemed bent on teasing Albert. "We're usually up before dawn and finish after dark." His gaze danced at the Easterner's dismay.

Asa Morrison forestalled Albert's reply. "We can keep up with you. If you work fourteen-hour days, Albert and I will be right there at your elbow. I want to experience every aspect of uranium mining."

Garnet reached for her water goblet and buried her face in the glass. She couldn't help but grin at Albert's appalled expression. As far as she knew, he'd never been up before the sun in his adult life.

A black-jacketed waiter interrupted their conversation long enough to take their order. When their orders had been placed, the men settled down for some serious discussion while they waited for their food.

"Tell me about your mine." Asa Morrison settled back in his chair as if prepared to spend the evening talking business.

The Cole brothers exchanged a glance.

"Our mine is located in the Rockies west of Denver, along Big Bear Creek," Cole spoke first. "In order to get the ore out to be processed, we have a four-day trip by pack mules to the nearest railhead, where the ore is loaded onto trains and transported to Denver."

"Refineries are being built here in Denver to lower the cost of processing. Until recently, pitchblende and carnotite ore were shipped overseas to be processed," Rafe said. "Shipping the ore to France cuts down on the profits. It makes economic sense to build processing plants on site."

"If we can get the finances, we could build our own refinery. Not having to transport the ore to Denver for processing will lower the cost of production and increase profits." Cole picked up the narrative where his brother had left off. "Also, we'd like to expand the mine and would need help financing that."

Asa Morrison nodded his graying, leonine head. "And that's where I come in. You need economic backing to build your processing plant."

The brothers exchanged another look.

Cole spoke for both brothers. "Our great uncle, Clint Logan, has offered to finance us, but we prefer to be independent of the family."

While the men talked, Garnet listened and watched her hosts. The Wild Wind brothers both possessed dark, exotic looks. What she'd earlier thought to be a tan on Cole's face she now realized was a natural deep, golden hue. What could be their family history?

She sipped her water and eyed the brothers over the rim of her glass, hoping to discover the keys that would unlock their secrets. Regardless of their Western background, their deportment told her they'd be comfortable in the drawing rooms of New York's socialites.

Garnet narrowed her gaze and imagined what Cole would look like dressed for work in the mine or riding one of his family's Quarter Horses. Without doubt, he could fill the role of miner or cowboy as well as gentleman.

Her thoughts switched to Albert. She tried to envision him in mining clothes or cowboy dress. Her imagination failed her. Albert's taste in clothing ran to dapper outfits, and since he hated horses, he seldom forked a saddle. She couldn't picture him in anything except the latest New York fashion.

Rafe's comment drew her back into the conversation. "The market for uranium is taking off. We're sitting on the cusp of a boom. You'd recoup your investment and make a large profit in just a few years."

An avaricious gleam glinted in Asa Morrison's eyes. Where there was a profit to be made, he was always interested.

The arrival of the waiter with their food interrupted their conversation. With her meal on the table, Garnet removed her gloves, laid them across her lap, and picked up her fork. The men dug into their steaks, and talking ceased. Only the muted murmur of other diners and the discreet clink of cutlery on china sounded.

When coffee had been served after the meal, Garnet's father withdrew a cheroot from his jacket pocket and lit it without asking if anyone minded. He leaned back in his chair and drew on his cigar while he watched the Wild Wind brothers through slitted eyes and a haze of smoke. He waved his cheroot aloft.

"I always want to be sure before I extend any money that all parties involved are in good standing. Therefore, I had both of you, as well as all members of your family, investigated."

Chapter 4

Silence descended. Garnet's gaze darted to Cole. The prisms from the chandelier above their table cast a rainbow across one lean cheek.

An expressionless mask had dropped over his face and hid his thoughts. He dipped his head in acknowledgment of her father's admission. Steel laced his tone when he replied. "I'm sure that's a wise business practice, especially in the East. And what did your investigators discover?"

Asa Morrison drew on his cheroot before he removed the cigar from his mouth and tapped the glowing end against the bowl of a crystal ash tray. He squinted at Cole through the smoke. "Your uncle, Clint Logan, is a distinguished Civil War general. He's also a retired three-term senator to the Colorado state legislature. The ranch your great uncle owns is well established. His holdings are diversified in cattle, horses, and oil. Clint Logan is well respected in both political and ranching circles." Asa paused.

"Your uncle's wife was born into the South Carolina planter society. Her family lost everything during the War Between the States. Clint Logan mustered out of the military during Reconstruction and purchased property north of Denver to raise remounts for the army. Later he branched out into raising cattle. Since oil was discovered on his land, he's gotten rich selling crude. Your parents run the horse side of the ranch, and your uncle's sons run the cattle and oil businesses."

Garnet's father tapped ash from the end of his cigar again and glanced back at the brothers. "Your cousin Flossie, Clint and Coral's oldest daughter, is married to a sitting Colorado senator. They reside in Washington, DC."

"That pretty much covers it."

Asa took another draw on his cigar. "Your mother is Clint Logan's niece. Your father is half Cheyenne. He was a Dog Soldier and chieftain when the tribes were fighting for their land."

Garnet caught her breath. Her speculations had been correct. Cole had Cheyenne blood.

"Will that be a problem for you?" Cole's low voice was smooth as warm honey, yet something about the stillness that hung over him made Garnet shiver.

Her father shrugged. "Not for me. I'm more concerned that you hold up your end of any bargain we make."

"I assure you, Rafe's word and mine are as good as any of your Eastern friends."

"It had better be."

A silent duel ensued while Cole's and her father's gazes tangled. Neither man seemed inclined to back down, so Garnet deemed it time to intervene.

"Mr. Wild Wind, tell me about your mine. Where do the men live who work for you? Do they bring their families with them?" Eager to hear about life at the mine, Garnet leaned forward.

Cole disengaged from her father and swung his glance to her. His expression softened. "Some of the men are married, and most of them have brought their families to the mining camp. We've provided cabins for the married men, and a bunk house for the single workers."

"Are there many women in the camp?"

"Over a dozen, but not all of them are the wives of miners. Some of them are women who do laundry for the single men." He paused to sip his coffee and set the cup down in the saucer. "Not everyone who lives at the camp works in the mine. One of the men owns a blacksmith shop, and a married couple runs the mercantile. We also employ a cook to feed the single men."

Garnet tried to imagine the camp, tucked high in the mountains, rough and elemental. "It must be exciting to be part of such a venture."

Cole caught her glance across the table. "Why don't you and Daisy come with us? You could experience camp life firsthand."

A surge of excitement coursed through her. "I'd love to. When do we leave?"

Her father frowned at her and shook his head. "You aren't going to the mine, young lady. A rough camp like that is no place for a respectable woman. You and Daisy will stay here in Denver. You can visit the shops and see a play. Denver must have a theater."

Garnet clamped her mouth shut. She wouldn't argue

with her father in the presence of Cole and Rafe Wild Wind, but she determined she wouldn't be left behind. One way or another, she'd get to the mining town. She yearned for adventure and for something more purposeful in life than attending soirees and the theater.

"How long will it take us to reach the camp?" Asa tapped ash from his cigar into a cut glass ash tray.

"A day's ride by train, then four days on horseback."

Albert straightened and looked aghast. "You mean the train doesn't go all the way to your mine? We'll have to travel by horseback?"

Rafe nodded. "Four days' ride and sleeping on the ground for three nights."

"I absolutely refuse to sleep on the ground. Can't you take a wagon, at least?" Irritation sharpened Albert's tone.

"We'll take two wagons full of supplies. You're welcome to sleep with the supplies if you can find room." Cole shrugged as if it didn't matter to him where Albert slept.

Albert subsided, though disdain turned down his mouth.

Garnet gave her would-be suiter a disgusted look. Once out of his usual element, Albert displayed more unpleasant attitudes than usual. She couldn't imagine being shackled to him in matrimony. Marriage to Albert would be a lifelong prison sentence she couldn't endure.

"When do we leave?" her father asked. "We can be ready to go in the morning."

"We'll leave on Monday. Rafe and I attend church on Sundays, but we'll head out on the Monday morning train."

"Church? What church do you attend?" Garnet perked up at the mention of church.

Cole told her the name of the church where he and his brother attended and countered with a question of his own. "Do you attend church, Miss Garnet?"

She met his curious look. "I used to. My mother and I attended church every Sunday."

Beside her, her father tensed. Mention of her mother was taboo, so she rarely had opportunity to talk about the woman who had given birth to her.

Cole's glance swept his dinner companions, then returned to her. "And did you leave your mother in New York?"

Garnet forced down a tortuous memory and the pain the image caused. She tried instead to give Cole a simple answer to an incident that had shattered the family and destroyed her relationship with her father. "My mother died when I was a little girl. Since she died, I haven't been to church much."

Her father made a strangled sound. Garnet ignored him and directed her attention to Cole.

Cole's sympathetic gaze rested on her face. His dark eyes expressed a compassion that warmed her to her core and brought a lump to her throat.

Her father's disapproving voice jolted her back to his presence. "Garnet, say good night and go upstairs. We men would like to discuss business."

Garnet sliced a peek at her father and met his cold glare. He wanted to be rid of her and the distressing memories she'd roused. A perverse imp of resistance made her draw out the moment as long as she dared. With unhurried motions, she pulled on her gloves and worked them over her hands. When she finished, she pushed back from the table and rose. Albert stood to pull out her chair.

She nodded at the Wild Wind brothers, who had also risen. "Good evening, gentlemen."

"Good night, Miss Garnet." Cole directed a heart-warming smile at her. His teeth flashed white in his dark face, and his eyes crinkled.

Rafe tossed her a grin. "'Night, Miss Morrison."

She glanced at her father. The glowing tip of the cheroot clamped between his teeth absorbed his attention. She didn't bother to address him. With an abrupt nod to Albert, she spun and flitted between the tables to the dining room's door, her shoulders squared and her chin high. Her father had dismissed her like a wayward child, but she refused to slink away. She might leave at his command, but she'd make her own statement in the process.

Chapter 5

"Daisy, hurry. We don't want to be late." Garnet swept out of the Palace's Grand Entrance and paused on the top step.

Daisy, dressed in her Sunday best blue cotton skirt and white blouse, scurried to keep up.

The taxi the desk clerk had arranged for them waited at the curb. The uniformed driver, who had been leaning against the motor car's side, sprang to attention and opened the back door with a flourish when the women drew near.

Garnet gave him the address of the church that the Wild Wind brothers attended, information she'd procured from the hotel staff, and slipped into the back seat. Daisy scrambled in beside her, and the driver shut the door.

Once the taxi was navigating Denver's streets, Daisy turned to her. "Miss Garnet, your father won't be happy to wake up and find you gone."

Garnet eyed her maid, whose anxious face reflected Daisy's apprehension about a possible scene with Asa

Morrison. "I left him a note letting him know where we were going."

"Yes, ma'am, but he still won't like it."

Garnet shrugged. "At home, he doesn't much care what I do, as long as I stay out of his way. Why should this be any different?"

"I don't know, but he sure has been watching you like a hawk ever since we left New York."

Daisy spoke the truth. Her father had been vigilant in his attentions ever since they'd left the city. "I think he's worried I won't come to heel and marry Albert."

Daisy frowned. "You know you'll have to give in to him."

Garnet shook her head. "Never! I refuse to marry that self-indulgent excuse for a man."

"I don't see that you'll have much choice."

"I'll think of something. I can't marry Albert. I won't!" Garnet shuddered. She twisted her gloved hands together. She untwined her fingers and smoothed her palm across her slim skirt. The apricot silk, covered by an overskirt of lace, draped across her knees. After a moment, she smiled and tipped her head toward Daisy. "Cole Wild Wind, he's all man. Beside him, Albert seems nothing more than a spoiled boy."

Daisy returned her smile. "That's a fact, Miss Garnet."

The drive to the church took them to Denver's western edge. The taxi rolled to a stop before a white clapboard-framed building, where a few motor vehicles, interspersed with horse-drawn buggies, lined up beneath a row of cottonwood trees nearby. A pointed steeple pierced the blue Colorado sky. Garnet eyed the simple structure. Could this be right? Given the brothers' social status, wouldn't they attend a more imposing church?

The stone edifice with its stained-glass windows and soaring, arched ceiling where she'd attended church with her mother seemed more fitting for men like Cole and Rafe Wild Wind. The parishioners of the cathedral she'd attended as a child had entered in solemn reverence and never dared to smile. A reserved nod toward acquaintances had been the accepted greeting, not the cheerful calls and conversations of the people who made their way toward this simple chapel. Perhaps the clerk at the Grande Palace had given her the wrong address.

The driver twisted about toward the back seat. "Is this the correct destination, ma'am?"

Despite her doubts, Garnet nodded. "Yes, it's the address I was given at the hotel."

A movement to her left caught her attention. Two tall, broad-shouldered men wearing well-cut dark suits approached the church. *The Wild Wind brothers.* She leaned toward the driver. "Sir, do you see those two dark-haired men going up the steps?"

The driver twisted back to the front and looked out the window. "Those two tall men who walk like they own the world?"

"Yes, those two. Will you please call them over?"

While the cab driver clambered out, Daisy turned a scandalized face to her. Her eyebrows rose toward her hairline. "Miss Garnet! How forward! You should wait for them to address you first!"

Garnet shrugged. "How else am I supposed to let Cole Wild Wind know we're here?"

"You could 'accidentally' encounter them on the steps after the service."

"I have no desire to wait until after the service to let Cole Wild Wind know I'm here when I could sit beside him during the preaching instead. If that makes me forward, then I'll just have to be forward."

"He may not like forward women."

"He likes me. I can tell." Garnet leaned around Daisy to look out the window. The cab driver had delivered his message, and the brothers were striding toward the taxi. Not wanting to appear too eager, Garnet sat back again.

A moment later, Cole Wild Wind bent down to peer into the back window on Daisy's side. "Miss Garnet and Daisy. What a surprise!"

Garnet angled forward again and smiled at him. "Since I haven't attended church in years, I thought it was time that I rectified my error. I hope you don't mind."

"Certainly not! Let me help you out." Cole straightened and sent a meaningful glance his brother's way before he strolled around the motor car to Garnet's side. He opened her door and thrust out a hand.

As she slipped from the vehicle, she lifted her head so that she could see beneath her hat's broad brim into his face. "Thank you."

Their gazes connected. Awareness sizzled through her.

"The pleasure is mine." Cole smiled down at her and placed her hand on his arm. "Shall we go inside?"

They paced around the front of the cab, where Rafe had assisted Daisy out of the motor car and now played the gallant. He'd tucked her hand in the crook of his elbow, and Daisy appeared dazed, as if a handsome statue had come to life and appeared at her side.

Cole halted beside the taxi and dropped his gaze to Garnet's face. "Do you have transportation back to the hotel?"

"I thought I'd ask the driver to wait and take us back after church."

He thumbed back his cowboy hat. The sun washed his face with its pure light, illuminating the lines fanning out from his eyes and the grooves bracketing his mouth. He directed toward her the full strength of his vitality.

Bemused by his potent forcefulness, Garnet couldn't help but stare. Compared to society's manhood in New York city, Cole Wild Wind appeared bold and capable. His toughness would be a match for her father's wiles.

"There's no need. You and Daisy can ride back to town with Rafe and me."

"Are you sure? We don't want to impose."

"You're not imposing. It's settled, then. I'll dismiss the driver." He released her hand and turned to the cabbie. After he paid the fare, he slipped his flat leather wallet back into his jacket pocket.

Garnet protested the money he'd spent. "You didn't have to do that." Intent on making good on the debt, she fumbled with the clasp of her beaded reticule. "Let me repay you."

Cole shook his head. "There's no need." He forestalled her efforts by placing her hand once more on his arm. "We'd better go in, or we'll be late."

The two couples climbed the wooden steps and entered the church. As they paused at the back of the sanctuary, awareness of her social position in contrast with the other worshippers made Garnet's face flame. The women wore simple cotton dresses or skirts, and cheap suits adorned the men. Her slim, apricot silk ensemble overlaid with masses of lace and pearl buttons, her kid leather ankle shoes, and her ridiculous wide hat with three ostrich plumes screamed wealth and privilege. She tugged on Cole's arm.

He halted and tipped his head closer to hers, his eyes questioning.

She leaned up on tiptoe to whisper in his ear. "I fear I'm a trifle overdressed."

"No one here will mind. Everyone will welcome you just as you are."

"You're sure?"

He nodded and led them to an empty wooden pew near the back, where he ushered her into the row. Rafe and Daisy settled beside them.

The hymns and preaching impressed Garnet with their simple sincerity. The music touched a wound hidden deep and rarely acknowledged, a wound she'd carried since her mother's death. The preacher seemed to speak directly to her. His message of Christ's sacrificial love soothed her soul, love she'd accepted as a child. How long ago that seemed!

At the end of the service, they rose for the final hymn. Garnet's throat clogged. She couldn't sing, but Cole's clear tenor voice moved her. He expressed what, in that moment, she couldn't.

When the service concluded, the brothers steered the girls toward Cole's touring car. When they reached the vehicle, Cole halted. The cottonwood trees cast a shifting shadow over his features. "What are your plans for this afternoon?"

Garnet glanced at Daisy. "We don't have any plans, do we, Daisy?" A breeze fluttered her skirt against her knees, and the ostrich feathers on her hat danced.

Daisy flashed her a hunted look. "I think your father wanted to talk to you."

Garnet made a dismissive gesture. "He can talk to me after we get back to the Palace."

Cole glanced across the women's heads to his brother. His expression communicated volumes. "Rafe and I would be pleased to escort you ladies to lunch, if that's agreeable with you."

"We'd love to join you." Eager to spend more time with Cole, Garnet accepted his offer without a second thought. She turned to Daisy. "Wouldn't you like to eat lunch with the men?"

Uncertainty crossed Daisy's face, as if someone of Garnet's social class asking her opinion was a novel experience. "I... I don't know. Is it all right for me to join you?"

Rafe took Daisy's hand and placed it on his arm. He smiled into her doubtful blue eyes. "Yes, Daisy, you can join us. Cole and I would be pleased if you'd honor us with your company."

For a long moment, Daisy stared back at him. "You really want me to eat lunch with you?"

"We do." Rafe gentled his voice, as if Daisy was a skittish mare he was trying to coax nearer.

Garnet held her breath, curious about Daisy's response.

Daisy wasn't accustomed to mingling with her "betters" or handling the attention of a male as handsome as Rafe. The whole experience must overwhelm her.

At last, Daisy lifted her head and smiled at Rafe. Her eyes glowed. "Yes. Yes, I'd be pleased to accept your kind invitation." The breeze loosened a golden curl from the bun at the back of her head, and she tucked it behind her ear, then adjusted the flat brim of her straw hat.

Rafe patted her hand. "It's settled, then." Reaching around her, he opened the touring car's back door. "In you go." As if Daisy were made of porcelain, he ushered her into the back seat.

Garnet and Cole shared a smile while he bent to open the front passenger door. With her skirts gathered in one hand, Garnet slid into the seat. Cole shut the door, then leaned into the open window. "Would you ladies mind if I put the top down? The weather is so fine today, it seems a shame not to enjoy it."

"Please, we'd love to ride with the top down." Garnet reached up to pull out the pins anchoring her hat to her coiffure. "With this large brim, my hat would fly right off my head."

With her hat on her lap, Garnet settled back against the seat's black tufted leather cushion and watched the brothers work together to put the top down. She smiled to herself. She couldn't remember when she'd enjoyed herself so much, and the afternoon was just beginning.

Chapter 6

Later that afternoon, the touring car chugged through Denver Park's wrought-iron gate and turned into a tree-lined parking area reserved for motor vehicles, buggies, and bicycles. The car rolled to a stop, and Cole cut the engine, then set the brake.

From the back seat, Rafe spoke. "I hope you ladies are ready to enjoy a boat ride on the lake."

Daisy clasped her hands beneath her chin. "A boat ride! What fun!" A shy smile tipped up the corners of her mouth, and she cut a sideways glance at her companion.

The men climbed from the vehicle and assisted the ladies out. Once again, Cole tucked Garnet's hand in his elbow and adjusted his longer stride to match her slower amble.

Beside them, Rafe and Daisy carried on a private conversation. Daisy giggled at something Rafe said, and his eyes glinted down at her. He captured her hand and placed it on his arm.

Garnet lifted her chin to scan the park beneath her

hat's wide brim. Boaters rowed across a placid lake, their laughter drifting shoreward. A grassy slope encircled the lake's perimeter, surrounded by a ring of trees wearing summer's lacy green. Families with children and courting couples strolled the paths alongside the water or sat in the wrought-iron benches that dotted the shore.

"This is beautiful!" Garnet sent Cole an appreciative glance. "I'm glad you brought us here."

"Denver Park is a popular attraction on Sunday afternoons."

"I can see why. What a delightful way to spend a Sunday afternoon."

They sauntered toward the water's edge, following Rafe and Daisy. When they reached the shore, Daisy glanced at Garnet with a dreamy expression. "Miss Garnet, isn't this the most wonderful place?"

"It's marvelous."

Daisy took a step closer to the water and stooped to plunge one hand into the wavelets that rippled along the sand. She clutched Rafe's arm for balance. When she raised her hand, water trickled from her closed fist and splattered into the lake. She sighed and stepped out of reach of the current that lapped toward her shoes. "It's a pure pleasure to do something just because I want to."

She still gripped Rafe's arm, and he patted her hand. "This afternoon is yours to command. What would you like to do next? We can stroll along the paths or go boating. And there are bicycles to rent." He cast a discerning eye at the ladies' outfits. "Although I don't think you're dressed for cycling."

Nibbling at her lip, Daisy glanced first at Garnet, then at Rafe. "Oh, I don't know what to say."

With a patient expression, Rafe waited for her to make up her mind.

Daisy cast a wistful look at the boaters out on the lake. "I've never been in a boat before. That would be a treat." She glanced down the path that wound its way beneath the trees. "And it would be fun to explore."

While Garnet and Cole kept their opinions to themselves, Rafe stepped into the breach. "Why don't we do it all? We can rent a boat. When we tire of rowing, we can explore the park."

Daisy's diminutive form quivered, and the eager face she turned to Rafe glowed. "Can we really?"

"We most certainly can."

"Oh, thank you."

They hurried to the shack where boats were rented. The men made the arrangements, and they clattered along the wooden dock with a set of oars in Cole's hands.

"This is our boat." Cole halted beside a white rowboat with a red stripe painted around the hull. With the oars blade-end down on the planks and the shafts tilted skyward, he grinned at his younger brother. "Well, little brother, it's been a while since we've handled a pair of oars. Do you think we can manage without tipping the ladies into the water?"

Rafe swept his cowboy hat from his head and scratched behind his ear while he pretended to contemplate his sibling's question. "I'm not sure. Perhaps we'd better just sit in the boat and enjoy the fine weather." With a playful grin, he settled his hat on his curls.

Cole's gaze met Garnet's. "Do you ladies dare risk your Sunday outfits to our less than skillful efforts?"

Daisy's smile vanished, and Garnet hurried to reassure her. "The gentlemen are roasting us, Daisy. I'm sure they're both quite competent oarsmen."

The brothers exchanged a sheepish grin.

Cole laid the oars on the wharf's planks and leaned down to pull the rowboat alongside the dock with its bow pointing toward the lake. "I'll hold the boat steady."

"And I'll help you ladies step down safely."

With Cole's hand on the gunwale to steady the little craft, Rafe stepped off the dock into the rowboat's belly. The boat rocked. He beckoned to Garnet. "Miss Garnet, you come first."

She gripped his hand and stepped into the vessel. Rafe held her in a firm grasp until the boat steadied. "You and Daisy sit in the stern." He guided her over the middle seat to the back of the craft.

Garnet lowered herself to the wooden seat in the stern and watched while Rafe pivoted to help Daisy.

Daisy hung back, her face pale. "Are you sure we won't tip over?"

Rafe waited with one hand outstretched. "You have my word as a gentleman. You're perfectly safe."

Another moment passed while Daisy dithered. When she didn't move, he gripped her about her waist and swung her aboard. Daisy squeaked and clutched his shoulders. He deposited her in the stern and steadied her when she swayed.

"There, you're in the boat, and you're not even wet." Rafe grinned down at her.

Daisy gave him a shaky smile and sat beside Garnet.

While Rafe loosened the line that anchored the craft to the dock, Cole leaped into the rowboat and settled himself on the middle seat facing the ladies. After he'd secured the oars in the oarlocks and rested the shafts across his thighs, he shrugged out of his suit coat and draped the jacket over his lap. A gold watch chain stretched across the front of his pin-striped waistcoat glinted in the sunshine.

Garnet watched him remove his gold cuff links and stuff them into a jacket pocket. He rolled his sleeves up to the elbow and glanced over his shoulder at his brother.

"Are you set, Rafe?"

Already settled in the prow, Rafe nodded. "You can cast off."

Cole pushed away from the dock with an oar blade, and then his long fingers wrapped about the oars' shafts. The boat shot away from the dock.

Garnet couldn't help but admire the way Cole's shoulder muscles bunched with each stroke and pull on the oars. She recalled the strength of those muscles when he'd whirled her from the path of the oncoming horse yesterday afternoon. Female appreciation shivered through her.

Beside her, Daisy gripped the edge of the planked bench, though her face had lost its pinched look.

"Are you enjoying this, Daisy?" Garnet sent a sideways glance at her maid.

"I feel like a bird flying over the water."

Rafe leaned around his brother. "You have a point, Daisy. Riding in a rowboat is a bit like flying."

Daisy glowed and loosened her grip on the seat.

Sunshine spangled the waves and scattered glitter across the rippled surface. A breeze offset the heat and fluttered the lace on Garnet's blouse. Voices of other boaters drifted over the water with tranquil geniality. Garnet closed her eyes and tipped her face up to the warmth, giving herself up to the moment's pleasure. If only they could sail forever, she needn't return to the hotel and the scene that awaited her when she faced her father.

She felt herself being watched and opened her eyes to meet Cole's gaze. A lazy smile curled one corner of his mouth, and his eyes crinkled. The unmistakable message he sent her betrayed his interest. The wordless communication charmed her, and she couldn't help but return his smile.

After a glance over his shoulder, he slowed his strokes as they reached the middle of the lake. He lifted the oars and let the craft drift, bobbing, on the water. Droplets dripped from the paddle blades and splattered onto the water's surface.

Garnet motioned toward the oars. "You seem to know your way around a pair of paddles."

Cole grinned. "I was on the rowing team when I was a student at the Rocky Mountain School of Mines."

"That would explain your skill."

"I've been known to win a few races during my university days."

"So you attended a university dedicated to mining?"

"Yes. After I figured out that politics or ranching wasn't for me and that mining interested me, I enrolled in the university."

"Here in Colorado, you have plenty of opportunity to put your education to practical use."

He shrugged. "Colorado is rich in ore. Taking advantage of the resources made sense."

Garnet steered the conversation to the men's trip to the mine. She had no intention of being left behind. "So you men are still planning to go up to the mine tomorrow?"

"Yes. We'll take the morning train."

Garnet dipped her hand in the water and pretended to be absorbed in the wavelets her fingers created. She adopted a casual tone. "How far will the train take you?"

As if he suspected her of priming him for information, Cole gave her a perceptive glance. "We'll take the Western and Mountain Railway to Indian Pass. That town is the end of the line."

"And from there you'll take your supplies by wagon?"

"We'll travel by wagon and horseback. As we mentioned last night, it's a four-day journey."

Thoughts of the discomfort Albert would suffer during four days on horseback and nights sleeping on the ground brought a grin to her lips.

"What?" Cole cocked his head. "By the way your eyes are glinting, I suspect you're up to mischief."

"Albert hates horses. And his idea of roughing it is sleeping in any bed away from his New York mansion."

"He's in for a shock, then." Cole shared her smile before he sobered and pinned her with a penetrating stare. "Whatever you're planning, you'd better think twice before you do it."

How had he guessed? A guilty wash of color heated her cheeks. "What makes you think I'm planning anything?"

"I know when I'm being pumped for information. And I suspect you're a headstrong young woman who doesn't like to be thwarted."

His accusation rang true. Beside Garnet, Daisy shrank against the gunwale as if to disappear.

Garnet swallowed. "I dislike being told to amuse myself at the shops or theater while you men have an adventure."

Cole narrowed his eyes. "We won't have an adventure. Denver may be civilized, but the mountains are still untamed. The trek to the camp will be dangerous. Anything could happen. Your father only wanted to protect you when he told you to stay here."

Garnet jutted her chin. "But you invited me to your camp."

"That was before I'd thought about the danger. And life at the camp is primitive. I doubt you'd enjoy the conditions."

Rafe interrupted them when he tipped sideways again to speak around his brother's shoulder. "In case you should wonder why Cole made me his business partner—aside from my good looks—I followed him into mining school and am as qualified as he is." Rafe poked Cole on the shoulder in playful raillery and grinned. "Now, big brother, it's my turn to impress the ladies with my prowess at the oars."

Time sped by in a whirl of banter, conversation, and smiles. When they finally returned to the dock and secured the rowboat, they sauntered along the shore and mingled with other merrymakers.

A nearby booth, painted in vertical stripes of red and white, offered refreshment. A gentleman with a curling mustache dispensed flavored ices. From another booth, the scent of popcorn mingled with funnel cake filled the air.

Cole cocked his head at Garnet. "Would you and Daisy care for an ice?"

"That sounds delightful."

Rafe touched Daisy's shoulder. "Daisy? How about you?"

"Oh, yes. Please." She beamed at Rafe.

The men stepped up to the booth and ordered four ices. Rafe offered one to Daisy, who took the treat from him with the air of a child on Christmas morning.

With a thoughtful air, Garnet watched the byplay. During their outing, Daisy had blossomed beneath Rafe's attention. Pleasure lent her features a prettiness Garnet hadn't noticed before. Though Rafe accorded Daisy all the courtesy a lady of his own station would expect, he never crossed the line into flirtatiousness. Garnet's opinion of him rose.

The couples ambled along the trail. Rafe and Daisy disappeared beneath the trees, leaving Cole and Garnet together. Busy with their ices, they strolled beside the lake in amiable silence. Bicyclists whizzed past, and children shrieked as they chased balls or played tag. Other couples paced beside the water.

"So," Cole said after they'd finished their ices. "Forgive me if I'm being impertinent, but what is the nature of your relationship with Albert Davies?"

Garnet halted in the middle of the path. His

unexpected question had scattered her thoughts, and she struggled to frame a coherent reply. "We're not engaged, if that's what you're wondering."

He pushed back the edges of his open suit jacket and propped his fists on his hips, frowning at her. "Actually, I was wondering if you're about to become engaged. Your father seemed quite emphatic on that point."

She glanced away and sighed before she looked up at him again. "My father views my marriage to Albert as the merger of two dynasties. Our marriage would make us one of the richest families in New York."

Cole looked pensive. "And what about you? I have the distinct impression you don't have much use for Albert. Are you willing to marry him for the money?"

His directness should have offended her, but the relief that she could clear the air on this point vanquished any insult. She shook her head. "Certainly not! No amount of money could make me shackle myself to him."

He tipped his head to one side and gave her a slow perusal, from the top of her plumed hat to her heeled kid ankle shoes.

Garnet ignored the impulse to squirm and returned his regard.

His stare flicked to her face. "I don't know much about ladies' clothing, but I'd wager that the outfit you're wearing came from Paris. A farm family out here could probably live on what it cost for six months. Could you forfeit all that if your father should give you an ultimatum?"

Garnet made a dismissive motion with one hand. "Mr. Wild Wind, if you knew me better, you wouldn't ask that. I have no intention of marrying Albert, money or not."

He gave a nod, as if confirming something in his mind. A smile warmed his eyes first and then tipped up the corners of his mouth. "Pardon me for treading on territory that's none of my concern, but I like to know the lay of the land. I don't want to poach on another man's claim."

Did Cole mean what she thought he did? Her breath caught.

"You intrigue me. You make me want to peel back the layers to figure out who you really are beneath all your polish." Cole's gaze traveled over her once more. "And who knows where that might lead?" He took her arm and turned her toward the trees. "We should probably get back to the Palace. Let's find Rafe and Daisy." He peered into her face. "And please call me Cole, at least when your father's not around."

Chapter 7

"Garnet, where have you been?" Asa Morrison rose from his comfortable chair before one of the fireplaces on either end of the Grand Salon and frowned at his daughter. "I found your note telling me you'd gone to church, but you should have been back hours ago."

Garnet came to a standstill between the Wild Wind brothers and stared at her father's florid face. Displeasure turned down his mouth.

Both Cole and Rafe stepped forward as if to shield her. Cole took the reproach upon himself. "Don't blame your daughter, sir. Rafe and I encountered her and Daisy at church. We took the ladies to dinner afterward, and then we went boating. If you must blame someone, then my brother and I are entirely responsible."

Albert, who had been sitting in a matching chair on the opposite side of the fireplace, leaped to his feet and glared at the Wild Wind brothers. "Garnet shouldn't be cavorting with other men. She's as good as betrothed to me."

Blood pounded in Garnet's ears, and her fingers clenched into fists as she whirled to face him. "Albert, don't be a ninny. You have no claim on me. I can enjoy the company of whomever I please." She lifted her chin and stared him down. "And I wasn't cavorting."

Albert opened his mouth to retort, but Asa Morrison forestalled him. "Perhaps we've been a trifle hasty, eh, Albert? If the brothers wish to show my daughter some of Denver's sites, then we shouldn't quibble over that. And since Daisy was along to act as chaperone, I'm sure it was all unexceptionable."

Albert subsided into sulky silence, though temper still mottled his face.

Asa spoke in a hearty voice. "Albert and I were just enjoying teatime." His arm swept out to encompass the Grand Salon. "Drinking tea is so civilizing, don't you agree? Would you care to join us?"

Over Garnet's head, Cole and Rafe exchanged a glance before Cole nodded. "Rafe and I would be pleased to accept your invitation."

"Garnet, would you take tea with us?" Her father turned a ruddy face toward her.

Suspicious of the olive branch her father had extended, Garnet declined. "I think I'll go upstairs. I'm a trifle weary." She held out a hand first to Rafe, then to Cole. "Thank you both for a delightful afternoon. I can't remember when I've enjoyed myself so much."

Cole squeezed her fingers, while his expression conveyed sympathy. "The pleasure was ours. Thank you for gracing us with your company."

In spite of her sudden exhaustion, she managed to

smile at him before she reclaimed her hand. With a tilt of her chin, she glanced at her father. "I'll take dinner on a tray in my room. Don't wait for me."

She pivoted toward the door. She felt the men's stares burning into her back until she stepped into the mezzanine and shut the paneled salon door behind her.

Upstairs, she reached the haven of the suite she shared with her father. She desired only privacy and the opportunity to regain her composure. She leaned against the door and closed her eyes, mourning the sabotage of her delightful outing. The scene in the Grand Salon had tarnished the afternoon's pleasure.

Her father hadn't wanted to offend the Wild Wind brothers before any contract had been signed, so he'd tempered his anger and attempted to smooth over his lapse. Otherwise, he might have taken Albert's side. The time spent with Cole, whose own sterling character exposed Albert's deficiencies, strengthened her resolve to never marry her father's business partner.

Daisy's cheerful voice intruded on Garnet's musings. "Miss Garnet, didn't we have a most splendid afternoon?"

Garnet opened her eyes to see Daisy standing in the bedroom doorway. She made an effort to match her maid's sunny mood. "Yes, we certainly had a splendid afternoon."

As she skipped into the suite's living room, Daisy's high spirits bubbled over. "That Rafe Wild Wind sure is something. He was so kind to me all afternoon when I know he didn't have to be." She halted in the middle of the room and clasped her hands. "He treated me like a real lady, though I know he didn't mean anything by it."

Garnet pushed off the door toward her maid, thankful

Rafe's courteous manners hadn't raised any false hopes in Daisy's impressionable bosom. "Rafe is a true gentleman. It didn't matter to him that you're my maid."

Daisy's lips puffed out in a sigh. "I know Mr. Rafe was only being kind, but he gave me a taste of how a lady is treated. I'll never forget this afternoon."

"Neither will I." Garnet patted Daisy's shoulder. "Now, I'd like to change into something comfortable."

After Daisy had assisted Garnet out of her dress and into an apricot silk nightgown and matching robe, Garnet gripped her maid's hand. "Daisy, I intend to be on that train tomorrow morning. I'm going to the mining camp. Can you help me?"

Daisy jerked back. Alarm pinched her features. "Miss Garnet, you heard what Mr. Cole said this afternoon. It's dangerous, and what about your father? He'll be furious."

"I'm sure Cole and Rafe can keep me safe. Besides, there are other women at the camp. If they live there, it must be safe enough. I don't mind the discomfort."

"Those other women aren't society ladies."

"What does that have to do with anything? I can handle whatever they can."

Daisy looked dubious. "You've only known luxury, not hardship. How do you know you can abide the living conditions? It sounded awful to me."

Garnet huffed. "I've made up my mind. Will you help me get ready? I'm not sure what I'll need."

"You'll still have to face your father. He'll have apoplexy when he sees you. I don't want to be there when he does." Daisy tapped her toe and folded her arms. "I'll stay here.

I'm sure I can find work cleaning rooms in the Grand Palace."

"Very well, stay here. But I'm going, with or without your help. I want to be useful at the camp."

Daisy sighed, and she turned toward the wardrobe. "I'll see what clothes you have that you can wear in a mining camp. And you can borrow my valise instead of taking your luggage. Wear my hat. Your father might not recognize you in my hat."

When the girls had packed Daisy's cheap valise with Garnet's things, Garnet dismissed her maid and curled up in a chair in one corner of her room. With her elbow resting on the chair's arm and her chin propped in her hand, she laid her plans. One way or another, she intended to be on the Western & Mountain train when it left Denver in the morning.

Chapter 8

Garnet paid the taxi driver his fare and turned into the railway station's shadowy interior. Would she encounter her father or Albert before she boarded the train? She tugged the brim of Daisy's plain straw hat lower over her bright hair and pulled the collar of her serviceable brown coat up around her ears. Perhaps if her father saw her now, he wouldn't recognize her.

With Daisy's worn valise in one hand, she trudged toward the ticket office on the righthand wall.

This morning she'd donned a utilitarian black skirt and a white cotton blouse, one of the few serviceable outfits she possessed. Daisy had packed her more durable clothing in the borrowed valise, but Garnet suspected her wardrobe would be inadequate for camp life.

Garnet hunched her shoulders and kept her head down as she plowed through the crowds. People either arriving or having just disembarked blocked her path. At the ticket window she addressed the agent, a thin middle-aged man whose moustache reminded her of a walrus. "How much is a ticket to Indian Pass?"

"That will be twenty-five cents, unless you're traveling first class." With a bony forefinger, the agent pushed up his wire-rimmed spectacles.

"No, coach will be fine." Garnet fumbled in her reticule for the coins and shoved the cash across the counter. "That's the Western and Mountain railway?"

"Yup. Ain't another train goin' up that way 'til next week." The agent scooped her fare off the counter and dropped the money into a tin cash box. He pulled a green ticket off the roll and pushed it toward her.

"Here you go, miss." He peered at her through his spectacles. "You ain't goin' up there by yourself, are you?" He looked over her shoulder as if searching for a companion. "Where's your husband?"

"I don't have a husband."

Concern puckered his forehead, and he ran a palm over his balding pate. "It's none of my business, but Indian Pass is no place for a lady. The town is full of miners and riffraff."

Garnet tried to appreciate his concern when all she wanted was a place to hide until she could board the train. "I won't be alone. My father is meeting me there." And what a reunion that would be when her father discovered she hadn't followed his instructions and stayed behind with Daisy. Last night's scene in the Grand Salon would seem tame by comparison.

Relief crossed the ticket agent's face. "Well, now, I'm glad to hear it. You stick close to your daddy while you're at Indian Pass, and you'll be all right."

Garnet thanked him and turned away, tucking her precious ticket into her reticule. Her safety didn't concern her. The Wild Wind brothers' patronage would be enough to protect her in the rough mining town.

The dim railway depot echoed with the clang and rumble of steam engines idling on the tracks and freight being loaded into baggage cars. The blended voices of passengers scurrying along the platform provided a muted counterpoint to the din. She kept her head down while she wandered along the platform in search of the train that would take her to Indian Pass. When she found the Western & Mountain locomotive and its coaches, she hid behind a nearby pillar to wait until boarding time. According to the schedule she'd seen in the ticket office, the train would depart in an hour.

She dropped the valise at her feet and peered around the pillar. A group of men near one of the baggage cars caught her eye. *Cole and Rafe Wild Wind.* Her father and Albert.

The Wild Wind brothers supervised the loading of their supplies onto the train from the bed of a mule-drawn wagon. Today, they wore denim jeans and cotton shirts, cowboy boots and hats. Garnet drank in the sight of Cole as he directed the unloading of wooden crates and canvas-wrapped bundles. He seemed as comfortable in his workman's wear as he had in the suits he'd worn every other time she'd seen him.

She turned her attention to her father. Asa Morrison stood with his head thrown back, a cigar clamped between his teeth and his hands braced on his hips. His elbows jutted. He'd pushed back the jacket of his sack suit, so the fabric billowed behind him. Her father's sharp brain must be analyzing the Wild Wind brothers and trying to find a way to manipulate them to his advantage.

Albert stood a little distance away, a bored expression on his face. His dapper suit and black top hat seemed more appropriate for New York city than for a rough mining town. Two trunks and a couple of leather valises rested at his feet. Didn't he realize how ridiculous he'd appear in the mining camp wearing his New York suits and his kid leather shoes? Maybe he'd fall into a mud puddle. A little dirt might humble him.

When the call came to board, Garnet took care to avoid the first-class carriage. With her head down and her shoulders hunched, she picked up her satchel and joined a group of working-class people headed for the passenger coach. The scene her father would enact should he find her made her mouth dry. Her heart pounded.

At last, she reached the coach. The porter tore her ticket in half and assisted her up the steps.

Inside, she hurried down the aisle and dropped into an empty seat near the middle of the car. She tucked her satchel beneath her and scanned her surroundings. She'd never traveled in the working man's world. Here, no private compartments afforded luxury. No roomy velvet chairs or tasseled curtains lent a genteel air. Worn, brown leather covered the straight-backed seats. Scuffed wooden floors showed the wear of countless feet, and grime stained the windows.

As Garnet watched her fellow passengers settle themselves, she envied their simple lives. *I could be happy, living like this.* If her father actually cut her off when she refused to marry Albert, she could be happy without money. Being without her father's wealth might be liberating.

A tall young man with a shock of sandy hair stopped beside her. He motioned to the empty seat on her other side near the window. "Is that seat taken?"

Garnet shook her head. "No, it's not."

"Do you mind if I join you?"

Garnet had hoped to avoid sitting near a window, but since allowing the young man to crawl over her to the window seat would be awkward, she chose to sit beside the window herself. "I can move over." She shoved her satchel to the space beneath the window seat and then scooted across. "There. You can have the aisle seat."

The young man dropped his lanky length into the seat she'd just vacated and grinned at her. He held out a calloused hand. "Gilbert Adams is the name."

She returned his smile and placed her hand in his. "Garnet Morrison." When he freed her hand, she tugged down her hat brim on the side facing the window. Perhaps the brim would shield her face.

"Why are you headed to Indian Pass?" Gilbert tipped his head to one side. His blue eyes assessed her. "You don't look like a laundress. Or a store clerk. Are you married to one of the miners?"

"No, I'm not married."

Gilbert studied her for another moment. "So, you're not meetin' a husband." Worn jeans clad his long legs, and the sleeves of his blue cotton shirt had been rolled up to display sinewy forearms.

"No." Garnet weighed her words, careful not to reveal too much about herself. "I'm meeting my father."

"Does your father work in the mine?"

She hesitated. "Nooo... but he has business at the mine."

"And he let you travel by yourself?"

"He doesn't know I'm coming. I want to surprise him." A hard knot settled in her stomach. *Surprised* couldn't describe how her father would react when she appeared in Indian Pass. He'd be furious. She stiffened her spine. He'd just have to accept her presence. She refused to remain cooling her heels in Denver when she wanted to be useful. The mining camp should offer her many ways to help.

Gilbert's appreciative gaze traveled over her face. "You'll be a delightful surprise."

"I'm not sure about that, but I'll definitely be a surprise."

The train whistle shrieked, and the car jerked. Couplings clanged. Steam billowed from beneath the engine and engulfed everything nearby. The whistle screamed again, and the train gathered speed. The station's gloom gave way to sunny prairie. Garnet relaxed against the seat and smiled to herself. She'd left Denver undetected.

She turned toward the window and stared at the unfamiliar terrain as the train left the plains around Denver. The locomotive chugged into the foothills and wound between the upthrust ochre hillocks. Pale green shrubs clung to the bluffs. Above arched the clear blue Colorado sky. The scenery, so alien from New York, captivated her.

"Where are you from?" Gilbert captured her attention again. "You're not from around here."

Garnet glanced at her companion. What should she do with him? In her world, society ladies never dealt with inquisitive young men to whom they hadn't been properly introduced and who asked curious questions. Perhaps she should have brought Daisy along. Daisy's presence would have discouraged Gilbert's inquisitiveness.

Garnet parried his question with one of her own. "What makes you say that?"

Gilbert squinted at her. His glance roamed over her face, her hair, her clothing. "The way you talk. The tilt of your head. And somethin' about you isn't quite right…"

Garnet decided not to be offended by his frankness. "I hail from New York city."

"An Easterner. I thought so."

"And what about you? Why are you going to Indian Pass?"

Gilbert settled in his seat and stretched his long legs into the aisle. "I'm hopin' for a job at the Wild Wind mine. I hear they're hirin'."

At the mention of the Wild Wind mine, Garnet perked up. "Why the Wild Wind mine? Aren't there other mines that are hiring?"

Gilbert's toffee-colored eyes gleamed. "The owners have a reputation for treatin' their workers fairly and payin' them well. I've never heard of a disgruntled miner quittin'. That's good enough for me."

When her rumbling stomach alerted her to the noon hour's approach, Garnet dug into the borrowed satchel for the lunch the Palace Hotel's cook had prepared. She pulled out thick chicken sandwiches made with fluffy white bread baked in the hotel's kitchen, deviled eggs, and apple cobbler redolent with cinnamon and brown sugar. A carafe of iced tea completed the feast.

When Gilbert saw the snowy linen napkins and the crested silverware that accompanied the food, he threw a suspicious look at Garnet. "You didn't buy that meal on a workin' woman's wages. Who are you, really?"

She stared at him, struck mute. Should she tell him who she was? She had no inkling of whether or not he was an honest man. Apprehension shivered down her spine.

He grabbed her hand and turned it, palm up, for his inspection. He glanced up at her, his eyes accusing. "You have a lady's hands. I'll wager you've never worked a day in your life." He laid her hand in her lap and waggled his fingers at her clothing. "Your clothes may be plain, but the fabric cost more than a workin' girl can afford."

Garnet thought it prudent to tell him at least part of the truth. "My father is a New York banker. He has business with the mine owners. And I told you the truth—I'm meeting him in Indian Pass. He doesn't know I'm coming."

Gilbert held her stare for several moments. "Is that why you aren't ridin' in the Pullman car?"

Garnet sighed. Smitten with guilt, she couldn't hold his gaze. She looked down at the paper-wrapped sandwich in her lap, then forced her attention back to her companion. "My father is riding in the Pullman compartment. I don't want him to see me until we get to Indian Pass."

Gilbert narrowed his eyes. "I see. Now I understand what you're doin' ridin' coach and tryin' to pass yourself off as a regular gal. You're afraid you'll be recognized. Your father wanted you to stay in Denver, didn't he?"

Garnet nodded.

He grinned. "I hope you don't mind if I hang around when we get to Indian Pass. I want to watch the fireworks when your father finds out you're on this train. It shapes up to be mighty entertainin'."

Chapter 9

Garnet stared at Gilbert. He might call her upcoming encounter with her father entertaining, but to her, it would be tumultuous. The scene might entertain half the inhabitants of Indian Pass. When her father's temper got the best of him, he didn't care what kind of exhibition he created.

Not sure of what to say, she thrust out the paper-wrapped sandwich she held. "Here. Have this. The hotel packed more food than I can eat."

Gilbert took the sandwich without demur. He tore away the wrapping and bit into it with gusto.

Garnet shared the rest of her lunch. When she'd packed away the remains, she stared out the window. Each clacking revolution of the wheels took her closer to Indian Pass. Determination stiffened her spine. She wouldn't be a meek mouse and return to Denver, even if her father wanted her to.

By the middle of the afternoon, the Western sun had

turned the coach into a stifling oven. Garnet wrinkled her nose at the odor of sweating bodies. Fretful babies wailed. Children quarreled. Two men in the seat behind her argued. She fanned herself with a folded piece of paper, but the fan only wafted torrid air in her face and did nothing to cool her. First-class travel hadn't seemed so hot when they'd crossed the plains. It had smelled better, too.

Gilbert motioned toward the window. "I'll open that for you if you want."

Garnet perked up. "Would you? Some fresh air would be delightful."

Gilbert stood and leaned over her, then flipped the window latch. With his fingers beneath the ledge, he shoved upward. The window creaked open with a protesting groan.

Fresh air poured in, and Gilbert sat back down.

Garnet drank in the clear mountain air and luxuriated in the draft until the engine belched black smoke. A dark cloud rolled backward, engulfing the passenger cars that trailed behind the engine. Acrid coal smoke swirled into the coach and rained grit all over her. Garnet's eyes stung, and the smoke's thick scent coated her mouth. A live spark landed on her knee. The cinder simmered on her skirt, burning a hole through the fabric. Garnet yelped and swiped the spark onto the floor.

Gilbert stomped it out with his boot. "I think I'd better close that window."

"Probably you should."

Gilbert leaned over her again as he slammed the window shut.

Garnet sighed when stuffy air once again enveloped

her, but she didn't want cinders all over her person. She brushed grit from her clothing and shook ashes from Daisy's hat. When she'd cleaned herself as best as she could, she settled down to endure the rest of the trip.

Her back ached, and her posterior grew numb. She squirmed, hoping to find a more tolerable position.

Gilbert cocked his head at her. "Are you findin' coach seating less comfortable than Pullman?"

Garnet lifted her chin and gave him an imperious glare, about to deny her discomfort, when the amused gleam in his eyes made her abandon her pretense. "Yes, these seats are most uncomfortable. I never knew what people who traveled by coach have to endure."

"I take it this trip has been enlightenin'."

"You could say that. I've never traveled by coach before."

"You haven't missed much." Gilbert grinned.

A thin, work-worn woman with three children sat across the aisle. A toddler perched on her lap and leaned against her bosom. The little boy's bony ankles hung from beneath his too-short trousers, and patches decorated his shirt. The other children, two little girls of about three and five, wore clean but threadbare dresses.

The little boy whimpered. The girls sat in quiet lethargy and stared at the world with hopeless eyes. Garnet's heart went out to the family.

Even with Gilbert helping her eat lunch, they hadn't consumed all the food the Palace cook had provided. Garnet dragged her satchel from beneath her seat and rummaged inside. When she'd extracted the leftovers, she gathered up the food and turned to Gilbert. "Please excuse me. I'd like to get out."

He obliged with grave courtesy and rose, moving into the aisle.

Garnet stepped past him and knelt beside the drooping mother. "Ma'am."

The woman turned faded blue eyes to her.

"If you don't mind, I have some leftovers from my lunch. I'd be pleased to give them to you and your children."

The woman's expression didn't change. She appeared not to have heard Garnet's offer. At last, she shook her head. "Thank ye kindly, lady, but I cain't take charity from a stranger."

"I don't mean for this to be charity. Your children are hungry, and I have more food than I can eat. If your children don't eat it, I'll throw it away when we get to Indian Pass. You wouldn't want all that food to go to waste, would you?"

The woman flicked a glance at Gilbert. "Your man don't want it?"

Garnet hid a smile and exchanged an amused look with Gilbert. "No, he's eaten his fill. All of this is left over."

The woman stared at the wrapped sandwiches and the eggs. The cobbler tempted with its cinnamon scent. The children fastened wistful gazes on the food. The toddler stopped whimpering.

Garnet laid the parcels on the seat between the little girls. "Please. I'll be very disappointed if the food should go to waste."

The mother looked up at Garnet. Gratitude filled her faded eyes. "Thank ye, lady. I'm ever so grateful."

Garnet squeezed the woman's bony shoulder and stood. She returned to her seat, and Gilbert dropped down beside her.

He leaned close to murmur in her ear. "'Your man' thinks you have a very kind heart."

By the time the train came to a shuddering, squealing halt in Indian Pass, the sun had dipped behind the granite-faced mountain peaks. Shadows stretched across the valley and painted the slopes with a monotone palette.

"Well, Miss Morrison, do you want me to stand as your champion when you meet your father?"

Gilbert's amused voice tore Garnet's attention from the view. She turned away from the window and met her companion's droll stare. The only thing guaranteed to make the upcoming scene more explosive would be for Gilbert to accompany her when she met her father. One glance at her in a strange man's company would turn her father apoplectic.

She shuddered. "Thank you for your offer, but your presence wouldn't help."

"Well, then, if I can't offer you protection, I'll take my leave. Thank you for the pleasure of your company and for sharin' your lunch with a starvin' man." With a wide grin curling his generous mouth, Gilbert rose and stepped into the aisle. He tipped his cowboy hat at her before he joined the other passengers shuffling toward the exit.

Garnet waited until the coach had emptied before she reached for Daisy's valise. With the handle in a tight grip, she squared her shoulders. As she stepped down the aisle toward the exit, she gathered her courage and tried not to dwell on the imminent encounter with her father.

She halted on the dusty street and gave her surroundings a curious perusal. Beyond the rolling valley where the town huddled, majestic granite peaks jabbed their sharp edges into the sky. Dark green pine, fir, and spruce trees clung to the mountains' upper reaches, while aspen dotted the lower slopes. Garnet sucked in a deep breath. Clear air spiced with resin wafted to her on the evening breeze and filled her lungs. In that moment, she fell in love with the Rockies.

A huddle of wooden buildings straggling along the railway comprised Indian Pass. Garnet didn't catch sight of either her father or Albert, so they must have already gone to whatever passed for a hotel.

She heard voices from the baggage cars at the rear of the train. Garnet turned toward the sound. Two buckboards drawn by teams of mules had been backed toward the baggage car. One was half full of crates, while the other one waited to be loaded. The Wild Wind brothers stood in the wagon's bed directing the unloading of their supplies onto the buckboard.

Relief greater than she should feel at the sight of Cole Wild Wind overcame her. She didn't question why his presence filled her with such comfort, but if Cole stood beside her, she could face her father. Her feet moved of their own accord and took her toward the buckboard. When she halted beside the vehicle, she tipped back her head to watch Cole help unload a crate.

Garnet stood there for several moments before anyone noticed her. Rafe saw her first. He caught his brother's arm when Cole passed by and nodded toward her. Cole flicked a glance in her direction. Although his expression didn't change, he froze.

Their gazes locked. Neither moved. At last, Cole broke the force holding them in thrall when he stepped around a wooden box. With one hand braced on the buckboard's side, he vaulted over the edge to land with a graceful thud before her. With narrowed his eyes, he ran a contemplative gaze over her. He hooked his thumbs in his belt, elbows akimbo.

"I almost didn't recognize you in that get-up." His voice didn't accuse or condemn, merely betrayed modest curiosity. "I assume you rode up here in the coach so your father wouldn't see you."

Unable to speak, she nodded.

"I can't say I'm surprised to see you here."

Garnet gulped. Cole didn't seem overjoyed to see her. Perhaps he wouldn't help her. She must have expected more of his chivalry than he was prepared to give. "I just couldn't stay in Denver. I want to see your mine. And I want to help. Surely, you can find something for me to do at your camp."

Seconds ticked past while his stare bored into her. "Your father won't like it."

She tried to smile, but her lips trembled. "That's an understatement. He'll be furious."

Cole didn't smile back.

"I promise not to bother you or get in the way. You'll never know I'm around."

He sighed and swept off his hat, ruffling his curly hair with his other hand. Settling his hat on his head and tipping down the brim, he gave her a pained look. "Garnet, there's no way I won't 'not know' you're around. Just your presence will be enough to distract me when I need to be focused."

Her name on his lips sounded like music. His confession made her heart thump, but she hung her head. "I'm sorry. I didn't intend to be a bother."

A large male hand beneath her chin lifted her head. "It's not your fault. You can't help how you affect me."

Their gazes collided, one blue and the other dark. Unspoken messages simmered between them. Garnet couldn't breathe. At last, one side of Cole's mouth curved up, the first smile he'd given her since she'd appeared.

His thumb stroked across her cheek. "What's this? Have you been playing in the cinders?"

"What?"

He touched her cheek again. "Here. You have soot on your face."

Mortified, Garnet swiped at her cheek with one gloved hand. "I must have gotten that when we opened the window."

Cole chuckled. "One never opens a train window." He gripped her upper arm. "Come along. You need to clean up before you meet your father." He pivoted and called to his brother. "Rafe, take over here. I'll be back later."

With Garnet trotting at his side, his long strides took them around the back of the train to a livery stable at the edge of town. At one side of the open double doors stood a water trough. They halted before the metal tank.

Cole dropped his hand from her arm and reached up to loosen the knot that fastened his red cotton bandana about his neck. When the neckerchief slid free, he folded it in half and dipped a corner in the trough. "Stand still." With his fingers clamped about her chin, he dabbed at the soot on her cheek.

While he scrubbed, Garnet took one glance at his intent face, then lowered her lashes. She couldn't look at him. With his head bent close to hers and his hands on her face, watching him seemed too intimate. After several strokes, he took a final swipe at her cheek. He stepped back and stuffed the neckerchief into his jeans back pocket.

"There. Now you don't look like a chimney sweep." He narrowed his eyes, perusing her with a critical gaze. "You'd better do something about your hair, though."

Garnet patted her coiffure, feeling for any stray strands. "What's the matter with my hair?"

"You look a bit windblown. And you're covered with soot."

Cole was right—she couldn't meet her father looking like a street urchin. She pulled out the pins and swept the hat from her head.

Cole snatched the headgear from her. "Here, I'll take care of your hat. You do something with your hair."

While Cole slapped at her borrowed hat, Garnet leaned forward and shook cinders from her pompadour. When she couldn't feel any more ash, she straightened. Her gaze fell on Cole.

He was turning her hat over and over, a speculative gleam in his eyes. He tossed her a glance. "This doesn't look like anything you'd wear."

"It isn't mine. I borrowed it from Daisy."

He perused her form again. "And your outfit? It can't be Daisy's. You're taller than she is."

"It's mine, but these are the clothes I wear when I go into the poor neighborhoods at home to help the children."

A beat of silence passed while he stared at her. "You go into the New York city slums to help the children?"

Garnet nodded. "So many children are starving. They suffer from illness and malnutrition. I do what I can to help."

"Does your father know?"

"He does, but as long as I take a man servant with me, he turns a blind eye. He doesn't like it, though. He'd prefer that I do my charitable work from a genteel distance, such as serving on a committee to raise money for the poor."

Cole shook his head at her. "You're full of surprises, but I have to admit, you've got grit."

"Thank you." Garnet struggled with her hair. Several coppery strands had blown free. She pulled out some of the hairpins and tried to refasten the loosened tresses.

Cole wrapped long fingers about her hand and tugged. "Here, let me. You don't have a mirror." He took the hairpins from her and stepped closer.

Though a quiver ran through her at his nearness, Garnet stood motionless. She felt his body heat. Her shoulder almost brushed his chest. His hands on her tresses were reverent while his fingers worked the loosened strands back into her pompadour and inserted the hairpins. Though she'd known him for only three days, the familiarity between them seemed comfortable.

He inserted the last pin and stepped away. "There. If you put your hat back on, you should be presentable."

She settled the borrowed hat on her head and secured it with the pins.

Cole gave her a final inspection and nodded. "Now, are you ready to meet your father?"

Chapter 10

With the moment of reckoning at hand, Garnet's knees wobbled, but she refused to give in to her fear. She tipped up her chin and stiffened her spine. "Yes, I'm ready. I guess I'd better get it over with."

Cole grinned down at her. "The worst he can do is to send you back to Denver."

"You don't know my father. He can make me wish I'd never been born."

"With me at your side, I doubt he'll do anything of the sort."

She flashed him a hopeful smile. "You'll stay with me?"

"As long as possible." He looked her over once more and nodded at the satchel by her feet. "What did you pack?"

"A couple of skirts and blouses just like the ones I'm wearing."

"Did you bring a jacket?"

Garnet frowned. "No, I didn't think to pack a jacket."

"In the event that your father allows you to stay, you'll need a warm jacket. Mountain nights are cold. And you'll need wool socks and more serviceable shoes than the ones you have on now. You'll also need to purchase a split riding skirt. What you're wearing won't survive four days on horseback."

She glanced down at her black skirt. He was right. She'd given no thought to what she'd need beyond a few skirts and blouses. Her shoulders slumped. "We haven't even left, and I'm already a burden to you." She sighed.

He shook his head. "You could never be a burden to me." Once again, something Garnet couldn't define flashed between them. "Now, don't poker up and get all missish on me, but you'll need to buy yourself a couple of thick flannel nightgowns."

Garnet caught her breath. For a gentleman to whom she wasn't married to mention sleepwear was a scandalous breach of etiquette. No man had ever mentioned such a personal item of clothing to her in her entire life. She flashed him an imperious look, about to launch into a severe set down.

He held up one hand, palm out, and slitted his eyes at her. "This isn't New York, Garnet. This is the West, and the wild Colorado mountains. We don't hold to such prudish notions as Easterners. If you're going to stay at the mining camp, it's my responsibility to see you're properly outfitted. You're such a tenderfoot, you don't know what you need. So, spare me the lecture about propriety, and let's find your father."

Before she could admit he was right, he snagged the valise with one hand and gripped her elbow with the other.

Then he steered her toward the row of wooden buildings that straggled along the street.

While they'd stood outside the livery, twilight had crept down the mountains and stolen through Indian Pass. Shadows painted the town and drained the buildings of color. Yellow lamplight spilled from the windows onto the boardwalk. A night bird called from the woods behind the livery, and crisp air with a bite teased Garnet's nose. She shivered in her long-sleeved blouse.

They passed a saloon with batwing doors. Garnet peeked over the tops as they passed. A press of humanity filled the room. A row of men garbed in jeans and wool shirts lined the bar at the opposite wall. A scandalous picture of a scantily clothed female hung on the wall beyond the bar. The tinny notes of a honky-tonk piano blared. The music, mingled with men's rough voices and women's shrill laughter, rolled outward. Liquor fumes, cigarette smoke, and the pungent scent of unwashed bodies hit her in the face.

Heat rose from her neck all the way to her hairline, and Garnet grimaced.

Cole chuckled. "Welcome to Indian Pass. You've just walked past the most popular building in town."

She expelled a breath. "Phew! It's worse than anything I could have imagined."

"A western saloon doesn't offer the kind of entertainment that you're used to."

A mercantile store rubbed shoulders with the saloon. Its blank windows stared into the street. They strolled past without speaking. Cole's bootheels rang on the boardwalk. The sound, solid and masculine, reassured Garnet. Cole had promised to stand by her, to shelter her through the coming storm. He'd be a bulwark against her father's anger.

The next building, a low, wooden structure that lacked paint, boasted two empty rocking chairs on either side of the door. A sagging porch roof cast dubious shelter over the rockers. Through curtainless windows, lamplight scattered onto the boardwalk. A faded sign beside the door identified the building as "Brown's Eatery."

Cole's hand tightened on her elbow. He tugged her to a stop and peered into her face. "Are you a praying woman, Garnet?"

The question pierced her. She met his questioning gaze. "I used to be, although I must admit that I haven't prayed in a long time. After my mother died, I had no one to encourage me to pray, so I got out of the habit."

"You might want to try it now."

Garnet peered past his shoulder at the eatery. "Is my father in there?"

"He and Albert are probably just finishing supper."

She took a deep breath, unsure of what to say.

"Would you like me to pray with you?"

Cole's offer took her by surprise. Her gaze flashed to his face. His mouth made a straight slash, though his eyes were gentle. Garnet surprised herself when she nodded.

With his head bowed, Cole launched into speech. After a startled moment, she closed her eyes.

Cole prayed as if his heavenly Father stood beside them. He asked for courage and grace for Garnet, for her father to be reasonable, and for wisdom.

When he finished, Garnet peeked up at him. "Thank you, Cole."

He smiled down at her and clasped her shoulder with a gentle hand. "Now, are you ready?"

"Not really, but I don't have a choice, do I?"

"I don't suppose you do."

She lifted her chin. "Let's meet my father."

With his free hand riding the small of her back, Cole urged her toward the door. He reached around her and swung the portal wide. They stepped over the threshold, and he closed the door behind them. Garnet stood rooted to the floor, though Cole's solid presence at her shoulder loomed in reassurance.

She darted a glance about the dining room. Several patrons, mostly men and a few women, sat at round tables covered with yellow oilcloth. Savory scents drifted from the kitchen at the back. Her stomach rumbled.

The low hum of conversation died. A lifetime of training buttressed Garnet against the scrutiny, when instead, she wished to hide behind Cole.

Gilbert sat at a table nearby. He tossed her a brief smile, but she didn't have a chance to respond before a man seated at a table on her left shot to his feet.

The man's chair scraped backward along the wooden floor, a man with a bull-like neck and a barrel chest. Her father. "Garnet! What are you doing here?" His bellow filled the room.

A heavy silence settled over the room. No one moved.

Garnet's stare locked with her father's. Anger mottled his face, and his walrus moustache quivered. Cole's hand touched her back again, and his strength flowed into her.

"I wanted to go with you to the mine." Somehow, she kept her voice steady, though her knees shook.

"I told you to stay in Denver."

"You did, but…"

Her father leaned forward and braced both hands on the table. "'But' has nothing to do with it." His chin jutted.

"I just couldn't stay in Denver with nothing to do. I want to be useful."

From his seat at the end of the table, Albert glared, but he didn't interrupt.

"A mining camp is no place for your social work. You should have stayed in Denver." He slapped both hands on the tablecloth, and his coffee cup rattled. "How did I get saddled with such an impertinent daughter?"

In spite of herself, Garnet jumped.

Once again, Cole's hand in the small of her back urged her forward. They approached the table where her father and Albert sat. Albert rose and swung his glare to Cole.

"I should send you back to Denver when the train leaves in the morning." Her father breathed heavily through his nose.

"Sir, if you don't mind me interrupting, I don't think you should send her back." Cole's low voice soothed. His tone brought order to the scene and made the point that every face in the room was turned their way.

Asa Morrison took the point. After a cold glance at the eavesdroppers, he returned his attention to Cole and lowered his voice. "Why not? She got herself here. She can get herself back."

"I could use her help at the camp."

Asa Morrison raised his eyebrows. "How can she help?

She's a society miss. I can't see how you can have much use for a society miss at the mine."

With his booted feet planted wide, Cole pushed his brown cowboy hat farther back on his head and hung his thumbs from his back pocket. He didn't glance at Garnet. "There are several families with children at the camp. We have a small school there, and I just lost our teacher. She returned to Denver to care for her ailing father. Perhaps your daughter could fill in while I'm searching for a permanent replacement for Miss Danby."

Afraid to move, Garnet remained motionless. Cole remained true to his promise and stayed by her side. Having a champion who advocated for her was a novel experience. Despite her father's ire, a warm glow filled her.

Her father stared off into one corner of the room, as if deciding what to do. After a long moment's deliberation, he swung his attention to his daughter. "Do you think you can be a teacher, girl?"

Garnet nodded. "I'm sure I can. I enjoy children."

Her father grunted and replied in a gruff voice. "Very well. You can go with us. But stay out of our way."

Relief made Garnet's knees weak, but she resisted the impulse to sit down. She remained ramrod straight. "Thank you, sir."

Her father pinned her with a wintry stare. "And what have you done with Daisy? She's not lurking about on the boardwalk, is she?"

"Daisy didn't want to come with me. She's signed on to be a temporary housemaid at the Grande Palace."

"At least I won't be paying her wages to sit in a hotel room." He stabbed his fork at her. "Have you eaten?"

She shook her head.

He motioned toward a chair. "Sit. I'll have the waitress bring you something to eat."

Cole pulled out the chair for her, and she lowered herself into it. For the first time since they'd entered the eatery, she realized her hands trembled.

Asa Morrison indicated the last empty place at the table. "Sit yourself down, Mr. Wild Wind, and join us."

Cole shook his head. "Thank you for the offer, but I left Rafe supervising the loading of our supplies onto the wagons. I need to get back and help finish up."

Her father narrowed his eyes at Garnet, then swung his gaze up to Cole. "Is there an extra room in that shack that passes for a hotel that we could rent for my daughter?"

"I'm afraid not. When the train comes in, the hotel fills up."

Asa turned to Albert. "Well, Albert. Here's your opportunity to demonstrate what a gentleman you are and offer your room to your intended wife."

Albert reared back in his seat as though the older man had suggested he rob a bank. "Where would I sleep? It's bad enough that I have to sleep in a bed that hasn't had the sheets changed since the last patron. Garnet should have thought of that before she sneaked up here. I'm under no obligation to give up my bed for her."

Since Cole stood behind her right shoulder, she couldn't see his face, but his body's abrupt stillness radiated a dangerous displeasure she could feel without looking at him. If she should look at him, he'd be white about the mouth, and his lips would be clamped in a straight line.

"Never mind. Keep your room. We wouldn't want to inconvenience you." Cole's low tone held a cold timbre that carried more impact than if he'd shouted. He pulled a room key on a short chain from his shirt pocket and proffered it to Garnet. "Here. You're welcome to use Rafe's and my room. We'll bunk down in the livery."

Garnet twisted to look up at him. "I can't take your room."

His mouth tipped up in a lazy grin. "Sure you can. Rafe and I should sleep with the wagons, anyway. Someone needs to guard our supplies."

Their gazes tangled. Cole's hand still stretched toward her, the key dangling from his fingers.

Albert snatched at the key and flung it onto the table. The key bounced on the oilcloth surface with a dull clang. "Don't be coy, Garnet. Take the key. Since Mr. Wild Wind is so anxious to play Sir Galahad to your damsel in distress, don't deprive him of the opportunity."

Garnet ignored Albert. She kept her gaze on Cole. "Thank you so much for all your kindness. I do appreciate it."

Cole inclined his head. "The pleasure is mine. Good night. I'll see you in the morning. And don't forget what I told you."

"I won't."

With a terse nod toward her father and cutting Albert as though he weren't present, Cole spun and strode from the room. The door slammed shut behind him.

Garnet stared at the closed door, feeling bereft. When he left, Cole had taken a part of her with him.

Chapter 11

Garnet paused on the boardwalk outside the mercantile the next morning and peered at the street. Excitement shivered down her spine at the sight of two wagons loaded with the supplies Cole and Rafe had purchased. The mule teams hitched to the traces stood slack-hipped and drooping. Several men gathered about the wagons while saddled horses waited at the rear.

Those wagons symbolized her bid for freedom. Adventure awaited. On this cold, sunny morning, anything seemed possible.

The battered satchel dragged on her arm. She'd purchased two split riding skirts, two flannel nightgowns, several pairs of wool socks, sturdy shoes, and a long-sleeved, moss green wool dress decorated with white daisies. With Cole in mind, she bought the most feminine gown the mercantile offered. She'd caught Cole's eye, so why couldn't she catch his heart, as well?

She snuggled the collar of her new sheepskin jacket around her ears. Her breath puffed out in a white cloud.

When she stepped off the boardwalk, hoarfrost crunched beneath her feet. The hem of her new, black, split riding skirt swirled about her calves.

With the satchel dragging on her arm, Garnet approached the cavalcade. She brightened as Gilbert's face smiled at her beneath a black cowboy hat.

"Mornin', Miss Garnet. I see your father has agreed to let you go to the minin' camp."

Garnet paused beside him at the lead wagon's near front wheel. "Mr. Wild Wind was able to convince him to let me teach school at the camp."

Gilbert nodded and squinted off in the distance, then swung his gaze back to her. "Your meetin' with your father was even more entertainin' than I figured it would be. It was dicey there for a bit."

"Mr. Wild Wind seems to have a way with my father. If it weren't for him, I'd be back on the train to Denver." She crinkled her nose at him. "What are you doing here?"

"Mr. Wild Wind hired me to drive one of the teams. He promised I could work in the mine after we get there."

"Then we both got what we wished for."

Garnet's attention strayed to the rear of the cavalcade, where Cole and Rafe busied themselves checking harnesses, the load distribution in the buckboards, and consulting with the men clustered about the equipage.

"Are all those men going with us?" She gestured toward the wagon.

Gilbert tugged his cowboy hat lower over his brow, and his gaze followed her pointing finger. "Yep. Some have been hired to provide security, and others are going to work in the mine. We'll have a sizeable group. No one should bother us."

Garnet cast him a curious look. "Why would anyone bother us?"

"Competition among the mines is fierce. And we're carryin' much-needed supplies. A rival mine owner could hire men to attack us and steal the cargo, then sell it. At any mining camp in the mountains, that cargo is worth four times what the Wild Wind brothers paid for it in Denver."

Garnet hadn't considered such a possibility. Law and order hadn't yet come to the Rockies. As Cole had told her last night, she really was a tenderfoot. She had so much to learn.

She turned her attention to Cole and watched his interaction with his employees. The men accorded him a respect mingled with camaraderie.

Gilbert nudged her arm with his elbow and drew her focus back to him. She turned with a question in her eyes.

He grinned at her. "Methinks the handsome boss has caught your eye. You can't resist watching him."

Garnet bit her lip. "I'm sorry, Gilbert. I don't mean to be rude."

He shrugged. "No matter. I'm just a lowly mine worker. Mr. Wild Wind is the owner and a much better match for you."

"You make me sound like a snob."

Gilbert thrust both hands up, palms out. "Nope, that's not how I meant it. Just stating facts."

The jingle of spurs interrupted the moment, and Garnet

looked toward the sound to see Cole stride toward her. He came to a halt before her, while Gilbert eased away.

She eyed him up and down. Today, he looked like the Western men she'd seen painted on the penny postcards in dime stores back East. A bright blue bandana encircled his neck. A short sheepskin jacket encased him in its warmth. A six-shooter rode low on his hip, with a gun belt slung about his waist. He looked tough, and capable, and ready for anything.

His eyes crinkled with the slow smile that warmed his expression. "Good morning, Garnet. I trust you slept well."

His smile lit a flame that spread its glow through her whole body. "I did. Much better than you, I'm sure. I hope Rafe wasn't too annoyed that you gave away your room."

Cole shrugged. "Rafe's a good sport. He would have done the same." He looked her over. "You're dressed for Rocky Mountain weather."

Garnet glanced at her sheepskin jacket and then back to Cole. "I took your advice and made some purchases after breakfast."

"You'll be glad you did, though you'll shuck that jacket before lunch. Are you ready to go?"

"I think so." She cast him a shy look. "I don't want to slow you down."

"If you can't make the whole day on horseback, you can ride in one of the wagons." He bent to pick up her valise, grimacing at the extra weight. "This weighs a lot more than it did last night. You must have bought out the whole mercantile."

She grinned at him. "I only bought what you recommended."

"Huh. When does a woman ever buy only what she needs?" He softened his jibe with a grin. "Here, I'll stow your bag in this wagon." He tossed the valise into the bed of the buckboard. "I bought a horse for you to ride. Come along and meet her."

Garnet trailed beside Cole to the horses waiting at the cavalcade's rear. A trim little bay mare stood at the edge of the group. She lifted her head and perked her ears at their approach.

Cole snagged the reins and led the bay to Garnet. "Meet Comet. She's a sweetheart. She'll do anything you ask and will go all day."

Garnet stroked the mare's blaze. "Hey, girl. We're going to be partners."

Comet flicked an ear and nuzzled the front of Garnet's jacket.

"Why don't you mount up? I'll adjust the stirrups for you. We'll be ready to leave as soon as your father and Albert show up."

"If you're waiting on Albert, don't hold your breath. He usually doesn't make an appearance before noon."

"If he intends to go with us, he'd better show up. We can't wait until noon. We're already behind schedule." With a loose clasp on her elbow, Cole urged her around the mare's head and halted by the horse's shoulder. "Should I ask if you've ridden astride?"

"No worries. I was one of those bold New York misses who packed away her sidesaddle when I left finishing school. I know what to do with a man's saddle."

"I can't say I'm surprised. Doesn't your father object?"

"Sometimes it's easier for him to pretend I don't flaunt the rules. My very existence is a trial to him."

Cole cocked an eyebrow at her.

Garnet shook her head. "That's a story for another day."

With a look that told her he intended to hold her to her promise, Cole flipped the reins over Comet's head. "Let's get you mounted." He gripped her waist and tossed Garnet into the saddle as though she weighed no more than a thistledown.

Garnet toed for the stirrups.

He laid a hand on her mare's shoulder and tipped back his head to look into her face. "While we're traveling, keep Comet between the two wagons. That's the safest place for you. I don't want to worry about your safety when I have other things on my mind."

They exchanged another glance that continued the silent conversation running beneath their verbal exchange. With her gaze locked on his face, she nodded. "I'll remember."

He seemed about to speak again when her father's voice cut through the quiet morning. "We're here, Mr. Wild Wind. You can leave now."

Garnet stared at her father. A bulky coat and a scarf buffered him against the cold. Beside him, Albert appeared as a sulky boy. His mouth turned down, and he hung back behind the older man as if loathe to approach the horses. His tweed riding habit and shiny English riding boots appeared ridiculous in this rough Western town.

Cole stepped around her mount's head and strode toward her father. "We were about to pull out without you."

"Leave without me? I don't think so."

Cole halted a pace from Asa Morrison. Fisting his hands on his gun belt, he stared the shorter man down. "Let's get one thing straight. You may be an important man in New York city and can call the shots there, but this isn't New York. This is the Colorado Rockies, and while you're traveling with me, you'll do as I say. If you can't follow my commands, then you can get on the train and go back to Denver. I'll not endanger this whole company because you can't take orders."

Garnet's gaze darted to her father. No man she knew had ever talked to him in such a manner. Biting her lip, she waited for the explosion.

A charged silence hung over the company. Seconds ticked past. Cole stood his ground, staring down his nose at the Easterner as if it mattered not one whit to him whether her father stayed or left.

Asa Morrison set his jaw. "Do you realize to whom you're talking?"

Cole shrugged. "You're just a man."

"I'm a very influential man. I don't take orders from anyone."

Cole's stare didn't waver. "Out here, you take orders from me."

"I can ruin you."

"I doubt that. Smart men in the East know we're on the cusp of a uranium boom and would be happy to partner with me."

A squawking from a pine tree disturbed in the silence as the two men faced off. Tension hung heavy in the morning air.

At last, Asa Morrison backed down. "Very well. You have

a point."

Cole gave an abrupt nod. "Take care not to undermine my authority. If you do, I'll send you back to Denver so fast you'll wonder what hit you."

Garnet let out a breath. Cole had bested her father in as decisive a manner as she had ever seen. She glanced at her sire and shivered at his expression. Cole had better watch his back.

Cole stepped around the banker and strode to Albert and towered over him. "Every morning, you'll get out of your bedroll at the crack of dawn. Otherwise, we'll leave you beside the trail. You'll take responsibility for yourself and your gear. Don't wait around for someone to serve you breakfast, or you'll go hungry. After today, tack up your own horse."

Albert's face flamed, and he backed away from the irate Western male towering over him.

Cole pivoted and motioned to Rafe, who held the reins of two saddled horses. "Bring them their mounts."

Rafe strolled toward the two city men, his spurs jingling. He handed the reins of a stocky buckskin gelding to Asa Morrison. He led the other horse, a staid-looking sorrel mare, to Albert. "Tansy should be a good match for you."

Suspicion crossed Albert's face. "This horse is for me?"

"Unless you'd prefer to ride in one of the backboards." Rafe waited for Albert to take the reins.

Albert stood rooted to the muddy street and eyed Tansy as if she were a venomous viper.

"Would you rather ride in one of the wagons? It doesn't matter to me." Rafe's indifferent tone sounded bored.

Albert darted a glimpse at the men gathered about him. None seemed sympathetic. Their leathery faces showed no kindliness. As if realizing for the first time his wealth and social position made no impression here, Albert swallowed and approached the stocky mare with reluctant steps. He stared at the heavy stock saddle. "Is this saddle all you've got? I want a real saddle."

"This is a work saddle. Out West, our horses work. If you want an English saddle, you'll have to go back to Central Park. An English saddle is adequate for a ramble through the park." An arctic bite froze Rafe's voice.

Albert didn't have a comeback. He took the reins from Rafe and lifted one shiny leather boot to the stirrup. With a grunt, he hoisted himself aboard and gathered the reins.

Tansy stood with her head hanging and her ears drooping. She appeared to be half asleep. When Albert squeezed her sides with his heels, she swished her tail and shook her head, but she remained rooted to the road.

Albert's lips clamped in a tight line, and he glared at Rafe as he heeled Tansy again. Still, the mare wouldn't budge. She closed her eyes.

Sniggers sounded from the men as they turned away and swung into their own saddles.

Cole approached a long-legged, showy black gelding who was tethered to the back of the last wagon. The gelding swung his head at the man approaching him and laid back his ears in warning. Cole smacked the reins against the horse's neck. Grasping the leathers and the saddle horn in one hand, he vaulted aboard without using the stirrups. He had just thrust his boots into the stirrups when the gelding exploded beneath him.

The miners scrambled to safety.

The finest display of horsemanship she'd ever witnessed filled Garnet with admiration. Despite the gelding's fierce attempts to unseat its rider, Cole stayed planted in the saddle. The horse leaped skyward and spun, landing with a jolt. Its glossy hindquarters bunched and thrust with each buck. Cole swayed with the horse but didn't lose his balance. At last, the gelding gave a final half-hearted crow hop and stood with legs spread, head down in submission. Cole gathered the reins and gave the signal to begin.

The mule drovers scrambled into their wagons and cracked their whips. Cole and Rafe trotted to the column's head while the guards on their mounts surrounded the wagons. Garnet urged Comet forward and swung her into position between the two buckboards. She glanced back to where Albert and Tansy stood. When the horse appeared to be in danger of being left behind, the mare plodded forward. Garnet twisted to the front and patted Comet's neck, thankful she rode a sweet and willing mount. Albert would trail along at the column's end, since he couldn't rouse Tansy out of her amble.

With the jingle of trace chains and bits, the squeak of saddle leather, and the thud of hooves, the cavalcade lumbered forward. A thrill shivered down Garnet's spine as the mountains reached out to her. The oddest sensation that she stood on the threshold of a momentous life change filled her. The mountains, the mine, the West itself, would change her. Just how her life would change remained a mystery.

Chapter 12

By the time Cole called a halt for the evening, Garnet almost moaned. Every muscle ached. Pain stabbed through her lower back and down her thighs. Unwilling to let anyone see her pain, she straightened her spine when she drooped over the saddle horn. Just as she gritted her teeth and prepared to swing her leg over Comet's rump, Cole materialized at her side.

"Here, let me help you. You're done in."

Garnet shook her head. "No, I can manage. You have more important things to do."

Cole didn't bother to argue. He grasped her about the waist and hauled her from the saddle. When her feet touched the ground, her quivering legs collapsed beneath her. He tightened his hold and held her upright.

She clutched his shoulders and hung on. Her head slumped forward to rest against his chest. She drew in a deep breath. "Just give me a minute. I'll be fine."

He snorted. "I doubt that. When is the last time you spent eight hours on horseback?"

In spite of herself, she giggled. "Today."

"You could have ridden in the wagon, you know."

"I wanted to prove I could manage."

"Well, you proved it, but you shouldn't overdo it on your first day. If you hurt tomorrow morning as much as I think you will, you'll ride in one of the wagons."

Garnet lifted her head and stared into his face. His head bent close to hers. His dark eyes, narrowed with concern, warmed with something else that touched a cord deep within her.

"Come on," he muttered in a husky tone. "Let's find you a place to sit." He curved an arm about her shoulders and propped her against his long length.

She grabbed at his jacket front and managed to hobble to where the men set up camp.

He lowered her to the ground. "Sit here and rest."

Garnet sighed and closed her eyes. She couldn't move even if a grizzly bear charged from the trees.

"Don't pamper my daughter. She asked for this when she stowed away on the train."

Garnet's eyes popped open at her father's voice. Asa Morrison stood spraddle-legged in Cole's path. The two men faced off.

"Your daughter's welfare is my concern, as is every person in this outfit. I'll do what I see fit." Cole brushed past the older man on his way to check on the stock.

Garnet ducked her head and stared at the ground. For her father to be subordinate to a younger man must gall him. How would a business partnership between those two ever work?

Albert collapsed in a boneless heap beside her, looking

as though he ached every bit as much as she did. She'd expected him to complain all the way up the mountain, but he'd kept to himself and not spoken to anyone.

Garnet shivered and drew her jacket closer around her. They'd climbed farther into the mountains, and even at dusk, the air nipped at exposed skin. The trail had been steep and rugged. The mules had put their shoulders to the harness and dug in their heels while the wagons lumbered behind.

Aspen trees, with their straight, ghostly trunks, shivered amongst darker conifers. Shadows bloomed beneath the evergreens and cast murky darkness along the mountain's sides.

The men busied themselves laying a fire, and soon, a blaze warmed the camp. Orange sparks spiraled upward on a rush of heat and vanished among the fir branches. Garnet held out her hands to the flames and rubbed warmth into her fingers.

The men remained alert. Each one had a six-shooter strapped about his waist and a rifle close at hand. Gilbert's comment about the possibility of being robbed hadn't been idle talk.

The trail cook set to work stirring up a batch of drop biscuits and beans, their fare for the night. The scent of biscuits tantalized, and Garnet's stomach rumbled.

She crawled closer to the fire. "Those biscuits smell delicious. How do you make them without an oven?"

The cook grinned at her and pointed at the pan where the biscuits browned. "You see that iron skillet over there? You can cook anything in an iron skillet."

Garnet looked doubtful. "If you say so."

"By the time we get to camp, you'll be amazed at what I can cook up in that skillet and that there pot."

The men didn't need a second call to supper, though they insisted Garnet fill her tin plate first. Silence descended over the camp, broken only by the scrape of spoons on tinware. Garnet kept an eye out for Cole, though both he and Rafe didn't appear until halfway through the meal.

As Cole dished beans onto his plate, a scream rent the evening. Garnet shot to her feet and whirled toward the forest. Her tin plate clattered to the ground. The hairs on the back of her neck stood up, though nothing moved in the darkness.

Cole halted beside her, plate in hand.

"What was that?" Garnet's voice shook.

"Cougar."

She slanted a glance up at him. "Cougar? It sounded like a woman."

"Cougars can sound like a woman screaming."

"Is it close?"

"Close enough." He peered into the gloom.

"Are we in danger?"

He tipped his head at her and smiled. "No, we're safe as long as we don't venture out alone. Cougars aren't likely to attack a group of humans, especially with a fire handy. And we'll keep the fire going all night."

Garnet let out a breath. "That's a relief."

Supper over, the camp settled down for the night. Without complaint, Albert spread out his bedroll beside the fire. While she watched the men spread out their blankets, Garnet realized she'd forgotten to bring a bedroll. She'd have to make do with sleeping in her jacket and enveloped in her horse blanket.

Cole materialized beside her, his hands filled with blankets. "Here, you might need these." He thrust the bedding at her.

"How did you know that I'd forgotten to buy blankets this morning?"

He grinned, and his teeth flashed white through the darkness. "You're a tenderfoot, remember? You don't know what you need."

Garnet hugged the gray wool bedding against her chest. "I'm really out of my element here."

Cole cupped her elbow and turned her toward the first wagon. "Don't worry about it. You'll catch on."

"I hope so."

They halted beside the buckboard's back wheel. Cole turned to her. "I figure you'll be more comfortable sleeping in a wagon."

"I don't want special consideration. I can sleep on the ground if necessary."

He shook his head. "Not an option."

"Why not?"

"Rattlesnakes. They like to cozy up to a warm human body in a bedroll."

Garnet squeaked. "Rattlesnakes?"

"You should be fine in the wagon."

She nodded, speechless.

He touched her shoulder. "Don't be afraid. I'll post guards tonight. You'll be safe from both two-legged and four-legged varmints."

Garnet turned and put a booted foot onto a wheel

spoke, then dropped her foot to the ground. She faced Cole again. "Tell me something."

He nodded, solemn.

"Why do you do it? Ride that black devil that tried to kill you this morning."

Cole thumbed back his cowboy hat and rolled his shoulders. "Diablo bucks first thing every morning, but I like the challenge. And once he admits I'm boss, he's a joy to ride. He has such heart and spirit. He'd do anything I ask him."

"And you get on that horse every morning, knowing you could get thrown?"

Cole's low laughter stroked over her nerve ends like velvet. "He hasn't thrown me yet."

Speechless, Garnet stared through the firelight at Cole. The flames drenched his face in a muted glow. "Are you a crazy man?"

With a dazzling smile and a courtly gesture, he swept off his cowboy hat and held it against his chest. "Sure. Western-style crazy."

She couldn't help but laugh. "If that's crazy, I like it."

He settled his hat on his head once more and flashed her a grin. "Who knows? Maybe tomorrow morning, Diablo will throw me."

Garnet shook her head. "You are crazy."

Later, settled in the buckboard on a hard bed of crates, Garnet stared through the fir branches at a black sky that burned with stars. With her thoughts full of a certain dark-haired mine owner, she smiled to herself. She couldn't imagine being anywhere else. Despite assorted aches in every muscle, she wouldn't give up this adventure for a king's ransom.

Chapter 13

On the evening of the third day, Rafe rode into camp with a mule deer slung over his mount's withers. He halted before the fire and slid the deer to the ground. "I thought everyone might appreciate a change from those beans you've been fixing," he called across the fire to Ben, their cook.

Ben waved a spoon at him. "What's wrong with my beans?"

Rafe grinned. "What's right with them?"

With only a token grumble, Ben dragged the deer closer to the fire. "You do know this means we'll eat late tonight."

"Deer steak will be worth the wait."

The cook Asa Morrison had hired to travel with them approached and stared down at the deer. "You can actually butcher this and fry it in time for supper?"

Ben rolled up his sleeves. "Watch me."

"Let me help. Two of us can get it done in half the time."

After filling up on roasted deer, everyone settled down to enjoy a few minutes of relaxation before turning in or going on guard duty. Gilbert pulled a harmonica from his pocket and treated them to a recital of western ballads. Garnet sat near the fire with her arms about her drawn-up legs, her chin resting on her knees. She watched the changing expressions flit across Gilbert's face as the many moods of his songs moved him. The stirring notes of the simple instrument touched her in ways that a concert hall performance didn't.

The campfire's flames snapped. Sparks whirled upward and vanished in the night's black void. Smoke added its scent to the tang of conifers. Even with her sore muscles, Garnet had enjoyed every moment of this venture. New York's drawing rooms seemed a continent away, and she hoped she didn't have to return any time soon.

A light touch on her shoulder drew her attention from the music. She glanced up.

Cole stood just behind her left shoulder. When he beckoned, she scrambled to her feet. He bent his head to murmur in her ear, "Walk with me?"

Delighted for the opportunity, she nodded and followed him away from the fire, conscious of her father's and Albert's stares on her back.

They strolled down the trail out of the campfire's light. When they could talk without being overheard, Garnet halted. "Is something wrong?"

Cole leaned his back against the trunk of a tall pine. With one knee bent, he propped the sole of his boot against the tree's bole. "I haven't had an opportunity to talk to you these past few days."

Garnet agreed. Since that first night and their conversation beside the wagon, he hadn't singled her out. She appreciated his discretion, though she'd missed his company.

"At least my father and Albert haven't been glaring at me."

Cole cast her a look that made her toes curl. "They'd better get used to my keeping you company. I'm not going to ignore you because they want you to marry Albert."

Though his admission warmed her heart, Garnet didn't want to talk about the men in her life. She changed the subject. "So, we should reach your mine tomorrow?"

He shrugged. "Barring accident or storm, we should arrive at the camp in the afternoon."

"Thank you for asking me to teach school. I'm sure that's the only reason my father let me come."

Cole turned his attention to her and studied her face through the gloom. "You were actually an answer to prayer. I'd been looking for a teacher to replace Miss Danby, but I hadn't found one. I seized the opportunity to give you a useful reason to be at the camp, and it met my need for a teacher as well." He hesitated, then gestured toward Garnet. "The camp is primitive. We don't have a real school yet. In the mornings, the eatery doubles as a classroom. On Sundays, we meet there for church. Rafe and I take turns preaching."

His information should have discouraged her, but Garnet refused to be dismayed. "I'll manage. Actually, I'm delighted you asked me to teach. How many students will I have?"

Cole spread his hands wide. "It may vary from day to

day, but usually about fifteen. I'm trying to encourage parents to let their teens stay in school beyond the mandatory age limit. Once the girls reach sixteen, their mothers stop sending them to class and start teaching them to keep house. The boys go to work in the mines. Perhaps you can help me show the parents that a good education will do more for their children than a job in the mines."

Garnet frowned. "I'll do my best, but I'm not sure I'm the person to teach them those things. My future doesn't depend on my ability to keep house or earn a living in a mine."

"I'm sure you'll be an inspiration, especially to the teenaged boys. I'd play hooky from the mine just to sit at a desk and look at you." His lopsided grin charmed her.

"And I'd rap your hands with a ruler to stop your daydreaming."

"Ouch! You won't be one of those teachers, will you?"

She brandished an imaginary measuring stick. "Most definitely. I'm a mean one."

"What is it about teachers and rulers? I had my knuckles rapped more times than I can count when I was a youngun'."

Garnet shook her head at him. "And I'm sure you deserved every slap."

He shrugged. "Rafe and I weren't very diligent students. Only our fear of our father's disapproval made us buckle down."

Garnet longed to know more about the man who had shaped their lives. Would she be prying if she asked?

Cole sent her a quizzical look. "What? I know you have questions."

"What is your father like? If you don't mind my asking." She crossed her arms and rubbed, trying to warm her chilled skin. The cold had penetrated her jacket.

"You really want to know?"

"Yes. I want to know all about you, what your home life was like."

A heartbeat of silence passed while they stared at each other through the darkness. Unacknowledged emotions sizzled between them. At last, Cole snagged her by the waist and pulled her close. "If you want me to tell you, come here. You'll freeze to death otherwise."

Garnet allowed him to draw her close. He settled her in front of him, her back against his chest, and curled both arms about her middle. His warmth engulfed her. She relaxed against his strength and savored the heat.

"There. That's better, isn't it?"

"Very much." She waited for him to speak.

The wind soughed around them. Evergreen branches swayed. An owl hooted.

At last, Cole spoke above her head. "Rafe and I have a younger sister, Lily." He paused as if to collect his thoughts.

Garnet waited. After a moment, his chest expanded beneath her back as he took a deep breath.

"I have a complicated family."

Thoughts of the tangled relationship she shared with her father reminded Garnet of her own family dynamics. "So do I."

"You know that I have Cheyenne blood."

"Yes."

"Our father was born when the Plains tribes still roamed the prairie, following the buffalo. The white man was just beginning to come West in greater numbers. A clash of cultures followed. My father is half white. His mother was a captured white woman who married my grandfather, Yellow Wolf, a chief of their village. She bore my grandfather two children before she was rescued by soldiers and taken back to white civilization."

The tale unfolded like one of the Western dime novels Garnet had read in her younger days.

"My grandmother had a young son by her white husband, who was captured along with her. Yellow Wolf loved his white wife, and he loved her son, Shane, as if Shane were his own blood. Yellow Wolf reared him as he would have a true Cheyenne. Shane was my father's half-brother. When my grandmother was rescued, my father and his sister were taken to the fort with their mother and Shane. My father, Wild Wind, hated living among the whites. After a couple of years, he ran away and rejoined the tribe."

Cole's voice drifted into silence. The wind soughed in the pine branches and filled the lull until his voice sounded in Garnet's ear again. "Tensions between the two cultures ended up in bloodshed. My father was a Dog Soldier leader."

Garnet twisted to look into his face. "What's a Dog Soldier?"

"Dog Soldiers were young warriors who were convinced the only way for the tribes to take back their land was to drive out all the whites. They raided ranches, stagecoach depots, and farms. They skirmished with the cavalry. Dog Soldiers were known for their fierceness and lack of mercy for their enemies. Wild Wind's name was feared among the white settlers. Adults whispered his name to their children to frighten them into obedience."

"Oh..." Garnet's mind whirled. She couldn't imagine Cole living one generation away from such violence, violence committed by his own father.

"While on a raid, my father's band of Dog Soldiers captured my mother. My father loved her. He took her to their village, where he courted her and planned to marry her. However, my mother was already in love with none other than Shane, my father's half-brother. Shane tracked her to the village and rescued her just in time to prevent her marriage to my father."

"But if she married your uncle, how...?"

Garnet heard the smile in Cole's tone as he continued his narrative. "My father tracked down Shane and my mother on their way back to the Slash L. Wild Wind challenged his brother to a fight. The winner would get my mother."

"This sounds like a penny Western novel."

Garnet felt Cole nod even though she couldn't see him.

"Shane won that fight, and he and my mother were married. They had six years together before he died in a blizzard. That spring, my father came to the ranch, not knowing that his brother had died. He had hung up his war bonnet and was trying to live in peace. He got a job on the ranch training horses. With my mother being widowed, he set about courting her again. He'd never stopped loving her all those years they were apart. They were married the next summer."

"And then what happened?"

"After they were married, they divided their time between the ranch and the reservation. My father was a chieftain in his village, and he tried to help his people adapt to reservation life. He taught them to raise cattle so they wouldn't be dependent on the government. While we lived on the reservation, he trained both Rafe and me how to track, hunt, and live off the land."

"That explains how you know so much about living in the mountains. I wondered."

"Rafe and I could both disappear into these mountains and never come out, and we'd still survive."

"I really admire that."

Cole continued his tale. "In 1887, Congress passed the Dawes Act. That effectively put a stop to tribal governance and took back much of the land that had been allocated to the tribes. There was nothing more my father could do for his people. He realized that bringing up his children in white society was the only way for us to prosper in the new era, so we moved to the ranch permanently. After that, we were brought up white. Both Rafe and I have a university education. We've toured Europe, but the West is the place we love."

Garnet sighed. "And you have a family that loves you."

"I have more family than I know what to do with. Cousins, siblings, aunts, and uncles. In-laws. And they all try to tell me what I should do with my life. That's one reason I spend so much time in Denver." Humor laced his voice.

"At least you have family." Garnet couldn't keep the wistful note from her voice.

"You have your father." Cole dipped his head and spoke into her ear.

"I suppose."

"He may bellow, but he loves you."

"I'm not so sure…"

"What makes you say that?"

Garnet stirred within the circle of Cole's arms. "Perhaps one day I'll tell you."

Wild Wind Mining Camp
Colorado Rocky Mountains
Summer, 1911

Chapter 14

Garnet pulled Comet to a halt and stared at the camp below.

Cole halted Diablo beside her. "Well, here it is. The Wild Wind mining camp. This will be a town one day." Pride filled his voice.

She couldn't speak. The sunny vista spreading before her took her breath away. Mountains whose jagged peaks poked holes in the sky surrounded a wide, rolling meadow that cradled the Wild Wind mine and the adjoining camp. Dark green conifers draped the mountains' shoulders with a shaggy mantle. Wildflowers flung a splash of color across the valley.

What Garnet guessed must be the mine stood on a knoll on the camp's far side. Nearer at hand, straggling along in rough order, was a stable and a corral, a tiny mercantile, and what she presumed to be an eatery. Small cabins dotted the field between the town and the mine. Like a piece of twine discarded in the meadow, a dirt track connected the mine with the buildings.

While they sat atop their horses, the second buckboard swung around them and continued toward the camp. The riders trailed along behind.

She glanced at Cole. "I like it. It's raw and new. I can feel the energy."

His self-conscious grin revealed that her opinion mattered more than she'd thought. His dark eyes reflected a vulnerability at odds with his confident character.

She wanted to touch his hand, which rested on his saddle's pommel, but she controlled the impulse. "This is your dream, isn't it?"

"Mine, and Rafe's. We're in this together."

"That may be, but the vision is yours."

Cole shifted in the saddle. "The idea was mine."

"And with your brother's help, you'll succeed." She smiled at him. "Your father must be proud of you."

"He is. He and my mother both. They've prayed for Rafe and me, but they let God take care of our futures. My father understands that my path doesn't lie on the Slash L training horses."

"From what I've seen, you would have been very good at training horses." She slanted a glance at him. "It must be something to have parents who pray for you."

"I've never known anything different."

"My mother prayed for me when she was alive." Melancholy filled Garnet's voice. The wind tossed a strand of bright copper hair across her face. She brushed it aside and tucked it behind her ear.

A light touch on her arm roused her from her memories, and she glanced at Cole. The compassion in his dark eyes touched her heart.

Tenderness filled his lean features. "I'm sure your mother committed you to the Lord's care when you were born. Her prayers are following you, even now. The Lord won't forget her prayers just because she's no longer with you."

His comforting words almost brought tears to her eyes. "I never thought of it that way."

"A mother's prayers are special." He swept the far-flung vista with a glance. "Someday, I hope to have a wife who will pray for our children."

To hear Cole speak of his future wife and children filled Garnet with mingled hope and doubt. Could he be considering her as a possible wife? Or was he warning her away?

He cocked his handsome head at her. "I'll race you to the camp."

The cavalcade's arrival created a stir. Those men who weren't working in the mine's belly spilled out of the mercantile, the blacksmith's shop, and the cabins. Greetings rang through the air. Women and children gathered on the boardwalk and stared at Garnet with bold curiosity. She smiled at them. Perhaps these ladies could be friends.

Albert crawled out of the saddle and dropped Tansey's reins. He staggered to the boardwalk and collapsed at her feet, his head cradled in his hands. "I hate horses. If I ever mount another horse, it will be too soon for me."

"Unless you intend to spend the rest of your life here, you'll have to ride again." Garnet's tone betrayed her lack of sympathy. She stared down at the top of his head and hoped she could avoid him during their visit to the camp.

Albert cut her a dispirited look over his shoulder. "You might show me a little pity."

"Why? You didn't do anything the rest of us haven't done."

Albert's caramel eyes flashed. "I just spent four days on the back of that uncooperative beast, and you can't spare me a moment's pity? I suffered all of this for you."

Their gazes clashed. Heat flared in Garnet's chest and spread through her body. "You didn't do it for me. You would have come up here with my father whether or not I came along. Don't try to make me feel guilty." She cocked her head and studied him.

His once-shiny English riding boots showed the scuff marks of the rough treatment they'd received during the past four days, and snags marred his tweed riding habit. He looked as out of place as a lily in a briar patch.

Albert shifted on the hard boards. Something ugly gleamed in his eyes and then vanished. One hand clenched atop his knee. "If you think your father will allow your hero to ride in and sweep you off your feet, think again." He swept the camp's rough buildings with an expansive gesture. "Your father wants more for you than this."

"What I do with my life and who I spend it with should be my own choice, not my father's."

"Your father won't let you squander your life here. This place is the end of the earth." Albert shuddered. "You're wasted here. You belong in New York, where you've been groomed to take your place as one of the premier socialites. You'll be an asset to my rise in the city's financial power structure."

Garnet stared at him as though he were a loathsome creature who'd crawled out from beneath a rock. Albert had just revealed a darker side to his character than she'd suspected existed. She'd always thought him merely indolent. "For my father, our union is about establishing a dynasty. For you, marrying me is to further your ambitions. For both of you, I'm just a pawn." She fisted her hands until her fingernails bit into her palms. "I won't marry you!"

Whirling, she stalked away. Her footsteps took her to where the men unloaded the buckboards. She tried to put her conversation with Albert from her thoughts and enjoy watching the men in their mundane task of unloading boxes and equipment.

On his way past with a small wooden box on one shoulder, Cole paused beside her and dropped her satchel at her feet, then lowered the box to the boardwalk. He smiled down at her. "Once everything is unloaded, I'll take you and your father to your quarters. You might like to rest a bit and clean up before supper."

She smiled back and swiped saddle dirt from her split riding skirt. "Yes, I could do with a change of clothes. I've worn these for four days."

Cole grinned down at her. "Welcome to life in the Rockies." He nodded at the café. "If you like, you could wait inside."

Garnet glanced along the boardwalk to the place where Albert had sat. Her hopeful suitor had vanished, so she wouldn't have to encounter him again. "Thank you. I'd like to wait inside. To sit on something that doesn't move will be a treat."

They shared a chuckle while she accompanied Cole to

the café. She stepped over the threshold while Cole held the door for her. Scattered square tables filled the room, covered by red and white checkered oilcloth. Matching ruffled curtains hung at the windows. A long, waist-high counter lined a space before the back wall. Beyond the back wall, a door opened into the kitchen from which savory aromas drifted.

Cole dropped her satchel beside a table. "Just rest here. I'll be back as soon as I can."

Garnet had just settled into a chair when her father sauntered into the eatery. He caught sight of her and crossed the room to join her. As he pulled out a chair, she tensed. Her father never sought her out without a purpose.

When he settled into his chair, he pulled a cigar from his jacket pocket and lit the end, then shook out the match. He put the cigar to his lips. After a puff or two, he squinted at her through the smoke. "You did well, girl. I must give you credit."

Garnet stared. Had her father just paid her a compliment? A compliment from him was rare and usually preceded a lecture, so she eyed him with caution. "For what?"

"You acquitted yourself well on our journey here." He jabbed the cigar at her. "You did much better than that puppy, Albert. Albert doesn't do well out of his element."

As she waited for her father to get to the real point of this conversation, Garnet declined to reply.

He took another puff on his cigar and tapped the ash onto the table. "Play the school marm while you're here, but don't forget all of this is temporary. You don't belong here. Your place is back in New York at Albert's side."

Garnet stared into her father's cold eyes. On the heels of her discussion with Albert, her father's decree sent icy fingers slithering down her spine. He meant every word. He really thought he could force her to marry Albert. Could he compel her into a marriage she didn't want?

She straightened her shoulders. She wouldn't allow him to intimidate her. "Let me remind you I won't marry Albert. I have no intention of shackling myself to him."

"And let me remind you, girl, that I'm your father. Any court in New York will back me. A parent's word regarding a minor child is law in the courts. You have no legal rights."

For the first time since her father had started mentioning a marriage between her and Albert, Garnet feared he might actually force his will on her. Dismay stabbed through her, though she refused to reveal her alarm. She tipped up her chin and glared.

He gave her a tight smile, which Garnet mistrusted more than his compliment. "Enjoy yourself while you're here. Have your fun. Let Cole Wild Wind squire you around. It suits me to have him occupied with you." Her father rested his hands on the table and leaned forward, his stare pinning her where she sat. He spoke around the cigar clamped between his jaws. "Just remember your future isn't with him. With his Cheyenne blood, he'll never be accepted into the best Denver society, even with his uncle's political connections. I want only the best for you, girl."

Garnet surged to her feet. "You don't want what's best for me. You don't care that a marriage to Albert will make me miserable. If you loved me, you wouldn't try to force me to marry a man I abhor." Her voice vibrated. Garnet whirled and ran for the door.

Her father's words followed her. "Just remember what I said. This time next year, you'll be a married woman. You may not think so now, but one day, you'll thank me for this."

The door slammed behind her. She strode across the boardwalk and halted beside one of the porch roof's support posts. With one arm encircling the pole, she leaned her head against the column. Tears burned behind her eyes. She'd been brought up to be an obedient daughter, but she couldn't reconcile herself to her father's edict. How could she submit to marriage with Albert?

She stiffened her spine and swiped at her eyes when the thud of footsteps and the jingle of spurs approached from the direction of the stable. To be caught in a moment of weakness made her want to sink into the ground. When the footsteps halted beside her, she kept her face turned toward the street.

"Garnet? Is something wrong?"

Cole's voice nearly undid her. She swiped at her cheeks again before she looked at him.

He curled his fingers about her upper arm. "Something is wrong. Can't you tell me?"

She closed her eyes. "I can't talk here."

"I'll take you to your cabin. Wait while I get your valise."

Cole vanished into the café and returned a moment later with her valise in hand. He placed his other hand on the small of her back and guided her toward the cabins. "I see your father found you."

She nodded but couldn't reply.

They passed a long, rough wooden building just past the eatery. "That's the bunkhouse for the single men." They stepped off the boardwalk onto the dirt track that led to the mine. Log cabins clustered along the trail. "Those cabins are for the married men. They each have their own home."

"How many married families do you have here?" In spite of the shambles of her personal life, Garnet couldn't help but ask. To have some female friends would be pleasant.

"About a dozen. I offer good benefits to married men hoping to entice them to work for me. Married men add stability. And I want families to settle here to help build the town."

Garnet began to see why Gilbert had wanted to work for the Wild Wind brothers.

Children played alongside the trail, and Garnet smiled at them. These children would be her students. Even now, she could start building relationships with them.

The track wound upward toward the mine. Two larger cabins stood on either side of the mine entrance. Cole motioned to the cabin on the left. "This one is mine, and the one over there is Rafe's."

Garnet cut him a sideways glance. "You're giving up your cabin for me?"

He halted at the bottom of the step and cast her an inquisitive look. "Of course. Where else would I put you?"

She shrugged. "I hadn't thought. I'm sorry you have to give up your home for me." She hung her head and scuffed the toe of her shoe in the dirt. "I really didn't think all of this through when I came here."

Silence fell between them.

"Garnet, look at me."

She lifted her head.

The expression on Cole's face made her forget her troubles, forget the possible marriage with Albert, forget everything except the man who stood before her.

Tenderness warmed his features, and a smile curled the corners of his mouth. "I'm very glad that you're here. Yes, you're a distraction, but I'm glad that you're not in Denver. I look forward to spending time with you."

"Really?" She'd had her share of interested males hanging about her in New York, but she'd always known her money had been an attraction. She'd assumed the men were more interested in her wealth than herself. With Cole, none of those doubts plagued her.

"Really. Before I met you, I'd never met a female who has interested me enough to spend more time with her. The more time I spend with you, the more I want to be with you." He curved his palm about her shoulder and forestalled her when she caught her breath to reply. "Don't say anything now. You're tired, and you're upset. Now isn't the time for us to have this discussion." He gestured toward the door. "Your palace awaits."

Garnet grinned in spite of her anxiety and climbed the steps. Cole reached around her to open the door, and they stepped inside. A curtainless window graced each of the four walls. A wood stove with a coffee pot resting on its surface filled one corner. An iron bedstead with a spooled railed headboard filled another, and a kitchen table and chair claimed the space beside the door. Though dust coated the furniture, everything had been left in an orderly condition.

Cole gazed about with a critical eye. "If I'd known a lady would be living here, I'd have tidied up a bit."

"You don't think this is tidy? You should see my room at home. Daisy stays busy picking up after me."

He brushed past her and deposited her satchel on the bed.

"Where will you sleep?"

Cole pivoted but remained standing beside the bed. "I'll put a cot in my office at the mine."

"A cot?" The image of Cole's long length trying to fit onto a cot made her smile. "It sounds mighty uncomfortable."

"I'll manage."

"Where will my father and Albert stay?" Her eyes widened as realization dawned. "Of course, Rafe has given up his quarters for them."

"Rafe has moved into the bunkhouse."

"We're causing you a lot of inconvenience."

"You're our guests, not an inconvenience." Cole moved toward her on silent feet. He lifted her hat from her head and sent the headpiece sailing onto the table. His big hands framed her face. "Now, tell me what has upset you."

The conversation with her father flooded back. With the words choking around the lump in her throat, she recounted everything her father had said. "He can't really force me to marry Albert, can he?"

Cole pondered a moment before he replied. His forthright gaze speared her own tremulous one. "I'm not a lawyer, although as a property owner, I've had my share of dealings with the law. Since the turn of the century, a father's rights over his minor children have sometimes been successfully challenged in court, although those cases are few. It would help if you had a mother to take up your case. Without a mother, all parental rights rest with your father."

Garnet closed her eyes. That didn't sound promising. Besides the disadvantage of not having a mother to take up her case, she missed the comfort of a mother's love. Her mother's death had left a hole in her life that had never healed.

Cole's voice brought her back to the moment. She opened her eyes and found comfort in the hands that cupped her face.

"I know a gentleman should never ask a lady her age, but in this case, your age is critical. When will you reach your majority?"

"I'll turn twenty-one next June."

"Up until you reach your majority, I doubt you could find a court that will challenge your father's rights. And if I were a betting man, I'd wager your father has a couple of judges in his pocket who would rule on his side." Cole's fingers tightened in her hair. "He aims to see you married before you turn twenty-one and can legally challenge him."

"Cole..." Her voice broke. "What can I do? I can't marry Albert!"

Cole drew her against him and enclosed her in a tight embrace. Her face pressed into his shirt, and her arms stole about his back. They stood in silence, clinging together. At last, Cole bent his head and murmured in her ear, "I know it doesn't look good, but we have a Heavenly

Father who knows all about your problem. He's stronger than your father. We'll pray about this. And in the meantime, I'll contact my solicitor in Denver to see what legal advice he can give me."

Garnet heaved a sigh torn from her soul. Cole's embrace soothed her, and his strength flowed into her. "Cole?"

"Hmm...?" He rested his cheek on her hair.

"At least we have my father's permission to spend time together. He told me to have my fun with you now, because by this time next year, I'll be married to Albert."

With a finger beneath her chin, Cole tipped up her face. "We'll make the most of this time. We'll have our fun." He ran his thumb over her lower lip. "And I'll do everything in my power to see that you don't marry Albert."

Cocooned in his embrace, Garnet almost forgot her fears. If anyone could protect her from her father's schemes, Cole Wild Wind was the man.

Chapter 15

With her fleece jacket buttoned to the throat, Garnet climbed sturdy wooden steps to the mine. The brothers had promised to give their guests a tour of the mine's inner workings, and she couldn't wait to see the source of their dreams. She opened the door and stepped over the threshold.

A reception area greeted her, brightened by the sun that spilled through the windows. A couple of benches where visitors could sit lined the walls. Straight ahead, a stout door guarded what she guessed must be the mine's inner workings. Cole's voice drifted from an open door on the left.

Garnet sidled to the portal and slid inside. This room, adorned only with a massive oak desk and chair before the window, a second chair in front of the desk, and a metal filing cabinet, must be the office. A camp cot had been pushed against the back wall. Her father and Albert filled the vacant area between the desk and the cot. She squeezed into an open space between her father and the brothers.

Cole shot her a brief glance. A smile flashed in his eyes before he returned his attention to her father. Rafe nodded in her direction. Her father ignored her.

In jumbled disorder on the desk lay several yellow rocks small enough to fit into her hand. Cole held one on his open palm. "Uranium is extracted from this yellow ore, carnotite. We use burros to haul the ore from the mine to the surface. Every week, mules transport the ore to Indian Pass, where the train carries it to Denver for processing. The expense of getting the ore to Denver eats into the profits."

He dropped the ore into her father's hand.

"To protect the ore, we're forced to hire guards. As you know, it takes us four days to reach Indian Pass, and another day for the ore to get to Denver. It's an eight-day round trip for the mules. They no sooner get back to camp when we load them up again and send them back to Indian Pass. If we built a refinery here at the camp, all that time and expense transporting the ore would be eliminated."

Asa Morrison tossed the ore into the air and snatched at the carnotite on its downward arc. He squinted at the yellow rock. "I see what you mean."

"The larger mining operations and the government-subsided companies are building their own refineries. We must do the same if we intend to remain competitive."

Her father passed the stone to Albert, who frowned at it and tipped it into Garnet's hand. He wiped his palm on his trousers.

She stared at the yellow ore cradled in her hand. A dull luster gleamed from the stone's rough surface. The rock felt warm, almost soft, as if it could be carved like clay. How much ore lay beneath the mountain? Did enough exist to turn the Wild Wind mining camp into a town? Cole and Rafe must think so, since they were investing their future in this yellow rock.

She laid the ore on the table.

"Now, if you're ready, we can tour the mine."

Excitement coursed along Garnet's nerves. She'd anticipated this outing ever since she'd boarded the train for Indian Pass.

The Wild Wind brothers pushed through the huddle of people and reached for steel mining helmets that hung from pegs on the wall. Cole took one down and handed the hat to her father. "Anyone entering the mine must wear one of these. A uranium mine isn't as deep as a gold or silver mine, but it's still dangerous."

He handed another helmet to Albert, and then turned to Garnet. "I think I have one small enough for you. Some of the teenage boys who work here aren't much bigger than you." Cole flashed her a smile and settled the steel hat on her head.

She returned his smile while she tried to adjust to the weight of the metal helmet pressing onto her scalp.

Rafe took a box of six-inch candles from a shelf and distributed the lights. "Each helmet has a clamp at the front that will hold a candle. That way, everyone will have his own light. You must be careful not to catch anything on fire."

Cole inserted a candle into the clamp at the front of her hat. "There. You're all set."

As they prepared to leave the office, Garnet glimpsed Albert's face. His complexion had turned the color of pie dough. Droplets of sweat ran from his temple and dripped off his jaw.

He swiped at the moisture.

"Are you all right?" She peered up at him.

"Of course. Why do you ask?" Albert hunched his shoulders and cast her an impatient glance.

"You don't look well."

"Don't fret, Garnet. I'm fine." Albert brushed past her and followed the other men from the office.

With a sigh, Garnet trailed behind the men. Rafe had opened the heavy door at the back of the reception area and was ushering her father and Albert into the mine's working area. Cole waited near the door, and she came to a halt beside him.

"Are you ready?" His eyes mirrored the concern in his voice. "Are you claustrophobic? Does darkness bother you?"

"I've never been claustrophobic before, but I've never been down in a mine before, either."

"The darkness in a mine is like nothing you've ever experienced. It's darkness so intense you can feel it. Not everyone can tolerate the conditions."

She managed a shaky smile. "I guess we'll find out if I can handle it."

"When we get inside, I'll light your candle. And there are lanterns, so that should help."

They crossed over into the earth's dank bowels. The

men had lit their candles. The flickering flames atop each helmet seemed a puny defense against the blackness. Garnet shivered, as much from the weight of the darkness as from the chill.

Rafe was speaking. While his brother talked, Cole struck a match and held the flame first to Garnet's candle and then his own.

"Most of the carnotite ore is found fairly close to the surface, which is why a uranium mine isn't as deep as a gold mine. We drill mostly straight into the mountain, with side shafts leading off the main tunnel. Feel free to ask any questions." With that, Rafe turned and led the group down the track that joined the working shaft that led to the surface.

"Be careful to watch your footing," Cole warned Garnet with a hand on her elbow.

The track wound down at a gentle grade. The deeper into the mountain they went, the more absolute the blackness became. Their candles threw feeble golden circles into the darkness, and the lanterns that hung from metal pegs spaced along the rock wall provided a muted glow against the blackness.

Garnet shivered again. The air grew colder. Her sheepskin jacket helped keep the raw temperature at bay, but she couldn't imagine spending hours in this stygian shaft. The mountain's weight pressed on her with a tangible force.

Disembodied voices floated up from deeper in the earth's belly, miners who worked in the darkness all day.

Garnet pointed at the narrow train tracks that lay in the tunnel's center. "What are these tracks used for?"

Cole nudged the metal rail with the toe of his boot. "These tracks are for the carts the burros use to transport ore to the surface," Cole replied.

By the time they reached the first station where new tunnels branched off on each side, Albert was gasping for breath.

Rafe stepped to his side. "Are you having problems breathing?"

Albert staggered to the tunnel's wall and braced a shoulder against the rock, then doubled over and braced his hands on his knees. In the candlelight, his expression had a green cast.

Rafe flagged down a man who had appeared at the entrance of one of the cross tunnels. "Joe, take this man back up top and make sure he sees the doctor."

At the end of the tour when they'd returned to the surface, Garnet yanked off her helmet and thrust the protective headgear at Rafe. She fled outside, across the porch's planked floor to the rail. Tipping back her head to the sun, she filled her lungs with deep breaths of fresh mountain air.

Behind her, the door opened and shut. Footsteps rapped across the porch and halted beside her. Cole. She slanted a glance up at him. "How do those men do it? How can they go down into the darkness every day?"

"They either get used to it, or they leave. Not everyone is cut out to be a miner."

Garnet gazed over the valley, at the meadow rolling away to meet the mountains on the far side and the lake in the center, somnolent in the sun. She drank in the scene's beauty, so welcome after the mine's blackness. She couldn't imagine being trapped beneath tons of earth each day, never seeing the sun or the majesty unfolding before her. She shook her head. "I couldn't do it." With one hand on the porch railing, she pivoted toward him. "But thank you for sharing your dream with me."

The slow smile that lit his face made her thankful she'd stayed with the tour and not left with Albert. In showing her the mine, Cole had shared part of himself. If only the brothers and her father could come to a business arrangement, she could stay here and be a part of his dream. New York city could fall off the eastern coastline for all she cared.

Chapter 16

Garnet caught her father at breakfast the next morning when she set her bowl of oatmeal on the table across from his seat. "Well, are you and the Wild Wind brothers going to be partners?"

He gave her a piercing stare and made her wait for his reply while he scraped his bowl clean with a piece of fluffy white bread. After he'd chewed and swallowed, he motioned for her to sit. "We each sent for our solicitors on this morning's mule train. When the lawyers get here, we'll draw up the contract."

Garnet's spirits soared. She wouldn't have to leave the camp. She could stay here and teach school. *And you can spend time with Cole Wild Wind.* Her heart whispered the words she didn't dare speak aloud.

Her father harrumphed. "That puppy, Albert, went back to Denver with the mules. He couldn't take the primitive conditions here."

Garnet schooled her expression to hide her relief at

Albert's defection. She didn't want to antagonize her father any further. "Is he going to wait in Denver?"

Asa crossed his beefy arms over his chest. "No. Once he gets to Denver, he'll take the train to New York. He's eager to get back to the city."

"Albert is a New Yorker through and through."

"He might as well get back to work as to cool his heels in Denver. He's more useful to me at the bank."

Having Albert on the other side of the continent suited Garnet just fine. If she never saw him again, she wouldn't care.

"Daughter."

Her father's voice shattered her thoughts of Albert on the other side of the nation and brought her attention to his face. His intent expression made her wary.

"I had good intentions in allowing you to come West on this business venture. I thought if you spent more time with Albert away from the social whirl, you'd come to see his finer qualities. Things didn't work out the way I intended. Albert didn't shine, I'm afraid."

Not sure how to reply, Garnet held her tongue. That Albert hadn't shined was a mild way of categorizing his behavior.

"Once you return to New York and see him in his element, you'll realize why I've chosen him to be your husband. He's everything a young woman of your station could expect in a spouse."

Garnet pushed away her bowl and rose. Her appetite had fled. "You still don't understand, do you? You've confused what you want with what I want. I don't want Albert, and I don't need your money."

Like a bulky bear rousing from its winter den, Asa shoved back his chair and lumbered to his feet. He planted both palms on the checked tablecloth and thrust his face toward his daughter. "You don't know what it's like to be needy, to depend on yourself for the food you eat or the clothes on your back. Every item of clothing you've ever worn, every piece of jewelry you own, even the roof over your head, has been provided by my money. Try living without my support, and see how long it will be before you crawl back and beg to marry Albert."

Garnet trembled with mingled anger and fear. Before she said something that would enrage her father further, she spun and fled.

* * *

After supper one evening, Cole caught her when she left the eatery. "Care to take a walk?"

She cast him a flirty glance. "Do you have romantical intentions, Mr. Wild Wind?"

He winked at her. "Most definitely, Miss Morrison."

"Well, then, I most definitely would care to take a walk with you."

They shared a grin and stepped off the boardwalk. Cole took her elbow. "Now that you have a week of teaching behind you, how is school going?"

Garnet thought of her students' eager faces, and she smiled. "So far, I haven't had any problems. I think they still view me as a novelty, so the children are on their best behavior."

Beneath the brim of his straw cowboy hat, Cole's eyes twinkled. "And have you had to rap any knuckles?"

"Not one. Even the teenage boys behave."

"They're probably trying to impress you."

"Whatever the reason, I'm thankful they're in class and not at the mine. Some of them actually seem to enjoy learning." She hesitated while they crossed the track and headed across the meadow. "Cole, would you be willing to consider me as your permanent teacher?"

He came to an abrupt halt and turned her to face him. "Why? What about your father?"

She met his questioning gaze, though she shriveled inside at the thought of her sire's threat. "My father has threatened to cut me off if I don't come to heel and marry Albert. I thought perhaps I could stay here and be the permanent teacher."

Anger flared in Cole's eyes before he banked the emotion to a low simmer. "I'll keep my opinions to myself, since I shouldn't insult your father, but if you need employment, Rafe and I would be happy to offer you the job of teacher. The pay isn't much, though, and the winters up here are tough. Once the snow hits, the mine is isolated until the trails clear in the spring. You'd be stuck up here all winter. Not everyone stays during the cold months, so you probably wouldn't have many students. I wouldn't blame you if you elected to spend the winter in Denver."

Garnet's shoulders slumped. "I couldn't afford to be unemployed during the winter. I'd have to stay here."

Cole brushed her jaw with a knuckle. "Never mind, we might get through this without your father cutting you off.

This is one more thing to pray about." He gave her a smile that warmed her to her toes. "Have you seen the lake yet?"

She shook her head.

He steered her across the meadow. "The lake is one of our local natural beauties you shouldn't miss."

"Then by all means, show me the lake. I don't want to miss a thing. Everything out here is much grander than I imagined."

"Oh? Have you had an interest in the West?"

Garnet halted and slanted a sideways look at him. The lowering sun, snagged by the jagged mountain peaks to their west, washed Cole's face in gold. The light illuminated the creases at the edges of his eyes and the grooves that slashed either side of his mouth.

He tipped down the brim of his cowboy hat. His eyes gleamed with interest, and he pinned her with a look that encouraged her to share her thoughts.

She grinned at him. "Living out here, you have no idea of how romantic the West sounds to us Easterners. Cowboys, Indians, the mountains and plains…" Garnet swept the meadow and the encircling mountains with a wide gesture. "All of this is like a fairy tale to us living in the East."

With lazy steps, they resumed their stroll, and their booted feet swished through the short mountain grass.

Garnet's gestures grew animated as she shared her enthusiasm. "I once saw Buffalo Bill Cody's Wild West Show when the troupe performed in Brooklyn. That day opened up a whole new world for me." She remembered the show, with its mock Indian battles, stagecoach robberies, and Wild West shootings, as if she's seen it yesterday. "Ever since then, I've wanted to visit the West. I read every Western dime novel I could find." She shrugged. "I have a drawer full of penny postcards of cowboys, Indians, and desperados."

Cole tipped his head down to her. "And did the West measure up to your expectations?"

"Oh, yes! The scenery is magnificent. And real cowboys are much better than the ones on penny postcards."

He shook his head at her. "You haven't met any real cowboys yet."

She surveyed him with an assessing eye. "No? You look like the real thing to me, cowboy boots, six-shooter, and all. And if I were a wagering woman, I would wager that when you aim, you hit your target every time. Your six-shooter isn't for show."

He tucked both hands into his jeans back pockets and shrugged. "My father was an exacting teacher."

They continued for several paces in silence before Garnet broached the topic of the upcoming partnership. "My father told me that you've agreed to terms of a partnership."

He nodded. "Our solicitors should arrive with the next mule train. When my lawyer arrives, I'll have a discussion with him about your legal rights. That wasn't a topic I wanted to commit to paper, so I decided to wait until I could discuss it with him in person."

Garnet met his gaze. "Thank you." She glanced away, looking over at the lake they had neared in their ramble. She sighed. "Sometimes, when I look at my father, I wonder who he is. He wasn't always so ruthless."

By mutual consent, they halted. The lakeshore curved

away in a gentle semicircle, ringed by weeds. The waves lapped with a lazy rhythm. A bird exploded from the reeds at the water's edge and whirred away over the grasses.

Cole shifted and hung his thumbs from his gun belt. "Tell me. What happened? What was it that soured your relationship with your father?"

His question snagged in her chest, and panic caught her in its suffocating clutches. Could she unburden herself to this man? Did she trust him enough to confide the details of something she'd hidden in the depths of her soul, even from herself?

Her breath panted in ragged hitches as horror spread through her like a smothering mist. "I... I don't know if I can tell you. I haven't told anyone."

Chapter 17

Cole waited without moving, his weight cocked on one hip. "You can tell me." His reassuring voice, smooth as warm honey, invited her to confide in him.

Garnet stared at him, then jerked her gaze to the lake. Her heart fluttered inside her chest like a bird trying to escape. She spun and stalked to the lake's edge. With her arms crossed, she gripped her elbows until her knuckles turned white. Could she open herself and share the burden she'd carried alone for so long?

A moment later, his footsteps approached from behind. He curled his hands about her shoulders, and he turned her to face him. "Garnet, what happened?" Tenderness filled his expression as he peered down at her.

She tossed him a piteous glance. "Please don't think ill of me. I couldn't bear it."

He squeezed her shoulders. "I could never think ill of you."

"You don't know what I did... I killed my mother..." She closed her eyes.

Would he hate her? Tell her what she'd done made her unworthy? She lifted her lids and peered into his face. Instead of the condemnation she expected, his expression revealed only compassion.

He stroked her jaw. "What happened?"

She gasped her tale in a breathy whisper. "I was four years old. Mama and I had been walking in the park that afternoon. My nanny was with us, and we were on our way home." Her breathing hitched, and she swallowed down the lump that clogged her throat. "I had a new puppy." She halted and shuddered. "I wanted to take the puppy with us. At first, my father said 'no', but Mama prevailed upon him to allow me to take the puppy on our walk."

Garnet struggled with her memories, memories she'd buried long ago. Once she opened the door on those recollections, the floodgates sprang wide and whirled her back to that long-ago day. In kaleidoscopic sequence, images flashed before her eyes. Pain clutched her chest as she became that child again.

Cole slid one palm down the side of her face. "It's all right. Take your time."

Her next words came out in a gulp. "The puppy got loose. He saw a squirrel, and he jumped out of my arms. I dropped the leash. He dashed across the sidewalk and into the street." Garnet heaved in another rasping breath and clawed at the collar of her blouse. "I ran after him and followed him into the street."

Wracked by tremors, she shuddered. "Mama chased after me. She was afraid I'd be run down by the traffic." A sob tore from her throat. "I was fine, but Mama was run over by a gentleman driving a phaeton. He was driving too fast, and he couldn't stop." Tears filmed her vision and made Cole's image swim. "I don't remember seeing it happen. One moment, I was a happy child. My day had been full of sunshine and love. The next, all I remember is people shouting and screaming, and my mother lying face down in the street."

Cole cradled her in his arms and rocked her as if she were still that terrified child.

"My father got rid of my puppy, and we've never had another dog." She clutched at his back, her nose buried in his shirt.

The wordless comfort he offered stripped away her defenses. Sobs erupted. She wept until she'd been wrung dry and had no more tears to shed. At last, he set her away and fished in his back pocket for a handkerchief.

"Here." He thrust the handkerchief toward her.

She took the hankie and dabbed her eyes. Hiccoughing, she pushed the hanky into his hand. "Thank you."

Cole waited until she could speak again.

"My father..." Garnet drew a ragged breath. "My father blamed me. He loved Mama very much, you see. From that day, he changed toward me. Now he can barely stand the sight of me. I'm told I resemble my mother very much."

Cole cut her a sharp glance. "You don't know what your mother looked like?"

She shrugged. "I was only four when she died, so I have very few memories of her. More like impressions, I think. My father had the servants remove every photo of Mama from our house, so I don't even have a picture of her. He got rid of every personal item she owned, all her clothing and jewelry. We were forbidden to speak of her. It was as if she'd never existed." She pushed away, and his arms slid from her. "My father's maiden sister came to live with us. My Aunt Belle reared me as a mother would have. I think she loved me, in her way, but no one could take my mother's place."

Garnet pressed her fists to her mouth. "When I was younger, I sometimes tried to get my aunt to tell me about my mother, but she was too afraid of my father to defy him."

"I can't imagine growing up like that."

"My mother's death left a black hole in our home. My father stayed away from the house most of the time. I didn't go to school or have friends because my father hired tutors for me. I grew up in a house full of servants and blaming myself for Mama's death."

"Your father had no right to saddle you with the blame for your mother's death. You were a child." Cole spit his words through clenched teeth.

"I was a child!" Garnet cried on a hitching breath. "Yes, I was just a child, but I felt the blame my father leveled at me. I grew up feeling responsible for his inability to love me. It was a relief to go away to finishing school." She took a step closer to the lake and stared over the placid water. "And now, here we are, and my father wants to marry me off to his rich bank partner."

Cole followed her. "I'll do my best to see that your father doesn't force you into a marriage you don't want."

She tipped her head and gave him a smile that trembled at the edges. "Perhaps it doesn't matter. I know

Albert doesn't love me, but it doesn't matter. I killed my mother. I'm not worthy of anyone's love."

For a moment, their stares locked. Incredulity crossed Cole's face before he swooped toward her and caught her by the upper arms. He dragged her against his chest and stared down at her with an intensity that made her quiver.

"Don't say you're not worthy of love! How can you think you're not worth loving? You're kind and caring. You're generous and fearless. You have a heart for others." His gaze roamed her face. "I know you have a heart full of love for some man special enough to win your affections. I intend to be that man."

Chapter 18

Garnet spooned a generous dollop of mashed potatoes onto a miner's plate. She hadn't asked her father if he objected to her helping with the evening meal, so his reaction when he noticed her behind the counter could be explosive. She darted a glance at the door. He hadn't yet entered the café, and the table in a corner he'd claimed for himself was still empty.

When Gilbert halted in front of her, a grin curled his mouth. "It's a pleasure to see your fair face this evening. I'm not surprised you're behind the counter."

Garnet brushed a gleaming copper curl out of her eyes. "I could say the same of you. Are you still glad that you're here?"

He shrugged. "Mining is what I do. I'd rather be here than anywhere else." He held out his plate to her.

She ladled a serving of potatoes onto his dish. "And I'd rather be here than anywhere else."

Gilbert took a step farther down the line, then paused

and looked at her over his shoulder. "Does your father know you're serving?"

She shook her head.

Humor laced his expression. "So can we expect to be treated to another family scene?"

She gave a mock shudder. "I hope not, but anything's possible."

He shook his head and moved down the line for a slice of ham.

As the miners passed her station, Garnet offered a smile with the potatoes, but her attention kept straying to the door. Apprehension about her father's reaction mingled with her eagerness to see Cole. Cole wouldn't skip supper, would he?

She'd taken special care with her appearance, although with her limited wardrobe, her choices had been few. She wore another of her slim, black skirts and a high-buttoned white blouse. Instead of the braid she'd adopted during her days at the camp, she'd tried to pin up her hair, though without Daisy's expert help, her heavy tresses kept slipping from the pins. With many of her curls tumbling about her shoulders, she looked like a waif who'd just endured a windstorm.

She froze with one hand suspended over a miner's plate when her father entered. He frowned at her, but he didn't make a scene. When he seated himself at his table without an angry outburst, her knees buckled, and she leaned against the counter.

Toward the end of the shift, when she'd abandoned hope of seeing Cole that evening, the brothers entered on a gust of chill air.

When Cole stopped before her, he slid an appraising glance over her. "I guess I shouldn't be surprised to see you behind the counter."

"I noticed that the ladies could use an extra hand with supper, so I volunteered."

Rafe nodded a greeting and held out his plate. "Evening, Garnet."

She returned his howdy and ladled potatoes onto his plate.

Cole remained rooted before her while his brother moved down the line. "I haven't had a chance to talk to you since my solicitor left, but I have some news for you. Can you drop by the office after supper? I'll be working late."

Garnet nodded, but unexpected shyness froze her tongue. Unlike the debonair New York gentlemen of her acquaintance, Cole's rugged manliness reached out to her. His smile scattered her composure to the four winds. She hadn't forgotten his declaration beside the lake, and she struggled to find where she stood in his affections.

"Then I'll see you later." With a touch of one hand to his hat brim, he moved on.

Garnet breathed again.

After the meal, she hurried to her cabin. How long she should wait before she joined Cole? The solicitors had come and gone, and since then, the brothers and her father had spent hours poring over plans for the refinery and the mine's expansion. Often, they worked late into the night.

She paused before a mottled looking glass tacked to the wall above a small table on which rested a white pitcher and wash basin. What should she do with her hair? She attacked the wayward curls, but the slippery curls kept sliding out of the pins. After a brief struggle, she gave up. Cole would have to take her just as she was.

She snatched her jacket off the peg by the door and shrugged into it, snuggling the collar about her ears. At the door, she paused and surveyed the cabin. Her clothes now hung on the pegs along one wall, and a canning jar full of daisies decorated the table. She'd added curtains to the windows. Her own feminine touch transformed the lodge into a home, yet, Cole's essence still lingered.

Garnet stepped outside and turned toward the mine. When she opened the door and stepped into the reception area, raised voices from inside Cole's office reached her ears.

The door to the office stood ajar. She held her breath and eavesdropped on the argument inside. She recognized both Cole's voice and her father's. Plans for the mine's expansion seemed to be the source of the disagreement.

"I'll not take chances with the safety of my men by allowing shortcuts with the construction. I want every safety feature installed that the engineers think necessary." Inflexibility laced Cole's tone.

A pause weighted the air before her father replied. "Do you know how much added expense all of those safety features will cost?"

"Taking shortcuts in construction isn't one place that I'm willing to consider expense. I'll not gamble with my men's safety."

"You'll cut deeply into our profits by including all those features. I won't sign off on it."

Another silence ensued. When he replied, steel threaded Cole's low voice. "May I remind you that Rafe and I constitute a majority in this business partnership? He sees things as I do. His vote will overturn yours. We can come to terms in other areas, but not in safety matters."

Garnet froze. Her father would be furious. He never allowed himself to be out maneuvered.

"Don't think you've heard the last of this. I can buy any engineer that you hire. See what happens to your safety features then."

Asa Morrison's reply sent a shiver down her back.

The office door flung open and banged against the wall. Her father stormed past her without a glance, while she tried to make herself invisible. The expression on his face terrified her. The outer door slammed shut behind him. The wall shook.

Garnet stared at the door. After a moment, she drew in a deep breath and tiptoed toward Cole's office. When she reached his sanctuary, she peered around the door jamb. Cole stood behind his desk with his back to her, his booted feet planted wide and his shoulders rigid. His hands were fisted on his gun belt, elbows jutting. She had just decided to retreat when he spoke.

"Garnet, you can come in."

She took a hesitant step over the threshold. "How did you know I was here?"

Cole pivoted. "My father was a Dog Soldier. He taught

me everything he knows. I heard you when you came up the steps."

She shook her head. "You're not like any other man I've ever known."

One corner of his mouth lifted in a small smile and chased the grimness from his face. "I hope that's a compliment."

"I meant it as a compliment. You being so different from the men in the world where I grew up is something I'll have to get used to." She stepped closer. "I heard your argument with my father. When he says he can buy any engineer you hire, he means it. You'll have trouble finding one who will include the safety features you want. He means to cut corners everywhere so he can to increase his profit margin."

"I already have an engineer."

"Not for long. My father will find a way to buy him or scare him off. Then you'll have to find another, and the next one will be under my father's thumb."

Cole stared across the room at her. A grim expression hardened his features. "I have no doubt your father will try to buy an engineer, but he may find he doesn't carry the same influence here that he does back in New York. We have mining safety laws now. The legal pressure may be enough to make an engineer hesitate about ignoring the laws."

"My father doesn't care about laws. Not if it costs him money."

Cole flexed his shoulders as if the responsibility he bore for his men weighed heavily upon him. "In the last twenty years, over fifteen hundred men have lost their lives in mining accidents. I don't want my men to add to those numbers due to a lack of safety measures."

Garnet stepped closer to his desk. "My father counts human life in terms of profit and loss, I'm afraid."

"Fortunately, my great-uncle Clint Logan still carries some influence in political and legal circles here in the state. Perhaps that will be enough to act as a deterrent to your father." Cole's mouth hardened. "And he still has to deal with me."

Garnet tipped her head to one side and studied him.

He lifted a quizzical brow. "What?"

"I'm wondering why you signed onto a partnership with my father. You and Rafe are so different from him."

A weighted silence settled over the office. The air between them sizzled. Cole rounded the desk and came to a stop a mere handspan from her. His expression softened. "I may regret taking him on as a partner. I have no doubt what I did may have been a mistake, since he's not a God-fearing man, but he has one thing I want." One large hand cupped her cheek.

Garnet caught her breath. She stared into his face, unable to look away.

He clenched his fingers in the coppery tresses that tumbled from its pins. "He has you. The only way I could get you is to have him as my partner. If I'd sent him away, you would have gone with him. Undoubtedly, he would marry you off to Albert." Cole curled his palm about her neck and tugged her closer. "That was something I couldn't allow. I wanted to keep you near me so we could spend time together, and I could offer you whatever protection is within my power." His other arm went about her. "I couldn't send him back to New York, so I took him on as a partner."

She bumped against his chest and clutched the front of his shirt.

He sifted his fingers through the tresses that had fallen from its pins. "So beautiful."

Garnet couldn't speak, mesmerized by the feel of his fingers gentle in her hair.

"You're beautiful, inside and out." His arm remained a vice around her waist, clamping her against him. His other hand slid from her hair to her cheek, and he trailed his fingers along her jawline. He stroked his thumb across her bottom lip. "I meant what I said beside the lake. I intend to be the man you spend the rest of your life with."

"But my father..."

He placed two fingers on her mouth to silence her. "Shh... Don't fret about your father just now. Let me tell you what my solicitor said. He confirmed what I told you. As long as you're a minor, your father has absolute rights over you."

Garnet's heart sank. "But this is the twentieth century. Surely, the law has been modernized to prevent a parent from forcing a daughter into a marriage against her will."

"That law isn't strictly enforced these days, but your father is within his rights in arranging a marriage for you. Should you take your father to court, you'd most certainly lose. Without a mother to take up your side, and with the judges I'm sure he has in his pocket, you would lose."

She dropped her forehead against his chest. "What am I to do?"

Cole stroked her back with his free hand, offering comfort. "We'll take advantage of our opportunities this summer, although we must be careful around your father. And we'll pray. We have a Heavenly Father who knows your circumstances. We mustn't lose heart. A way to free you will present itself."

Garnet sighed. She spoke into his shirt, her face still pressed into her chest. "Sometimes I wish I'd been born into wealth. Then my father wouldn't have ambitions to marry me off to a rich man. I could marry whomever I please."

Cole's knuckles beneath her chin tipped her face up to his gaze. She stared into his resolute features. "If you'd been poor, I never would have met you." His eyes crinkled in a smile, and his dark curls gave him the appearance of a mischievous schoolboy, at odds with his aura of power. "We'll get through this." Both hands framed her face, and doubt flashed across his features. "I haven't asked you… Do you want me to be the man you spend the rest of your life with?"

Did she want to spend the rest of her life with Cole? Garnet hadn't known him long, but she admired him more than any other man she knew. His upright, God-fearing character drew her, and she trusted him. Did she love him? Perhaps not yet, but Cole would be easy to love. She'd risk her future with him before any other man.

She curled her fingers about his wrists. "Yes, I'd like to spend the rest of my life with you."

His eyes gleamed as he tightened his fingers in her silken tresses. "Then let's seal our agreement with a kiss."

One glance at his face warned her of his intentions. His head dipped, and his mouth came down on hers. He hadn't declared his love, but Garnet forgot his omission, forgot her father and Albert, as Cole's kiss told her more than words of his love.

Chapter 19

Garnet stepped forward as the conversation between the Wild Wind brothers and the refinery's construction supervisor concluded their conversation. A wicker hamper, filled with a jug of tea and a plate of cookies, dangled from one hand and bumped against her knee. Her pulse hummed through her veins at the prospect of seeing Cole.

Cole had taken one step toward the refinery when he saw her. He halted, and his slow smile slid over her like warm molasses. Her cheeks heated as she returned his look. Her father's harrumph recalled her to her errand.

She set the hamper on the grass near the refinery's frame and flipped back the lid, then withdrew a pitcher and dented tin mugs from the basket's depths. After she'd poured tea into each cup, she approached her father with a mug of chilled tea.

"Would you care for some tea, sir?" Since her mother's death, she'd addressed her father as "sir." The papa she'd adored had vanished, to be replaced by a cold stranger.

Her father grunted but took the mug and drank with

gusto. Garnet moved on to Rafe, who grinned at her when he took the tea.

"You're spoiling us, although I shouldn't complain. I'm parched." With his free hand, he swept his cowboy hat off his head and swiped his forearm across his forehead. He settled his hat on his head and peered at her beneath the brim. "You're saving us from heat stroke."

She returned his grin. "Ha! I should leave you to your own devices and let you survive on a drink from the water barrel like the rest of the men."

Rafe's dark eyes twinkled down at her. "You wouldn't be so cruel as to deprive us of your tea or lemonade."

Garnet made a face at him and returned to the hamper to fetch the last mug, along with the plate of cookies. She offered cookies first to her father and then to Rafe. With the other men absorbed in their snack, she drew close to Cole, who had watched the byplay from a little distance. He stood with one hip cocked, his thumbs hanging off his jeans back pocket.

Garnet halted with her back to her father and held out the battered tin mug toward Cole. When he reached for it, he circled her fingers with his longer ones. His touch seared her, and she hissed in a sharp breath. Her gaze settled on his face. They exchanged a long look, while he smiled down at her.

"Thanks." His fingers slid from hers and curled around the mug. He brought the cup to his mouth and eyed her over the rim.

A delicious shiver wracked her at the message his look conveyed.

Cole guzzled his tea and reached for a cookie. "Molasses. My favorite."

"I baked them myself. Fanny is giving me lessons." Satisfaction at the simple accomplishment filled her. In New York, she never went near the kitchen except to confer with the cook about the weekly menu. If she'd so much as mentioned a desire to bake cookies, Cook would no doubt have expressed his horror in voluble French and stormed out.

Cole raised his eyebrows. "You baked these?"

"All by myself."

He reached for another cookie and examined the sweet from all angles. "You're full of surprises. I didn't know you could bake."

"She can't," Asa Morrison growled around a mouthful of cookie. "All my daughter can do is plan menus."

Garnet wheeled toward her father and jutted her chin. "I baked these cookies myself. You can ask Fanny."

Her father frowned at her, his bushy eyebrows drawing together over his nose. "I have no idea who Fanny is, and I have no desire to find out."

"Fanny is one of the miner's wives. She works in the kitchen. I've been helping with the meals, and she's been teaching me to bake."

"I don't know why you bother. You don't need to cook." Her father's cold gaze settled on her face. "Albert has an accomplished chef who will take care of all your meals."

Garnet clamped her mouth shut. She could have done without a reminder of Albert.

Rafe reached for another cookie from the forgotten

plate she held. "Well, I think these are delicious. You have a fine touch."

Stepping forward, Cole snatched another sweet off the platter and popped the confection into his mouth. "That stove is cantankerous. I'm amazed that you women can bake anything."

Garnet appreciated the brothers' efforts to smooth over her father's irritation, and she managed to smile at them. "Old Henry sure enough is cantankerous. It's near impossible to get the temperature right." The many struggles she'd had as she learned how much wood she needed to get Old Henry's temperature just right had almost defeated her.

"Old Henry?" Rafe quirked a dark eyebrow.

Garnet laughed. "Old Henry is the kitchen stove, named after a miner who was known for his cantankerous ways."

Rafe seemed about to reply when he glanced beyond Garnet's shoulder. His eyes narrowed. She twisted to scan the valley behind her but saw nothing that warranted a second look. Whatever had caught Rafe's attention had apparently vanished, and Rafe said nothing. Garnet gave a mental shrug. She gathered up the mugs and repacked the hamper.

With their break over, the men drifted toward the half-finished refinery. Cole tossed her a warm look filled with promise before he turned to her father. He jabbed a finger at a section of the frame structure that lifted bare ribs toward the Colorado sky.

Rafters stabbed a sharp silhouette against the blue expanse arcing overhead. The refinery's support posts and roof joists outlined the building's rectangular framework and gave evidence of its final shape. Rhythmic pounding fractured the afternoon's air as carpenters hammered nails into posts and beams. The scent of freshly sawn lumber sweetened the air.

Garnet watched as her father and the brothers halted near the building. Her father propped his hands on his hips and leaned toward Cole, who gestured again. Cole hadn't carried tales to her, but she knew her sire too well. She didn't need Cole to tell her that Asa Morrison had muscled his way into every decision between the brothers and the building supervisor. With a sigh, she turned away and trudged to the eatery with the hamper in one hand and an ache in her heart.

After supper, Garnet sought out Cole. Perhaps they could stroll by the lake. She found him in the stable, currying Diablo's glossy hide. Rafe stood outside the stall, his back to her. He gestured as he murmured to his brother in tones too low for her to overhear. She halted.

Inside a roomy box stall, Cole was propped against the gelding's shoulder, one arm draped over the horse's back and the other arm slack alongside his thigh. A currycomb dangled from his fingers. His narrowed eyes looked stormy. At her approach, Rafe glanced at her and fell silent.

"It's all right." Cole tipped his head toward her. "I have no secrets from Garnet."

"Someone has been spying on us." Rafe picked up the conversation where Garnet's appearance had interrupted him. "This afternoon I saw a flash from the mountain across the meadow, as if light had glanced off a mirror or a pair of field glasses."

Cole's expression turned thoughtful. While he contemplated his brother's information, barn swallows dipped and soared in the rafters above them. Their shrill cries pierced the silence. "We'll check it out tomorrow. If someone is watching the camp, we need to be aware of it."

Garnet glanced from one brother to the other. "Why would anyone spy on your camp?"

Cole swiped the currycomb along Diablo's side as he replied. "Competition is fierce among the uranium mine owners. It's not unusual for them to spy on the others to know what the competition is doing."

"This needs to stay with the three of us. No one should know what we're planning." Rafe propped both hands on his hips.

Cole stepped from the stall and bolted the door latch. He laid the currycomb on a shelf beside the stall, then moved close to Rafe and Garnet. He cocked his head at his brother. "Rafe, tomorrow morning you and I will take Garnet riding. We'll put out word that we're taking a break from the construction and are showing Garnet the beauty of our mountains. If you can remember where you saw the flash, we should be able to locate where the intruder spied on us."

Rafe shifted his weight to his other leg. "The carpenters might wonder why we're taking a day off when we've been pushing them hard all summer, but I don't think they'll be suspicious. They're just hired men, anyway."

"My students will enjoy a holiday." Garnet would miss their seeing their little faces, but having a chance to be with Cole more than made up for the time lost with the children.

Cole tipped his head toward her. "Will your father suspect anything?"

Garnet's gaze roved over his face. She wished her father were a less devious man. "I don't know. It depends on what he's been up to. I did warn you not to trust him."

"You did." Cole crossed his arms. "Do you know why he went to Denver for two weeks last month?"

She shook her head. "He doesn't confide in me. I have no idea."

The brothers exchanged glances. Cole looked grim. "He didn't tell us, either. He just said he had business in Denver."

"My father will undoubtedly take advantage of your absence to implement some of his ideas on the refinery. Perhaps he'll be so relieved to have you two out of his way, he won't wonder what you're up to."

Chapter 20

Rafe turned his gelding toward a spot along the shoulder of one of the mountains that ringed the valley. Evergreen trees mingled with the quaking aspen spilled down the mountain's side to grow in haphazard fashion along the meadow's edge. They rode into the shade beneath the trees and within minutes began a diagonal trek along a steep escarpment.

Garnet kept Comet close behind Diablo as her mare clambered after Cole's gelding. The horses' hooves dug into the soil, and they thrust their shoulders into the grade. Garnet clung to the saddle horn when Comet scrambled upward over a rocky ridge, her shod hooves striking sparks on the stone.

After a slow, grueling climb, they reached a level clearing. Through a space between evergreen branches, the mining camp could be seen nestled in the emerald valley.

The men swung down from their saddles and ground-hitched their horses. After a slow perusal of the clearing's floor, they squatted on the far side of a downed log to examine several objects on the forest floor. They murmured in tones too low for her to hear.

Garnet dismounted and dropped Comet's reins, then snatched off her cowboy hat and fanned herself with it. She might need her jacket at night, but the daytime temperatures made her wish she could take a dip in the lake. With her face lifted to the breeze that whispered through the spruce trees, she let its draft cool her heated skin.

The men rose to their feet. Rafe moved off to the clearing's far edge, his attention on the ground. Cole beckoned to her, and Garnet strolled to his side.

"What do you see?" She halted near him and squinted at the forest floor. Short, withered grass intermingled with lichen-covered rocks covered the soil. She saw no evidence to tell her who might have been there.

Cole pointed to several cylindrical white objects scattered amongst the stones on the far side of the mossy log. "Do you see those?"

"They look like cigarette butts."

"They are. Someone sat up here long enough to smoke several cigarettes. Do you see where he sat?" Cole pointed to a spot on the log. "The moss has been bruised there."

Garnet took a step closer to the downed log and peered at its weathered surface. The moss had been crushed at the spot Cole indicated.

Cole gripped her elbow and guided her to the clearing's center. Squatting, he parted the spikey mountain grass. "And here. This stone has been overturned. The lichen has been scraped off one side."

Her gaze followed his pointing finger. The signs Cole and Rafe had sighted betrayed a man's presence, like a message written on the soil.

Cole stood and cupped his hand about her elbow again. He drew her to where Rafe stood at the clearing's edge. "The spy tied his horse here." Cole tipped his head toward a spot on a fir branch where the needles had been broken. "The ground is marked with hoofprints, and the horse left droppings."

Garnet stared at him. "Is this what your father taught you?"

The brothers shrugged.

"One of the things." Rafe's tone indicated their father had passed much more knowledge than simple tracking on to his sons.

"What a wonderous talent. I'm so impressed!" She looked from Cole to Rafe and back again to Cole. She couldn't keep the admiration from her voice. "Your father must be a very special man. I'd like to meet him."

The brothers, so alike in looks and physique, exchanged glances and grinned.

"Our father is formidable," Rafe said. "But I must admit, he's putty in our mother's hands."

Garnet smiled at the image. Her heart yearned for a marriage such as the brothers' parents seemed to share.

Cole stepped closer and curled one hand about her shoulder. "I intend for you to meet both our parents." He tugged her closer and propped her against his side.

With her face tipped up to his, she splayed her hand across his chest.

He dipped his head until their noses almost touched.

Garnet thought he would kiss her, but when Rafe cleared his throat and turned his back to them, Cole squeezed her once before he turned her loose and stepped away.

"Well, little brother, what do you think?"

Rafe pivoted and shoved back his cowboy hat. "I think we should follow the tracks to see where they'll lead us."

"I agree. Let's mount up."

Three hours later, they pulled up on a rocky ridge. The mountains stretched before them, wrinkled and broken. Conifers darkened their shoulders. Already dusted with snow, the ridges' craggy spines speared the sky. In the limitless blue above them, an eagle rode the air currents.

On the far side of a high meadow, a jumble of buildings butted up against the shoulder of one of the mountains.

For long moments, no one spoke. At last, Cole broke the silence. "Well, well."

Garnet turned her head in his direction. "What is it?"

Rafe settled himself deeper against his saddle's cantle and stacked his hands on the horn. "That, my girl, is our competition. The Colorado Mining Company, one of the biggest uranium mining operations in the state."

"So they're the ones who sent someone to spy on you?"

Cole shrugged. "It appears so. The question is, why now?"

"Do you think my father had something to do with this?" Garnet's opinion of her father sank even lower. Disappointment that he could possibly betray the Wild Wind brothers churned in her stomach.

"I'm suspicious of anything your father does when I can't see what he's up to." Cole's grim tone revealed his concern.

"We should post guards." Rafe cocked his head at his brother. "But we'll need to keep it quiet, though, so as not to tip our hand."

"There are a few men whom we trust that we can pull out of the mine." Cole sighed and slumped in the saddle. "Thank you, Rafe, for not saying 'I told you so.' You were against bringing Asa Morrison into our partnership, and for valid reasons. You only gave in to my pressure because you knew the real reason I wanted him for a partner."

With a glance at Garnet, Cole reached across the distance between their mounts and laced his fingers between hers.

Rafe frowned at his brother. "Much good it will do your romance to have Asa Morrison as a partner. He's made it plain that he plans to marry Garnet to Albert Davies."

"I know that, but I don't intend to allow it."

Rafe raised his eyebrows. "And how do you propose to prevent it?"

"I'm working on a plan."

"It had better be a good one."

Garnet pulled her hand from Cole's. "Please, can we talk about something besides Albert Davies?"

The brothers fell silent.

She hung her head. "I'm terribly sorry my father has caused you so much trouble. His ambition has overtaken his scruples, I'm afraid. He did have scruples once, before my mother died."

Rafe's expression lost its grim lines. "Garnet, please don't blame yourself. Your father is entirely responsible for his actions."

The old sense of unworthiness gripped her. She tried

and failed to keep her voice from shaking. "But it's my fault that my mother died, you see. You could say I'm indirectly to blame for my father's actions."

Rafe cast a questioning glance at his brother.

Cole shook his head and sidled Diablo closer to Garnet's mare, head to tail. His knee bumped hers. He curled an arm about her shoulders and tugged her into his embrace, tucking her head into the curve of his neck. With his mouth close to her ear, he murmured endearments intended to console her. "Garnet, sweetheart, I thought we had this settled. You aren't responsible for your mother's death. You didn't make her run into the street without first checking for traffic. Nor are you responsible for your father's underhanded business practices. He's a grown man who makes his own decisions."

Garnet closed her eyes. Cole's arm about her soothed her bruised spirit. She nestled into his embrace, loving his strength and the support he offered. She laid her palm against his cheek, but she couldn't speak.

"Garnet? Are we agreed on this?"

She hesitated, then nodded.

"Good. No more blaming yourself." He pressed a kiss to the side of her face and tightened his arm about her before he tipped her back into her saddle. With his expression settled in forbidding lines, Cole swung Diablo about. "Let's head back. We have a long ride to the camp."

Chapter 21

With a folded dishcloth, Garnet pulled the baking dish from Old Henry's depths and laid the tin pan on the wooden counter beside the stove. The scent of molasses and cinnamon wafted beneath her nose. Today, she'd made warm gingerbread for the men's afternoon snack.

Fanny leaned over the pan and pressed a finger to the cake's center. "This seems just right. Done, but still moist. You're turning into a real cook." She straightened and tucked a stray curl behind her ear. "You're spoiling those men."

Thoughts of how much Cole enjoyed the treats brought a smile to Garnet's lips. "They deserve a little spoiling."

Fanny shrugged. "As long as you don't mind fighting Old Henry every day." She cast a dark glance at the cast iron stove.

"Old Henry and I have come to terms." Garnet's eyes gleamed. Never having had many women friends, she enjoyed Fanny's banter.

While she waited for the gingerbread to cool, Garnet

pulled a platter from the shelf along the back wall and carried it to the counter. She laid the plate beside the gingerbread pan to fill with gingerbread slices later.

Several other women had arrived to help prepare the evening meal. Her father's chef had already staked out a place at one end of the work counter and was slicing a cut of elk into steak strips, so the women worked around him. Garnet scrubbed potatoes in the metal sink beneath one window and hummed while she worked.

Her thoughts flitted to Daisy. How was her friend faring in Denver? Over the summer, they'd exchanged a few letters, and Daisy seemed content to await their return to Denver. Garnet had fallen in love with the Colorado high country and the mining camp. She wouldn't trade places with Daisy for any amount of money.

Garnet smiled to herself as Cole invaded her imaginings. She treasured their time together as Cole shared himself with her, and their daily Bible study and prayer time brought a special sense of closeness.

Fanny paused beside her and cast a concerned glance out the window. "The new tunnels are almost done. I'll be glad when the blasting is finished." She turned to Garnet and laid one hand on the sink's edge. "I know the bosses are careful, but using dynamite worries me."

Garnet patted Fanny's shoulder. "Cole and Rafe are concerned about their men's safety and won't take any chances. The crew they hired to do the blasting are experts. And now that the refinery is almost complete, all the ore the men will extract from the tunnels can be processed here." Except for the installation of the final pieces of machinery, the refinery was finished.

"I know Mr. Cole and Mr. Rafe are careful, but I just can't help but worry about my Ed." Fanny sighed and turned away to the counter to peel carrots.

Garnet leaned over the sink to peer out the window. If she tilted her head to one side, she could see the mine's working entrance and the reception room door. Cole had told her he'd be down in the mine today, but he'd promised to be out of the shafts by the time she brought her snacks.

She'd just straightened away from the window and picked up another potato when a low, rumbling explosion ripped through the afternoon. The kitchen shook, and the floorboards trembled. For a moment, she froze. Cole had told her that no blasting had been scheduled for today. Something was wrong.

A despairing cry from one of the women sounded behind her and jolted Garnet from her stupor. She jerked toward the sink and leaned over the rim to peer out the window, one hand pressed against the pane. Her heart stopped at the sight that greeted her. Dust and debris billowed from the mine's working entrance. Glass had blasted from the office windows. Men, blackened with grime, staggered from the tunnel into the light.

Cole! Where had he been when the explosion happened? Had he still been in one of the shafts? Garnet swallowed her panic and whirled from the sink. Her trembling fingers struggled with the bow that tied her apron about her waist. After a frantic struggle, the knot came free, and she tossed the smock over the sink's rim. She plunged into the group of women bolting from the kitchen. All of them had husbands in the tunnels.

On the boardwalk, they joined the throng who stampeded toward the mine. Men spilled from the mercantile, the stable, the refinery, and the cabins. Hemmed in by the tide of humanity that surrounded her, Garnet darted along the track and up the incline to the mine. Her breath rasped. She stumbled and fell to her knees. One of the mercantile clerks tripped over her and thumped her in the back with his boot. He leaped to his feet and hauled her upright before he plunged into the crowd and disappeared.

They reached the mine. Survivors still spilled from the earth's dark belly, gasping and coughing. Shouts beat against Garnet's ears. Whorls of acrid smoke drifted from the shaft.

She clawed her way through the mass to the front and halted near the front of the crowd, her hands pressed to her mouth. Her frantic gaze caught no sight of Cole. Some of the women gave glad cries when they found their husbands among the survivors. Gilbert staggered from the entrance. A part of her mind registered the fact, but she forgot about Gilbert in her search for Cole.

A tall man sprinting from the refinery caught her attention. Garnet swung her head toward him, but the man who charged up the slope toward the mine was Rafe. At the entrance he paused and took stock of those men who had reached the surface before he plunged into the tunnel. He battled his way against the tide of men who straggled from the depths and vanished into the shaft.

Garnet caught sight of her father. He ambled up the knoll and halted some distance from the chaos. Pulling a cigar from his jacket pocket, he lit the cheroot with an air of absorbed detachment. When the end glowed, he clamped the smoke between his teeth and surveyed the scene through narrowed eyes. At that moment, she almost hated him.

She picked her way between survivors and stalked across the hillside to come to a standstill before him. With her hands fisted on her hips, she glared at her sire. "How can you stand here and look so indifferent? Don't you care that men are injured, and some may have died?"

Asa Morrison turned his attention from the mine and regarded his daughter through half-lowered lids. After a long moment, he removed the cheroot from between his teeth. "Should I beat my breast and wail? What good would that do?" He shrugged. "Accidents happen."

Garnet snatched the cigar from his hand and flung it to the ground, then stamped out the sparks. "Yes, accidents happen, but the least you could do is look like you care. And the doctor needs help. Why don't you do something constructive?"

Her father stared at her as though she had two heads. "Why should I get myself in a tizzy over a few injured men? Leave their care to others of their own station. More men will come to replace those who have died." He swept the scene with a wide gesture. "Men come, and men go. That's the way of the world." Asa stretched out one hand toward Garnet in a placatory gesture. "I'll make sure the widows want for nothing and that the wounded are cared for. That's what my money can do. I'm not a heartless monster, Garnet. I'll do what I do best—give the widows and their children financial support and pay for the care of the wounded."

Garnet caught her breath. Tempted to say something she'd regret later, she fisted her hands and clenched her teeth, then spun and stalked away. When she neared the shaft, she halted to watch wives search for their husbands.

One woman, with her children clustered about her skirts, ran forward and threw her arms about her husband, who had collapsed to his knees. He appeared to be burned, but at least he lived. The children hugged their father and cried. Other women, not finding their loved ones, wept. Their sobs tore at Garnet's heart.

The stream of survivors who lurched from the mine had reduced to a trickle.

While Garnet stood on the slope drenched in autumn sunshine and fretted for Cole's safety, two revelations burst over her. She loved Cole, and she couldn't live without him. What she'd felt first as respect and then affection had developed into love. He'd become such an important part of her life that she couldn't imagine a future without him. Her heart settled into a slow thud against her ribs. Had she lost him before she could tell him that she loved him?

She closed her eyes against the horror around her. The verses she and Cole had been studying came to mind and brought her a measure of peace. The Lord had known the explosion would happen and had allowed it for His own purposes. Cole was in the hands of the Heavenly Father whom he loved. Whatever happened, she had to believe this afternoon's events had occurred in the Lord's sovereignty. The thought comforted her, and she sent a silent prayer heavenward.

Garnet turned in a slow circle to see how she could

help. She spied the camp doctor going from one man to another. Picking her way through the debris and men stretched out on the grass, she hurried to his side. "Dr. Fletcher, what can I do to help?"

Dr. Fletcher peered at her through his spectacles and tugged his shapeless hat farther down over his balding pate. "I could use some hot water and bandages. And if you could bring me some things from my clinic, I'd appreciate it." He tore a sheet of paper from a notepad in his black bag and wrote out a list of ointments and medications. "Here's the key to my medicine cabinet."

Garnet snatched the key and the list from his hand. She thrust them both into the pocket of her black skirt and hurried to his office. When she'd completed her errand, she ran back up the slope to where the doctor stooped beside a man with a broken arm.

She lost track of time while she trudged at the doctor's side, helping where she could. Dust smudged her skirt. Blood smeared the front of her blouse. She didn't notice. Her hair had come loose from its pins and tumbled about her shoulders. With an impatient gesture, she bundled the wayward strands back and tied them with a length of twine.

With her attention on the injured, she'd almost forgotten about Cole. She'd just finished helping the doctor bandage a miner's burned hand when she stood and stretched out the kinks in her back caused by too much stooping. Her gaze snagged on the mine's entrance where two tall men halted, a makeshift stretcher made of planking carried between them. A man lay unmoving on the stretcher.

One of the men wore a miner's hard hat. The candle

clipped to the brim still burned, its light diffused by the sunshine.

Garnet's breath caught. *Cole!* He was safe! Overjoyed at seeing him alive and uninjured, she took two steps toward him and willed him to look at her.

As if he felt her gaze, Cole swung his head toward her. The look they exchanged charged the air between them and set Garnet's nerve ends to tingling. For long moments they stood unmoving. Their gazes devoured each other. Her pulse hammered in her ears and drowned out all other sounds.

The man who held the other end of the stretcher spoke, interrupting their silent communication. *Rafe.* He'd found his brother, and together they'd brought out another injured man. Cole nodded at whatever Rafe had said. They picked their way down the slope toward Dr. Fletcher and Garnet and came to a halt beside the doctor.

"Here's another one for you." Cole's voice rasped, and he coughed.

Dr. Fletcher motioned toward a grassy level spot off to one side. "Put him over there."

The three men moved toward to the spot the doctor had indicated. Garnet trailed behind. Rafe and Cole laid their burden on the ground and straightened.

Cole rolled his shoulders and turned toward Garnet. She wanted to touch him, to clutch him close and rejoice in his safety, but she contented herself with looking at him instead. Dirt blackened his face. His flannel shirt sported a tear along one shoulder seam, and muck stained his jeans, but to her loving eyes, he'd never looked better. "I was so afraid I'd never see you again."

His gaze burned over her. They yearned toward each other, but they didn't touch. "I was in another tunnel on this side of the explosion."

"Praise God."

He nodded. "I can't stay. The main tunnel is blocked, and there are miners trapped down there. I have to organize a crew to try to dig them out."

With one more long look, he spun. Together, he and Rafe organized a crew of uninjured men. Armed with pickaxes and crowbars, the rescue team strode to the mine entrance and disappeared into the darkness.

Chapter 22

Garnet offered a meat sandwich to a weary miner, and a smile of thanks lit his begrimed face. She moved on to the next man, and the next, until she'd distributed all the sandwiches in her basket. Before she returned to the kitchen to restock her hamper, she paused to rest her over-worked limbs and scanned the scene. The activity outside the mine resembled organized chaos overlaid by a sense of grim urgency.

Several crews had worked all evening to clear the blocked passage, spelling each other in shifts while they rested and ate. Now, darkness cloaked the camp, broken by the torches' flickering orange light. Overhead, multitudes of stars glittered down from a satin ebony sky.

With her empty basket dangling from one hand, Garnet trudged down the hill toward the eatery. She passed women on their way back to the mine with hampers of food or pitchers of water to share among the men who had just emerged from the mountain's depths. Even those ladies whose husbands were trapped did their bit and ignored their fear over the men's unknown fate.

Garnet swept the slope with a glance, but she didn't spy her parent. He'd returned to his cabin shortly after their confrontation, and she hadn't seen him since.

When she reached the kitchen, Garnet packed her basket with more sandwiches, then wrapped two sandwiches in individual paper packets and included a piece of gingerbread in each one. These packets she placed on top of the other food. Perhaps she could find someone to deliver the sandwiches to Cole and Rafe, who hadn't taken a break since they'd led the rescue team into the mine.

Back at the scene of the explosion, she distributed sandwiches to exhausted men who'd come up for food and a much-needed rest. She kept an eye cocked for anyone who seemed about to return to the tunnel. When a disheveled, dirty man get to his feet and plodded up the incline, she hurried to his side.

"Excuse me, sir."

The man turned a hollow-eyed face to her. A tired smile lifted the corners of his mouth. "Garnet. You're keeping busy."

She peered at him through the flickering torchlight, trying to see past the grime that smeared his face and the exhaustion that furrowed his cheeks. "Gilbert? I didn't recognize you."

"I don't wonder." He recoiled when she reached a hand toward him. "Don't touch me. I'm filthy."

She laid a determined palm on his arm. "You're going into a mine that's been compromised to rescue other men. To the women whose husbands are trapped down there, you're a hero." She thought of her own father, sheltered in his cabin and removed from the grubby reality of the explosion, convinced his philanthropy would be enough.

Gilbert stared at her. "Has anyone told you you're an angel?"

She huffed. "No. I'm sure my father would disagree with you."

"What does your father know? I say you're an angel."

Garnet couldn't hold back a smile. "Thank you, Gilbert." Standing on tiptoe, she pecked his filthy cheek. "And you're a good man." She rocked down onto her heels. "How many men have been lost?"

His expression turned somber. "We've already uncovered two bodies. I'm sure we'll find more. And if we don't break through before the men who are trapped run out of air..."

She swallowed around the sudden lump in her throat as she shared his urgency. "Will you break through in time?"

"We hope so."

"Aside from the fatalities, how bad is it? Be honest, now. Can the damage be repaired?"

Gilbert's mouth turned down, and he shrugged. "Probably, but at great cost. Repairs will set the Wild Wind brothers back a pretty penny."

Garnet blinked back tears. Cole's and Rafe's dream had gone up in a blast of flames and smoke. She couldn't begin to imagine the cost or guess what her father would do. If he deemed the cost too great, would he pull out of his contract with the brothers? If he did, he'd haul her back to New York and Albert.

    She shook off her gloomy thoughts. "I won't keep you. I know you're in a hurry to get back to work." She fished the wrapped packets from her basket and offered them to Gilbert. "These sandwiches are for Cole and Rafe. They haven't come up for food, so I'm sending the food to them. Could you please see that they get it?"

    Gilbert took the packets from her and stowed them in his jacket pockets. "The Wild Wind brothers sure are lucky men to have an angel like you seeing to their welfare."

    Garnet's face heated. "Someone needs to look out for them."

    Gilbert flicked her jaw with his knuckles. "I wish I had an angel looking out for me." Without giving her an opportunity to reply, he brushed past her and climbed the knoll to the mine entrance.

    Bemused by his comment, Garnet watched him until he disappeared into the tunnel. She shook her head and turned toward the group of men resting on the grass. With thoughts of death and ruin casting a cloud over her, she forced herself to offer hopeful smiles to the men as she dispensed sandwiches. She prayed for the men who struggled to clear the shaft and for the women who would soon learn they'd been widowed.

* * *

The sun perched on the jagged mountain peaks the next morning when a cheer from the mine roused Garnet. Exhausted from hours of helping Dr. Fletcher and feeding the men, she'd slumped onto the ground, fallen into a fitful doze, unmindful of the frigid night air. The shout breathed excitement into everyone who remained outside the entrance. Garnet scrambled to her feet. Beside her, Fanny rose, and the two women shared a hopeful glance. They clasped hands in a tight grip and strained to see the survivors.

Ragged, stained, and disheveled men appeared at the shaft's lip. They staggered and blinked in the light, but they cheered and pumped their fists in a triumphant gesture. They'd been rescued in time.

Fanny spied her husband among the survivors. With a glad cry, she wrenched free of Garnet's clasp and plunged up the incline to meet her man. Joyful tears filled Garnet's eyes as Fanny met her husband and flung her arms about his neck. For Fanny, today would be a day of celebration rather than grief.

Behind the men who had been trapped came those who had worked so hard to free them, with Cole and Rafe among the last to emerge. They stood at the top of the knoll and stared at the people milling about below. Somber expressions masked their faces. The women whose husbands hadn't appeared huddled together in the forefront. After a pensive moment, the brothers walked down the slope toward the women.

Garnet's heart went out to the poor ladies who had lost their husbands. She watched in misery as Cole spoke to the widows. A grievous cry sounded when he broke the news. The women clutched each other as if their support was the only thing that kept them on their feet.

Friends of the women, those who had been fortunate

enough to have their husbands return to them, stepped forward and gathered around their newly bereaved sisters. The brothers turned the widows over to the care of their friends and continued down the slope.

Rafe tossed an exhausted nod to Garnet. "Thank you for the sandwich and the gingerbread. I'd completely forgotten to eat until Gilbert gave me the food." Without giving her an opportunity to reply, he plodded toward the single men's bunkhouse.

Cole halted beside Garnet. She studied his features. Dawn's rosy light shone on him with merciless clarity. He looked ten years older than he had before the explosion. Sweat plastered his curls to his head. His gaunt eyes stared out of a haggard face grimed with dirt. Filth caked his shirt and jeans.

She laid a sympathetic hand on his arm. "I'm sorry about the men you lost, but at least you saved the ones who were trapped."

He gave a jerky nod and replied in a voice raspy with fatigue and mine dust. "I'm going to take a bath and then sleep for twenty-four hours. After that, we'll talk."

Chapter 23

"Do you mind sitting on the grass?" Cole waited in silence for Garnet to respond.

"I don't mind."

He shrugged out of his jacket and spread it on the ground. "Here, sit on this."

Garnet sat with her arms about her drawn-up knees. Cole stretched out beside her on the spiky mountain grass, burnished now with autumn's golden hues. He reclined on one elbow, one leg cocked, and a wrist draped over his knee. With narrowed eyes, he stared over the glimmering lake, withdrawn into an unapproachable stillness.

A sharp breeze spiced with the scent of autumn leaves wafted off the mountains and eddied around them. Garnet sucked in a lungful of tart air, then slanted a sideways glance at Cole. He'd been uncommunicative since he'd awakened after sleeping around the clock. He'd lost the haggard look he'd worn yesterday, and he seemed refreshed, but he'd been distant despite her efforts to draw him out.

Perhaps during the meeting the three men had held in Cole's office that morning, her father had refused to help fund repairs to the mine.

She took a deep breath and risked a rebuff. "Cole, please look at me. Share your troubles with me."

When he gave no indication he'd heard her, she almost despaired. She tried again. "Cole, talk to me."

He swiveled his head to stare at her. The black torment in his eyes cut her to her soul.

"It's my fault those men died. I should have seen it coming." Bitterness hardened his voice.

"How could you have foreseen that? You couldn't have prevented such an accident."

He pinned her with a self-condemning glare. "The explosion was no accident. Rafe and I are sure it was sabotage."

"Sabotage?"

"Yes, sabotage." He glanced over the water and ran a finger down the bridge of his nose. "I noticed several odd things but didn't piece everything together until after the blast. There was something off about one of the men whom Rafe and I hired to dynamite the new tunnels. He hired on at the last minute, and none of the other crew members knew him. The day before yesterday, I noticed him hanging about the area where the explosion occurred. There wasn't a blast scheduled for that day, so I should have paid more attention to the fact he was there. Now he's gone missing. He hasn't been seen since right before the explosion."

Garnet curled her fingers about his forearm. "Do you think he's connected to the people who have been spying on your camp?"

Cole covered her hand with his palm and tipped his head toward her. "Rafe and I both think he's somehow connected to the Colorado Mining Company. That company is known for its ruthless business tactics."

"Perhaps they're trying to force you to sell."

"That's what Rafe and I believe. I hope you won't be offended when I tell you we didn't share that bit of news with your father." Cole searched her face with an earnest gaze.

"I'm not the least bit offended. I told you not to trust him." She met his look with a direct one of her own. "What does my father say?"

"This morning he didn't comment except to request an estimate of the damage and the cost to rebuild."

Garnet struggled, without success, to keep the bitterness from her voice. "Everything is about the profit margin with him. I hope he doesn't decide the cost outweighs the potential profit and pull out of your agreement."

Cole sat up, both knees cocked, and slanted his shoulders so he could look Garnet in the face. "I don't think he will. He gave no indication of doing that."

"I know your mine will be a success if you can rebuild. Your camp will become a town, and you and Rafe will give jobs to a lot of families."

He splayed his hand against her cheek. He speared his fingers into her hair, and "You don't know what your words mean to me. Your support is balm to my spirit." His tender voice spread over her like warm rain. "Having you as my wife beside me will give me courage to forge on, no matter the challenges." He traced a path over her lower lip with his thumb.

Their gazes snagged and held. Garnet couldn't look away from the tenderness in Cole's eyes. Where his palm cupped her face, the warmth of the caress told her of his love.

She curled her hand about his wrist and leaned her cheek into his palm. "You make it sound so easy. I want to be your wife, but..." Her words trailed into silence.

He stroked along her jaw. "Something will work out. We'll find a way to be together." He clasped her hand and rested their entwined fingers on his thigh.

"What will you do now?"

"Tomorrow, we'll have a funeral for the men who died."

Garnet squeezed his hand. "I know burying those men will be hard for you, but you mustn't blame yourself. You aren't to blame for the explosion any more than I'm to blame for what my father does."

Cole gave her a crooked smile. "I guess I should heed that advice. After all, it's the same advice I've been giving you."

"And very good advice it is, too."

A companionable silence fell before Garnet prodded him to continue. "And what then?"

"The men will dig out the debris and clear the tunnel. Rafe and I will go back to Denver. Before we order new equipment to repair the mine, we'll hire a Pinkerton agent. If we can apprehend the man who caused the explosion, it will make it easier to prove that the Colorado Mining Company is behind the sabotage."

"What will happen in that case?"

Cole pulled a blade of grass and twirled it between his fingers, his gaze on the spinning stalk. After a moment's contemplation, he glanced at Garnet and tossed the stem away. "You must realize that the justice system out here isn't as developed as it is in the East. Situations like this don't always end up in court. Most often, especially away from the city, conflicts are settled between the two parties."

She caught her breath. "Like in a gun battle? As in the Wild West?"

"These days we try to avoid that kind of violence. It may mean we'll meet directly with the owners of the Colorado Mining Company and resolve things that way."

Garnet mulled over his words.

He rested his wrists on his cocked knees and clasped his hands. "The problem is that this time of year, we're going to encounter bad weather and snow. The trail to the camp is closed for most of the winter. It probably will be spring before we can complete the repairs."

"I'm sorry about that."

Cole shrugged. His muscles bunched beneath his flannel shirt. "The men who stay at the camp will do as much as they can, but if we don't get the supplies up here before the trail closes, they can't finish until transportation commences again in the spring." He leaned closer. "You'll come back to Denver with Rafe and me. And your father, too, of course."

"Denver seems like a world away."

Cole took in the lake, the valley, and the mountains with an encompassing glance. "Yes, it does. Up here, none of that matters. Nothing outside of this valley matters."

"Although it does. The world still goes on."

He curled his free hand about the back of her neck and burrowed his fingers beneath her hair. Garnet closed her eyes in pleasure.

"Come Christmastime, we'll go to the Slash L. Christmas is the one time of year when my mother expects both Rafe and me to be at the ranch."

Garnet's eyes popped open to encounter Cole's face inches from her own. "It must be nice to have family who wants you to be with them for Christmas."

"The whole family gets together for Christmas. I may be an adult, but my mother would skin me alive if I didn't show up for the holidays."

"It sounds delightful. After my mother died, my Christmases were dreary affairs. I couldn't wait for the holiday to be over."

"You'll have to experience a Slash L Christmas and meet the whole family. My great-uncle Clint and Aunt Coral live there all year round now. My siblings will be there, as well as assorted cousins and their spouses. You'll have more family than you'll know what to do with."

"I can't wait."

Cole's gaze grew warm. "I want you to meet my parents. They'll love you."

"You can't introduce me to your parents the way I think you're planning! One hint of marriage, and my father would pack me back to New York on the next train."

Cole grinned at her with a naughty schoolboy air, as if

he were about to do something he knew the teacher had forbidden. "I won't do anything to jeopardize our relationship or get you into trouble with your father, but I'll take my parents into my confidence. I don't want you to leave the Slash L without them knowing I intend to make you my wife."

Denver
Winter, 1912

Chapter 24

Garnet pushed through the dress shop's glass door and stepped onto the brick sidewalk. Daisy followed close on her heels. Packages wrapped in brown paper filled their arms.

She'd been back in Denver for a week. The brothers and her father had dived into meetings with engineers and suppliers. She'd seen very little of the men.

"Daisy, have we forgotten anything? I think we have everything we'll need to go ice skating with Cole and Rafe this afternoon."

A frown puckered Daisy's forehead. "We bought coats, and gloves, and scarves, and fur hats."

Garnet grinned. "And boots, and warm socks, and wool skirts. And of course, skates. It's a good thing I didn't spend any money this summer while I was at the mining camp. I've used up almost all my teacher's salary on this shopping trip, but I still have my quarterly allowance if we need more clothes."

"We didn't bring any winter clothes with us when we came West. We had to buy everything, so it's no wonder you spent a lot of money."

A clock in a nearby church tower chimed. Dismay arrested Garnet's attention. The time was later than she'd thought. "We'd better hurry, or we'll be late. I lost track of the time while we were shopping. Cole and Rafe are meeting us in an hour."

Pedestrians jostled along the sidewalk. A burly man wearing a dark wool topcoat and a bowler hat bumped against her as he strode past. In the street, motor car horns blared. The vehicles jostled for space with bicyclists and horse-drawn carriages. The din beat at Garnet's ears, and she longed for the mining camp's peace and the wind's music soughing through the evergreens.

They hurried along the sidewalk, past shops, banks, and brick government buildings. They were two blocks from the Grande Palace Hotel when Garnet came to an abrupt halt. The gentleman strolling behind her sidestepped to avoid a collision.

She grabbed Daisy's arm. "Daisy! Isn't that my father over there?"

"Where?" Daisy craned her neck.

Garnet nodded in the direction of a gentlemen's club on the corner. "He's standing in front of that brick building. He seems to be meeting someone. They're shaking hands."

A cluster of pedestrians briefly obscured her view before Garnet saw her father again. Asa Morrison stood outside a two-story brick building. A fan-shaped window above the lintel endowed the establishment with an elegant touch. The words "Denver Gentlemen's Club" painted in gold cursive script on a white sign proclaimed the building's function.

As Garnet watched, her father greeted a tall man in a dark frock coat and top hat. The man replied, and Asa Morrison swept an arm toward the club. His companion nodded, and the two men entered the building.

Daisy peered after them. "That was your father, all right."

"I wonder who that other man is, and why are they meeting?" Garnet frowned at the closed door. "I don't like it."

"Are you going to tell Mr. Wild Wind?"

Garnet looked at Daisy's earnest face. "I think I should. I'll tell him while we're skating." The furtive air her father had displayed disturbed her. "My father is up to something." She shook her head to clear away the worrisome thoughts. "Cole will know what to do, but right now, we'd better get back to the hotel."

When they reached their suite at the Grande Palace, they dumped their parcels on the sitting room sofa, and Garnet made shooing motions toward Daisy. "Daisy, take your things and get ready. You don't have time to dress me. I can manage on my own."

Daisy gathered up her packages and whisked herself off to her own room.

Garnet changed her clothes in record time. She tossed her morning dress across her bed and left her silk stockings and shoes strewn across the rug, then wriggled into her skating outfit. Hurrying to the pier glass in the corner, she viewed her image with a critical eye. The dark green wool skirt swirled above her ankles and had enough drape so it shouldn't hinder her skating, yet the style still gave her a straight, slim silhouette. Her wool jacket of matching green and buff plaid fell just above her knees, and the lace of her cream-colored blouse peeked out between the jacket's wide lapels. She smiled at her reflection. Cole should be pleased she once again resembled a fashionable young lady instead of the disheveled castaway she'd appeared to be at the mining camp.

A soft rap sounded on the suite's outer door, and Daisy called out. Garnet turned away from the mirror and scooped her fur hat off the bed, then hurried into the sitting room.

Daisy stood just inside the door, an anxious expression on her face. "How do I look?"

Garnet circled her friend, assessing Daisy's appearance. She'd purchased a complete skating outfit for her maid, something similar in style to her own ensemble, yet not so fine as to make Daisy appear pretentious. The pale fawn-colored wool of her straight skirt and fitted jacket complimented Daisy's fair coloring. A wool turban perched atop her blonde chignon, and leather gloves completed her costume.

Tossing aside social convention, Garnet hugged her maid. "You look splendid. You'll do Rafe proud." She flicked Daisy's filigree earrings with one finger. "And these earrings provide the final touch."

Daisy colored a becoming pink. "Do you think Rafe will notice?"

"He'd have to be blind not to notice. Truly, you look beautiful." Garnet smiled, yet uneasiness flickered through her. She walked a fine line, dressing Daisy up for outings with the four of them. For both Rafe's sake and Daisy's, she didn't want Daisy to look like a servant when the couples socialized, yet she didn't want the girl to spin dreams of a future with Rafe.

Daisy gave her a diffident smile. "Thank you so much for buying me these clothes. This outfit makes me feel like a real lady."

"You should wear pretty things when you're with Rafe."

"Rafe treats me like a lady."

Garnet met Daisy's gaze. "Rafe is a true gentleman. He would never treat you as less than a lady, no matter what you wore."

Garnet pulled her own white fur turban over her hair, patting the low knot of coppery tresses coiled below the hat's rim. Every hair seemed to be in place. She reached for her gloves, which rested on a lamp table and picked up her skates. "Let's meet our escorts."

Cole and Rafe were waiting for them when they entered the hotel lobby. Garnet's gaze locked on Cole's when she stepped off the elevator. He speared her with an ardent look, and the world receded. He took her hand and drew her close.

"You're a vision of loveliness." Cole's husky, murmured words warmed her heart, words to be recalled later and treasured. She valued them more than her jewels.

"Thank you." Garnet indicated his woolen topcoat and

dark trousers. He no longer wore the jeans and flannel shirt that had been his costume at the mining camp. No six-shooter rode along his thigh. "You look like a fine gentleman tonight, but I miss the cowboy I knew back in the mountains."

He touched the fat pompadour at the nape of her neck. "And I love your hair all twisted up in that knot thing, but I also miss the hoyden I knew at the camp whose hair flew wild about her head. Your hair looked like it caught fire from the sun."

Rafe interrupted the moment with a less-than-tactful cough. "Daisy and I are ready to leave if you two can stop casting sheep's eyes at each other."

Cole tucked Garnet's hand into the crook of his elbow and punched Rafe on the shoulder. "Just wait until it's your turn to cast sheep's eyes, little brother."

Rafe snorted. "No sheep's eyes for me, thank you very much." With Daisy on his arm, he swung about and led the way outside. A dark blue motor vehicle waited at the curb instead of Cole's green touring car. "I'm the chauffeur today. Daisy, in you go up front with me." Rafe opened the front passenger door and settled her inside.

While Cole held the back door for Garnet, she climbed into the vehicle and scooted across the black leather seat. When Cole slid in beside her, he snuggled her close. Twining his fingers through hers, he rested their joined hands on his leg.

After they chugged through the arched iron gate that fronted Denver Park, Rafe parked his motorcar at one side in a space allocated for such vehicles and horse-drawn buggies. With skates in hand, the couples strolled toward the lake, now a solid silver sheet. Some skaters already raced across the ice, while other people huddled about a snapping log fire on the shore or ambled along the paths.

Rafe slowed his stride to match Cole's and Garnet's slower amble. "Isn't Daisy a picture today?" He grinned at his skating partner. "I told her she was a fair picture for any man's eyes."

Daisy's cheeks flamed at the compliment.

"I agree," Cole commented. "We're two of the most fortunate men here. We have the loveliest ladies in the park as our companions."

Garnet chuckled at their teasing. "You two have kissed the blarney stone, but we don't mind, do we, Daisy?"

Daisy laughed, a light, tinkling sound. "Certainly not." Her smile vanished. "But Rafe, you may be sorry you have me dragging on your arm. I'm not a very good skater."

If Rafe minded not being able to indulge his skating skills, he didn't let on. Daisy's palm rested on his forearm, and he covered her hand with his. "I won't regret a thing. Just being in your company is pleasure enough." He smiled down at her. "I can teach you to skate, and you'll be skimming along with everyone else before we leave."

Excitement shone in Daisy's blue eyes. "Do you really think so?"

"Of course. All you need is a little practice."

At the lake's shore, they stowed their shoes in a locker provided for that purpose and donned their skates, then stepped onto the ice. Cole gripped one of Garnet's gloved hands in his and curled his other arm about her waist. Leaving Rafe and Daisy behind, they pushed off.

Legs pumping in unison, Cole and Garnet skimmed

across the ice. Their skate blades scrunched the surface with each stroke and sprayed ice slivers in their wake. Garnet's breath plumed in a white vapor, and the cold air stung her cheeks. Her eyes sparkled. When they reached the other side, Cole swung them about. With an abrupt pivot, he brought them to a halt. They collided, and Garnet laughed as they grabbed for each other and steadied themselves.

"Thank you for bringing me here. I love to skate."

"Rafe and I skated a lot as boys. We still do when we can. You and Daisy provided the perfect excuse for us to play hooky from mine business this afternoon to go skating."

"I hope Rafe isn't too disappointed he can't stretch his legs. I'm sure he'd prefer to fly. Daisy was right. She'll slow him down."

Cole curved both arms about Garnet's waist and pulled her against him. Eyes gleaming, he grinned down at her. "Rafe's a good sport. He doesn't mind, and to tell you the truth, he enjoys Daisy's company. By playing the gallant knight, he becomes a hero in Daisy's eyes. Every man wants to be a hero for a pretty girl."

Garnet gripped his shoulders to steady herself. "Rafe has been very kind to her. He makes her feel like a princess. Back in New York, no gentleman in his position would jeopardize his social standing by associating with someone like Daisy."

"It's not the same out here. We weren't brought up to distinguish these social differences. My great-uncle Clint and great-aunt Coral were wonderful examples of treating each person as an equal."

"I can't wait to meet them."

With one arm still about Garnet's waist, Cole steered them toward a clump of willows growing along the bank. The trailing branches hanging over the lake's edge provided a small private cocoon. He spun them to a stop beneath the trees and pulled her into an embrace, his hands locked at the small of her back. He lowered his head and rested his forehead against hers.

"I've been wanting to do this ever since we left the camp." Angling his head, his mouth took hers.

Garnet's eyes drifted closed, and she lost herself in the wonder of his kiss. Her arms stole up to curl about his neck.

When at last he lifted his head, his gaze roved over her face, and his arms tightened about her. "Your lips are sweet. I could feast on them."

She laughed. "Such flattery! You're a smooth-talking man. My aunt warned me about men like you."

"Huh!" His eyes narrowed. "But this smooth-talking man loves you, so you should have no worries on that account. Have I told you yet that I love you?"

Garnet thought back to their summer days at the mining camp. He hadn't actually said the word "love," though he'd made his affection plain in other ways. "I don't think you have."

"How remiss of me! Let me make up for my lapse." He dropped a kiss on the end of her nose. "I love you." He trailed light kisses across her cheek. "I love you." As he drew her closer to him, about her, Garnet felt his muscled strength along her whole length. She tangled her fingers in his hair.

"And I love you." Her throat closed. The enormity of her declaration sobered her. To love a man enough to spend the rest of her life with him through the difficult times as well as the good stole her breath. She cleared her throat and tried again. "I love you, Cole Wild Wind."

A chill breeze gusted across the lake, ruffling Garnet's skirt and running icy fingers over the back of her neck. The afternoon sun pierced the willow's branches and painted shadows across Cole's face. No matter what happened in the future, this private moment the two of them shared would be forever imprinted on her memory. "Do you know when I first realized that I loved you?"

He shook his head, his dark eyes fixed on her face.

"I knew I loved you when you went back into the mine to rescue the men who were trapped. I didn't know whether I'd see you alive again, and that was when I realized I loved you."

"At least something good came from that explosion." He took her mouth again.

When he lifted his head, she rested her forehead against his shoulder. He slid his hand beneath her pompadour and curled about the back of her neck. He spoke above her head in a voice like velvet.

"This smooth-talking man is going to marry you."

Her heart contracted. He seemed convinced that her father would relent and allow them to marry. For this moment, she could play along. Indulging in a little harmless fantasy couldn't hurt.

She peeked up into his face. "So, when do you propose we marry?"

"I think a June wedding would be good, don't you?"

"I like that. June it is."

"We could be married in the chapel at the Slash L. That's the traditional place for our family to be married. Unless, of course, you'd prefer the wedding to be in New York." His intent tone spun a magical illusion that seemed, in that moment, possible.

At the mention of the city, Garnet shuddered. "Not New York. I'd rather be married at the ranch, with all your family there."

"Then that's settled." He grinned down at her and placed a kiss on the corner of her mouth, then another one at her temple. "Kissing you could become a habit."

"I won't complain about that." She palmed his cheek with one hand. His dear, handsome face shone with the love he professed. "You're a good man, Cole Wild Wind. The finest man I know. And I'll never tire of your kisses."

"Well, then, who am I to deny you?" With that, he dipped his head for another kiss. When he broke off the kiss, a sober expression marked his features. "I think I should talk to your father. I want to do things properly. I'll ask for his blessing on our marriage and convince him that you'll lack for nothing."

Mention of her father doused Garnet's joy. Fantasy gave way to reality, and she stepped out of Cole's arms. "I doubt you'll be able to change his mind. He wants to establish a dynasty with another banking family, a union that will elevate us without peer in New York society."

Cole seemed undaunted. "We'll keep praying. I feel sure we'll be together."

Garnet recalled the scene with her father and the stranger. She lifted her gaze to Cole's face. "I have information you should know. When Daisy and I were shopping this afternoon, I saw my father meet a man I'd never seen before."

Cole's expression sharpened. "What did the man look like?"

Garnet's forehead puckered in concentration. "I didn't get a good look at his face. He was tall and seemed younger than my father. He was wearing a hat, so I couldn't tell what color his hair was."

"That could describe a lot of men, but it also could be Craig Buchanan, one of the owners of the Colorado Mining Company." Grimness tightened Cole's mouth and lent an edge to his voice.

"The same company that spied on your mining operation? The one who probably blew up your mine?"

Cole nodded. "The very same. I wonder what business your father could have with our competition?"

For a long moment, they both contemplated the possibilities. At last, Cole shifted and shook his head. "Rafe and I will discuss this. And I think we need to have a talk with your father."

Garnet shivered, but she tried to be optimistic. "Perhaps my father just met him for a drink. He does that sometimes."

Cole smiled down at her and brushed her jaw with his knuckles. "Perhaps. His meeting could have an innocent explanation. I'll ask him." He glanced across the ice, where the lowering sun cast long shadows across the silver expanse. "We should find Rafe and Daisy. A mug of hot chocolate would warm us up. Then we'll find a nice restaurant and have dinner before we take you back to the Palace."

"That sounds like the perfect ending to a perfect afternoon."

"But first, give me one more kiss."

Chapter 25

With laughter bubbling in her chest, Garnet exited the restaurant through the door Cole held open for her. They stepped onto the sidewalk with Rafe and Daisy close behind.

Garnet turned an amused face over her shoulder and sent Rafe a saucy look. "I can't believe you played such a trick on your teacher."

Rafe chuckled. "It was actually Cole's idea, but we were both guilty." He glanced at Daisy, strolling beside him with her hand tucked into his elbow. "Daisy, you must have played a trick or two on your teachers when you were in school."

Daisy looked aghast. "Not me! I never did such a thing."

Rafe tweaked a curl that dangled at her temple. "Never? Surely you must have done something naughty in your school days."

Daisy's brow puckered. "Well, I passed notes to my friends when the teacher's back was turned."

"There! I knew it!" Rafe bumped her with his elbow. "I knew you had it in you!"

Daisy's face glowed at the back-handed compliment, and she beamed up at him.

Garnet faced ahead. Cole reached for her hand and laced his fingers through hers. The smile he gave her warmed her to her toes, and the possessive gleam in his eyes made her feel cherished. She smiled back at him and forgot the cold air that nipped at exposed skin.

While they'd eaten dinner, the sun had slid behind the mountains, and now darkness blanketed Denver's streets. Streetlamps spilled pools of golden light across the sidewalk, interspersed by stretches of gloom. Brick and granite buildings loomed along both sides of the roadway, whose blank windows stared through the dimness.

Rafe had parked his motorcar a little distance from the restaurant. They'd almost reached the parked vehicle when a blur of motion from a side alley caught Garnet's eye, and Cole shoved her away. Thrust off balance, she thudded to her knees and skidded along the walkway. Her hands scraped the pavement. Her knees burned, and her palms stung, but she scrambled to her feet.

Rafe had pushed Daisy away, and the smaller girl stood at the sidewalk's edge, clutching her arms about her. After one glance, Garnet turned her attention to the men.

An obsidian shroud between two streetlamps veiled the area where they stood, but she could make out Cole and Rafe's dark shapes struggling with three men. Twilight camouflaged the fight, but grunts and the thwack of flesh against flesh sounded in the murk.

Daisy leaped toward to Garnet, and the two women

huddled together while the shadowed forms grappled in a mass of writhing shapes. At the abrupt gleam of lamplight glimmering off a metal blade, Garnet's breath hissed through her teeth. One of the thugs had drawn a knife. Cole launched himself at the man and pinned him to the ground, anchoring the attacker's wrist against the sidewalk. He pounded the mugger's wrist against the pavement until the knife spun across the walkway.

Rafe shook himself free from one of the other attackers and scooped up the dagger. With a vicious thrust, he stabbed upward toward the man closest to him. The man leaped out of reach, and as quickly as the assault had begun, it ended. Two of the assailants faded back and vanished up the alley from which they'd come. Cole jerked the third one to his feet by the scruff of his neck and shook him.

"Who hired you to attack us?" His voice grated through clenched teeth, and his chest heaved.

The thug squirmed and lashed out with a booted foot. Cole danced out of reach while he kept an iron grip on the villain's neck. Rafe wrenched the mugger's arm up behind his back.

"Talk." Rafe leaned into the man. "This wasn't a random attack. Who sent you?"

The thug resisted. When Rafe increased the pressure, the man squealed. "All right, all right. I'll tell you." He panted. "A stranger paid me and my friends money to attack you and your brother...supposed to make it look like a robbery."

"Who was this stranger?" Cole said.

The mugger shook his head. "Never saw him before. Didn't give no name."

"What did he look like?" Rafe jerked the man's arm up higher between his shoulder blades.

With a hiss between gapped teeth, the captive went up on his toes. "Blond. Heavy set. Good dresser, like a fancy man. Talked smooth, ya know?"

Cole and Rafe exchanged glances.

"Anything else we should know?" Cole shook the man again.

"We'd get paid extra if we killed one o' you."

Cole gripped his captive's jaw and held his head immobile. "We're going to let you go, but only so you can tell whoever hired you that you failed. Tell him if he wants something, to meet us face to face and man to man. No more attacks in the dark. Got it?"

The other man exhaled. "Got it."

The brothers turned their erstwhile assailant loose, and he sprinted up the alley.

Silence descended when the thud of the mugger's footsteps had faded. With the attack over, tremors shook Garnet's body. A hot rush of tears filled her eyes, but she blinked them back.

The brothers spun toward the women. Cole opened his arms and enfolded Garnet in a tight embrace.

After the anxiety of the previous moments, the comfort he offered came almost as a shock. Garnet curled her arms about his back and hugged him close. With her face buried in his shirt front, she snuggled against his chest. His heart thudded with reassuring beats beneath her ear.

He stroked her hair. With his mouth close to her ear, he

murmured, "I'm all right. I'm fine. Remember, I was trained by a Cheyenne Dog Soldier. It would take more than a couple of half-rate thugs to kill me."

Garnet sucked in a shuddered breath. "It all happened so fast."

"They hoped to take us by surprise." Cole laid one cheek against the top of her fur cap and rocked her.

Garnet closed her eyes and clung to him.

When her trembling had ceased, Cole shifted her toward one of the streetlamps and cradled her hands in his. With his head bent, he examined her palms. "I must apologize for shoving you away. My only thought was to get you away from our attackers. I didn't mean to knock you down."

"You have nothing to apologize for. I realized you were protecting me."

He ran a thumb over her shredded gloves. "I owe you a new pair of gloves. And you're bleeding. Does it hurt?"

Though her palms stung, Garnet didn't want to admit as much. "A little."

Cole pulled a handkerchief from his jacket pocket and dabbed at her palms.

Garnet winced while he wrapped his handkerchief about her hand. When he finished, she looked around for Daisy.

Rafe and Daisy stood near the curb, Daisy enfolded in Rafe's arms. She burrowed against him, her shoulders shaking, and he patted her awkwardly. Rafe and Cole exchanged a man-to-man look.

Daisy pushed away from Rafe's embrace and swiped at

her cheeks. "Please forgive me. I forgot myself for a moment."

Rafe pulled her against him in a one-armed hug. "You've done nothing to forgive. Any man would be honored to comfort such a pretty lady."

Daisy sniffled. "You're too kind."

With his arm still about her shoulders, Rafe urged her toward his motorcar. "You need to sit down." After he'd opened the front passenger door, he eased her onto the seat and dug into his coat pocket for a handkerchief. Squatting in the motorcar's open doorway, he thrust the handkerchief into her hand. "Here, dry your tears with this."

Daisy took the proffered handkerchief and dabbed her eyes. "Thank you. I'm sorry to be such a ninny."

"You're no such thing. It's not every day you witness a knife fight."

On the ride back to the Grande Palace, Garnet huddled against Cole's side and clutched his hand, while she tried to quell the tremors that shivered through her.

Asa Morrison was seated in a carved mahogany chair reading a newspaper when they trooped into the Palace's Atrium Lobby. As they approached, he peered at them over the paper's edge. When they halted before his chair, he laid the periodical aside and stood. He thrust his hands into his trousers' pockets, surveying the brothers' disheveled condition and Garnet's torn skirt with a critical perusal. "What happened?"

Cole eyed the older man with a watchful air. "We were attacked by three men after dinner."

Asa Morrison didn't comment. His expression gave

nothing away, but he continued to study the Wild Wind brothers. "Do you think it was random? A gang looking for money?"

"We don't think so. We were targeted."

Garnet caught the guarded tone in Cole's reply.

Asa Morrison stared at them, his gaze flicking from one brother to the other. He rocked back on his heels. After a moment, he reached into his waistcoat pocket and extracted a cheroot. He busied himself lighting the smoke, then clamped the cigar between his teeth. After a couple of puffs, he pulled the cheroot from his mouth and jabbed it at Cole. "Any idea who would target you?"

"We have our suspicions."

"And that would be?"

For long moments, Cole didn't reply. A dangerous stillness enveloped him. Tension rolled from him in waves. "Perhaps you can answer that better than we can, sir."

Anger flared across the older man's face. "What is that supposed to mean?"

"You tell me."

Rafe stirred. A wave of tension resonated from him as well. Suppressed emotions roiled beneath the surface of the atmosphere. The air simmered.

A trio of hotel guests, clad in evening finery, strolled through the Atrium Lobby toward the Grand Entrance, while a well-dressed family with several children entered from the street. The children's noisy chatter broke the strain.

Asa Morrison scowled as the children's babble faded up the stairs. "I don't know what bee you have in your bonnet, boy, but you're way off base. I had nothing to do with that attack." He gave them another once over. "Were either of you hurt?"

"We weren't hurt." Rafe clipped off his words. "The ladies could have been injured. The thugs took us by surprise."

Garnet's father slid a glance at his daughter and Daisy. "Are you girls all right?" He indicated Garnet's skirt. "Your skirt is torn, and your hands are bleeding."

"That's my fault, sir." Cole clasped Garnet's elbow as he explained.

Garnet spoke up. "I'm fine, sir. Daisy and I were frightened, but Cole and Rafe got us out of the way."

Asa offered his hand first to Cole and then to Rafe. "Thank you both for protecting the ladies. I think whoever attacked you underestimated you." He put the cheroot to his mouth for a puff and then waved it at Cole. "Perhaps I should hire bodyguards for the ladies. Do you think they're in danger?"

"If it will set your mind at ease, hire bodyguards, but the girls weren't the target. Rafe and I were the intended victims." Cole motioned to himself and Rafe.

Garnet's father swung toward her and gave her shoulder an awkward pat. "You and Daisy go upstairs and ring for the hotel nurse. Those injuries should be seen to."

As she and Daisy excused themselves and headed for the elevator, Garnet overheard her father's comments to the brothers. "We should discuss a strategy to protect the women. You two can take care of yourselves, but I don't want my daughter and Daisy harmed. And I'd like to set up a very important meeting tomorrow morning. A gentleman wishes to meet with you to discuss a possible business transaction."

Garnet continued toward the lobby elevator. What kind of business transaction could the mystery gentleman wish to conduct? She thought back to the man she'd seen with her father that afternoon. Somehow, she knew he had to be connected.

Chapter 26

"Something tells me that you don't frequent this confectionery shop very often." Garnet tossed Cole a teasing grin over her shoulder as he seated her in a spindle-legged white metal chair.

"What makes you say that?" He skirted the round glass-topped table and lowered himself into a chair opposite her.

"I don't think you eat many sweets." A flick of her fingers encompassed the shop's interior. "And I just can't picture you here."

Cole surveyed the confectionery's décor and brought his gaze back to Garnet's face. Though his eyes twinkled, his features remained deadpan. "You don't think red silk wallpaper and crystal chandeliers are my style?"

"Uh-huh. My imagination doesn't stretch that far." Garnet shrugged out of her coat.

A smile cracked his impassive expression. "I heard about this place from Rafe. He's brought a lady friend or two here and assured me that women find this shop very romantic."

"Rafe's been here?" She shouldn't be surprised. She'd sensed when she met him that Rafe might be a ladies' man.

"Sure. Rafe's very popular with the girls."

Garnet hesitated over her next words. "Cole, Rafe won't hurt Daisy, will he? Daisy hasn't had much experience with men, especially one like Rafe."

Reaching across the table, Cole took both her hands in his and sent her an earnest look. "Rafe likes to flirt, but he never leads a lady on. He keeps things light, and women know not to expect too much from him. In Daisy's case, Rafe will guard her heart. He understands that she's inexperienced about men." Cole paused. "If you want the truth, I think Rafe may be a little sweet on her. He's spent more time with Daisy than he has any other girl."

"Truly?"

"Rafe hasn't confided in me, but I know my brother well." Cole peeled off her leather gloves and laid them aside, then reclaimed her hands. "Enough of Rafe and Daisy. They'll sort themselves out." His eyes crinkled. "I finally have you all to myself."

"We don't have our chaperones this afternoon." Garnet squeezed his fingers. "Did you have anything to do with that?"

Cole slid his hands from hers and thrust them up, palms out. "I had nothing to do with our lack of chaperones. Rafe decided to take Daisy skating again after luncheon, so the two of them are occupied. I took advantage of the opportunity to spirit you away before anyone was the wiser."

When their order had been taken, Garnet leaned forward and pinned him with an inquisitive stare. "Now, tell me about that business meeting my father arranged for this morning. I'm about to expire from curiosity."

Cole settled back in his chair. "The session was with one of the owners of the Colorado Mining Company, most likely the man your father met yesterday afternoon. He offered to buy out our mine. It seems your father has been meeting with the owners of the Colorado Mining Company, hoping to broker a sale."

Garnet shook her head. "Isn't that unethical?"

"Let's say it's a bit on the shady side."

"But why? What did he hope to gain? And do you think he was involved with the mine explosion and the attack on you and Rafe?"

The waiter arrived then with their hot chocolate.

When the waiter had served them and departed, Garnet swirled her spoon through the mound of whipped cream atop the liquid. She sipped and watched Cole over the rim of her teacup.

He traced a finger around his cup's gold rim, a thoughtful expression on his face, then met her gaze. "Your father insists he's innocent in both incidents."

"Do you believe him?"

Cole shrugged and sipped his own drink. He lowered the cup to the table and scrubbed a hand down his face. "Yes, I believe him."

"If he's innocent, why did he try to arrange a sale?"

"I think he decided he could better his investment by

arranging a sale of our mine and then joining with the Colorado Mining Company. The Colorado Mining Company is a big-time outfit compared to us. We're just a small competitor they'd like to swallow up, so your father could make a lot more money by joining forces with them."

Garnet mulled over what Cole had told her. "Do you think they'll plot anything else against you and Rafe? For them to try to get you killed is serious."

Cole pushed his cup aside and gripped Garnet's hands again. "We made it plain that we're not interested in selling our mine and won't be pressured to do so. We have no proof that the Colorado Mining Company was behind the explosion or the attack on us, but Rafe and I made it plain we'd sworn out affidavits with our solicitor. Should any other incidents occur, or if either one of us should die in an 'accident,' then the affidavits would be used in court. I think that will make an end of these incidents."

"I hope so." Garnet squeezed his hands.

Cole leaned closer, his face inches from her own. "Enough of that. I have something personal to tell you."

Garnet studied his countenance, so dear to her. Her vision traced the squint lines that fanned out on either side of his eyes and the grooves that bracketed his mouth. Her gaze roved over the strong blade of his nose and the curl that hung over his brow. Each feature blended with the others to create the whole of the man she loved. Surrendering to an urge to touch him, she pulled one hand free and palmed the side of his face. "Oh? Something good, I hope."

He captured her hand again. "I think so." He paused and allowed the suspense to build. His eyes twinkled.

"Well?" She let him draw out the moment.

"My mother called me today."

"There's a telephone at the ranch?"

Cole shifted his legs beneath the small table and stretched them out to one side. "We don't have electricity there yet, but we have a telephone to conduct ranch business."

"I see. So why did your mother call?"

"She asked me to pick up a few Christmas gifts for my father. She can't buy his presents in September when they come to Denver to shop. He never lets her out of his sight."

Garnet frowned. "Doesn't he trust her?"

"It's not my mother he doesn't trust." Cole drew his eyebrows together. "You have to understand the Cheyenne mentality. He takes very seriously his role as protector. He doesn't consider Denver to be safe enough for my mother to go about town without him."

Garnet mulled that over. "That's not so very different from how I live. I always take a maid or another family member with me whenever I leave the house."

"So you see how my mother needs Rafe or me to buy our father's Christmas presents for her." Cole lifted one of Garnet's hands to his mouth and kissed each knuckle.

His tender gesture captivated her. She couldn't look away from his mesmerizing gaze.

"Garnet." His thumb stroked over her hand where his lips had kissed.

"Hmm?"

"I told my mother about us."

His words shattered the moment's romance. Garnet

jerked her hand free. "You what?" She pinned him with a glare.

"I told my mother everything about our situation."

"But my father..."

"She knows about your father and his plans for you, but she'll be discreet. She won't spill our dreams." Cole ran his thumb over the back of her hand. "She knows from personal experience that if the Lord wants us to be together, He'll make a way. I firmly believe that the Lord intends for us to be together."

Cole's optimism encouraged her. "You really think so?"

"I do. My mother is looking forward to meeting you when we all go to the Slash L for Christmas. She's been praying for a wife for me for a long time."

Panic fluttered inside Garnet's bosom. "What if she doesn't like me?"

Optimism mingled with love lit Cole's expression. "Mother can't help but love you. Now, finish your hot chocolate. We have some Christmas shopping to do."

Slash L Ranch
Christmas, 1911

Chapter 27

From the back seat of Cole's dark green touring car, Garnet peered at the treeless plains around her. They'd left the flat area around Denver behind, and now the dirt track wound through rolling bluffs and ridges miles northeast of the city.

A towering spruce tree that had been cut from the mountains and shipped to Denver by train had been strapped to the back of Rafe's motorcar.

"Evergreens don't grow on the plains," Cole had said while the brothers examined the straps that secured the tree to the motorcar. He adjusted the tree's crown over the vehicle's roof and added another leather strap. "Our mother grew up in New England, where she always had a Christmas tree. After she came West, she missed that tradition. Now Rafe and I always bring a tree to the ranch when we come for the holidays."

Garnet and Daisy watched from the sidewalk by the Grande Palace's front steps as the men checked the bindings and loaded their luggage.

From the other side of the car, Rafe adjusted a strap and winked at Daisy. "Did you pack your boots? There's no snow yet, but I promise we'll have a white Christmas."

Now Garnet peered out the motorcar's back window at Rafe and Daisy, who followed in Rafe's vehicle. Rafe and Daisy were laughing and seemed to be enjoying each other's company. Perhaps Rafe was sweet on Daisy, after all.

Late in the afternoon, they crested a knoll. The track dipped down to a basin, and Garnet got her first sight of the ranch nestled in the valley below. The Slash L resembled a small town.

When they rolled past a sprawl of buildings outside the compound's encircling adobe wall, Cole tipped his head to the left. "That's the headquarters for the cattle side of the ranch. We have housing for the married men, a bunkhouse and a cookshack for the single cowboys, a commissary, blacksmith shop, barn, and corrals. We even provide a school for the children that doubles as a church on Sundays."

From his place in the front seat, Asa Morrison cast an assessing eye over the well-kept property. "Your uncle seems to have a thriving business here."

"Ranching is always a risk, what with the ups and downs of the beef market, weather, and predators, but Uncle Clint is a canny businessman. That, and God's blessings have made the Slash L what it is today."

They chugged beneath an arched sign with the words *Slash L* burned into the wood and entered the compound. Inside the wall sprawled the main house, a white clapboard structure fronted by a wide porch with spooled white railings. A horse barn and corrals to the left of the house shared space within the compound. Horses in the corrals lifted their heads to watch the humans who had just arrived.

A large gray dog who looked to be part wolf bounded off the porch and greeted them with loud *woofs*, tail wagging.

Cole brought his touring car to a stop before the front steps, and Rafe halted his vehicle behind Cole's. The dog circled the motorcar and planted large paws on Cole's door, his nose pressed against the window.

"That's Brutus." Cole indicated the canine with a wave of one hand. "He's supposed to guard the property, but he's not much good at that. I think he'd open the door for a burglar instead of chasing him off."

The reunion between Cole and the dog brought a smile to Garnet's lips. When Cole shoved open the motorcar's door and climbed out, Brutus greeted him with happy yips and wild tail-wagging. He reared up and plopped his paws on Cole's shoulders, licking Cole's face with sloppy enthusiasm. Cole ruffled the dog's fur and pushed him away. "I love you, too, but go on with you."

Cole opened the back door and gripped one of Garnet's hands. She slid across the seat and stepped out. Before she could sidestep, Brutus bounded toward her and planted his paws on her shoulders. Garnet staggered backward, and Cole wrapped an arm about her to prevent a collision with the touring car. With his other hand, he grabbed Brutus by the ruff and shoved him away. "Down, you beast. Don't you have any manners?"

Tongue lolling, Brutus whirled and gamboled to Rafe's

motor vehicle. Rafe had just helped Daisy from the cab when the dog launched himself at her. Rafe whirled Daisy aside and intercepted the dog's leap. All Brutus's considerable weight landed on Rafe's chest. "Off, you mutt!" Rafe shoved the canine away.

Brutus whoofed a rumbling bark and galloped in a mad circle about the compound.

Brutus's barks had alerted the family of their arrival. As Cole and Garnet rounded the front of his touring car, people spilled outside onto the porch. Garnet halted. Cole had told her he had a lot of family, but with her limited experience, she couldn't imagine such a reality. The group congregating on the veranda gave proof to his words. She gave him a sideways glance. He caught her look and shrugged.

He bent and murmured in her ear, "I warned you."

Her father joined them. "This whole crowd belongs to you?"

Cole nodded. "Every one of them."

They mounted the porch steps, with Cole's hand at the small of Garnet's back.

Rafe and Daisy followed. Daisy seemed overwhelmed and clung to Rafe's arm. Garnet cast a brief glance over her shoulder. Daisy looked enchanting in a fawn wool coat and matching cap over a slim blue skirt and ruffled blouse. Garnet had purchased the outfit so her friend would have no concerns about her appearance when she met Rafe's family.

The introductions passed in a blur. Before they'd even entered the house, she'd met numerous cousins and siblings. Jake, a tall, sandy-haired man who was several years older than Cole, greeted her with grave courtesy.

"Jake, this is Garnet and her father, Asa Morrison, my business partner. Jake is my older brother."

As she shook Jake's hand, Garnet recalled that he was Cole's half-brother from their mother's first marriage. "I'm so pleased to meet you. Cole tells me you run the Quarter horse breeding program."

They exchanged brief pleasantries before Cole urged her forward with a hand beneath her elbow. They halted before a tall woman. Her slim, stylish dress of turquoise satin, beaded and tucked at the bodice, flattered her slender figure. Coiffed in a simple French braid, only a few silver strands gleamed amongst her curly chocolate tresses. *Cole's mother.* Garnet's tongue stuck to the roof of her mouth.

"Mother, I'd like you to meet Garnet and her father, Asa Morrison. Mr. Morrison is our business partner. Garnet, Asa, my mother, Della Wild Wind."

Cole's mother thrust out her hand first to Asa Morrison.

The banker took Della's hand and swept her with an appreciative glance. "I'm charmed to make your acquaintance, Mrs. Wild Wind. Thank you for opening your home to Garnet and me this Christmas."

"We couldn't allow you to languish in Denver when we have room for you here." Della withdrew her hand and turned to Garnet. "Garnet, I'm so pleased to meet you. Thank you for coming." Cole's mother enveloped her in a warm hug. "We'll talk later," she whispered.

Garnet could only nod before they moved along the line. Behind them, Rafe and Daisy stopped to greet Rafe's mother. Curious as to how Mrs. Wild Wind would receive Daisy, Garnet kept half an ear tuned to the conversation behind her.

Not by so much as the flicker of an eyelid did Della Wild Wind show dismay when her son introduced her to the small young woman clinging to his arm. Rafe's mother welcomed Daisy into the bosom of the family with the same warmth she'd extended to Garnet.

With Daisy's greetings over, Garnet turned her full attention to the man who loomed just outside the door. This had to be Wild Wind, Cole's father. She would have recognized the family relationship without an introduction.

Cole's father had passed his height on to his sons. His hawkish face, with its pale bronze coloring, hinted at his Cheyenne heritage. A black, low-crowned cowboy hat covered his dark hair. A soft green wool shirt and denim jeans couldn't conceal his muscled frame. An essence of watchful stillness surrounded him, which underscored his commanding presence. He greeted Garnet and her father with grave civility, extending a hand first to Asa Morrison.

"Welcome to the Slash L. I understand you are doing business with my sons."

"Yes. They've taken me on as a partner."

While the men chatted, Garnet watched in silence, melding what Cole had told her about his father with what she now observed. Her vivid imaginings conjured up an image of the fearsome warrior Wild Wind had once been.

Wild Wind turned his attention to her. With an instinct that warned her this man respected a show of courage, she lifted her chin.

With a hand still cupped about her elbow, Cole introduced her. "Father, this is Garnet."

Wild Wind took her hand. "My wife is a she-bear. You are a wounded cougar cub, but you will grow to be a strong lioness. My son will walk your trail beside you."

Garnet cut a glance at Cole. How much of her history had he confided to his parents? Cole shook his head at her. He hadn't betrayed her secret.

What insight did Wild Wind possess that he could discern what she'd kept hidden? "I feel as though I'm just beginning my journey."

"The trail ahead will not be easy. Do not be afraid or turn aside. You will need the courage of the cougar to stand by your choice."

Aware of her father's speculative scrutiny from one side and Cole's support on the other, Garnet well understood Wild Wind's warning. "Thank you. I hope I'll have the courage to make the right choice."

"The right choice will bring the sunshine to your heart. The wrong choice will bring a cold wind to your spirit."

Garnet studied Wild Wind's inscrutable face, feeling somehow connected to this man who had seen into her soul. She nodded.

"Your hair is like the flames of nighttime's campfire. It reflects the fire in your heart. The fire will warm those you love and consume your enemies."

Enemies? Did Wild Wind refer to her father and Albert?

Cole's father didn't seem to expect a reply. He squeezed her hand and withdrew his own.

Cole swept a hand toward the door. "We have more family inside."

Wild Heart

As they stepped over the threshold into the foyer, her father groused. "What was that all about? The man was talking in riddles."

Garnet didn't bother to reply. If her father hadn't guessed Wild Wind's meaning, she didn't intend to enlighten him.

To their right, a double door opened into a spacious parlor whose windows looked out onto the veranda. Furniture of excellent quality dominated the room, though the style harked back to the Victorian era. The jewel-toned Aubusson carpet showed the wear of countless feet, and the upholstered medallion sofa and the Lincoln rocker had the well-loved look of old furnishings.

Several people crowded the room, but two caught Garnet's attention. Directly across from the door in front of a Franklin stove stood an imposing, silver-haired man with a lean Yankee face. Despite his age, he stood erect with no hint of stooping. This must be Cole's great-uncle, Clint Logan, who had been a Civil War general. Beside him stood a petite, gray-haired woman whose classic bone structure had carried her quiet beauty into old age. Her stylish costume draped a still-slender figure.

Cole urged Garnet into the room and toward the couple standing before the stove. "Uncle Clint and Aunt Coral, let me present to you Mr. Asa Morrison, my business partner, and his daughter, Garnet." One hand indicated Garnet's father, while his other rested on Garnet's shoulder. "Asa, Garnet, my great uncle, General Clint Logan and Great-aunt Coral."

Before Garnet had recovered from so many introductions, a woman of middle height and gentle beauty, her sorghum-colored hair caught back in a fashionable pompadour, swept to Garnet's side. Lines framed dark eyes that sparkled, and a smile teased her lips. She gripped both of Garnet's hands with impulsive familiarity and pulled her aside.

"I know your head must be whirling. Our family can be overpowering when we're all together."

"I do feel a bit overwhelmed." Which cousin could this be? "Cole told me he had a lot of family, but I never expected quite such a clan."

"That's Cole's excuse for staying in Denver most of the year." The woman's smile widened to an irrepressible grin. "I'm Flossie, Clint and Coral's daughter. That would make me Cole's second cousin."

Cole hadn't mentioned Flossie. "I wondered. I'm still figuring everyone out."

Flossie chattered on. "We live in Washington, DC. My husband has a government job, so we stay in Washington most of the year, but we always spend a month at the Slash L during the Christmas holidays."

At Garnet's right, Rafe introduced Daisy to Clint and Coral Logan. Flossie's next words snapped Garnet's attention back to Cole's cousin.

"We must have a gossip session later. You're the first lady friend Cole has brought to the ranch, and I want to know all about you."

Had her father heard Flossie's declaration? Garnet peeked at her father to see if he'd reacted, but he was still engaged in conversation with Clint Logan. For Cole's family to speculate on her relationship with him within her father's hearing would only provoke him. "Actually, my father is his and Rafe's business partner. I only came West to be with my father."

Flossie sent her a sly grin. "Deny it all you want, but I saw the way my cousin looked at you. He's never looked at another woman like that."

Loud thumps accompanied by the voices of young people sounded in the foyer and interrupted Flossie's interrogation. Cole's cousin turned toward the group who spilled into the parlor. "Here comes the younger set with the Christmas tree. It's a tradition for the young men to bring in the tree and set it up. Everyone will decorate it after dinner."

"Really? That sounds like a lovely tradition." Garnet couldn't keep the wistful tone from her voice.

"Didn't your family have Christmas traditions?" Flossie looked appalled.

Discussing her lonely childhood with Cole's gregarious cousin offset some of Garnet's gloomy memories. "My mother died when I was young, and my father didn't keep Christmas. It was just myself and the servants during the holidays."

Flossie stared, her eyes rounded in disbelief, and she squeezed Garnet's hands. "No Christmas! You poor thing. Well, here you'll find out what a real Christmas is like. We do Christmas in a big way on the Slash L."

Garnet glanced at the laughing young people as they set up the tree Rafe had brought. "I can see that. I plan to enjoy every moment."

Cole halted at her shoulder and pecked Flossie on the cheek. "I see you've met Garnet."

Flossie cast an arch look at Garnet. "I introduced myself. We're going to be great friends."

"Just don't talk her ear off. I know you, Flossie."

Flossie tweaked his chin. "I can't help it if I like to talk. Conversation is how one gets to know people, and I think I should get to know Garnet. What aren't you telling us, cousin?"

Cole tapped his cousin's nose. "You'll know when I'm ready to tell you. Now don't pester Garnet for the details." Cole glanced at Garnet. "Rafe and I will get your luggage, and then we'll take you up to your rooms. You'd probably like to rest a bit before dinner."

"Actually, a rest does sound good."

When their luggage had been fetched, the brothers led their guests upstairs. The merry din from downstairs followed them to the second floor.

Rafe cocked a thumb at the stairs. "I hope you don't mind the ruckus. There's no peace and quiet here when all the family comes home."

"We don't mind," Garnet said. "Do we, Daisy?"

"It reminds me of home." Daisy raised her glance to Rafe's face. "I have six brothers and sisters."

"Then you should be used to the hubbub."

Garnet's father didn't comment.

Rafe turned the crystal knob on the door of a room at the head of the stairs and swung the door wide. "Daisy, this room is for you. You'll be right across the hall from Garnet." He ushered her into the room and deposited her tapestry satchel just inside the door.

Cole opened the door of the room on the other side of the hall and motioned for Garnet to precede him. "This room used to be my mother's. Now our family has rooms in one of the new wings."

Garnet stepped past him and entered the room. The furnishings evidenced a woman's touch, and Garnet felt Della Wild Wind's essence remained.

Cole touched her shoulder. "Your father will be right down the hall. Rest now, and I'll come for you when dinner is ready."

She nodded. The hungry expression in his eyes told her he wanted to kiss her, but with her father lurking in the passage, a kiss would have to wait. She blew him an air kiss, and his lips quirked at the corners. Snatching kisses with so much family about would be challenging.

Chapter 28

The angel stared up at her with painted blue eyes. Garnet dangled the ornament by its ribbon and admired the colorful glasswork.

Cole appeared at her side, a glittering gold star in his hand. He stood so close to her that the buttons on his woolen waistcoat brushed her shoulder.

She swished the glass angel in front of his face. "I'm guessing this ornament is older than I am. With all of this—" She waved a hand at the children running about the parlor and the laughing teenagers who strung popcorn garlands about the tree. "How did this beautiful angel survive?"

"That angel is one of a set that Aunt Coral brought with her from her plantation home when she and Uncle Clint left the South. There were a dozen altogether, but I think we only have half that number left."

A golden-haired sprite in a gingham frock ricocheted off Garnet's leg. With a squeal, the child barreled across the room, a freckle-faced youngster in overalls in pursuit.

"I can't imagine how even six angels could survive." Garnet tracked the children as they gamboled amid the boxes of decorations. With a contented sigh, she turned once again to the tree.

The evergreen had been set up in a corner of the room between the wood stove and a piano on the adjacent wall. A tall, young man whom Garnet guessed to be about Daisy's age was helping her friend wind a popcorn garland about the tree. Daisy looked flushed, and her blue eyes glittered.

Garnet nudged Cole and inclined her head toward the pair. "I think Rafe has competition. Who is that young man?"

Cole flicked a glance at Daisy and her companion. "That's Trystan, Flossie's oldest boy." He grinned. "Rafe had better look to his laurels."

Even as he spoke, Rafe sauntered toward the tree and halted beside Daisy. He dangled another spun-glass ornament before her face. "When you finish with that popcorn, I'll help you with this angel. We'll hang it high enough that the little ones can't reach it."

Daisy turned a laughing face to him. "You need my help with an angel?"

Rafe gave her an easy grin, with a hint of something more serious behind it. "Hanging an angel takes two people. You don't know that? Your Christmas traditions need polishing, my girl."

Daisy flushed a becoming pink and sneaked a peek at Trystan.

Cole and Garnet exchanged a look, and Cole bent his head close to her ear. "If angels require two people to hang them, then we'll hang yours together after I put this star on the tree." Reaching up, he affixed the sparkling golden star to the evergreen's top. Once he'd secured it to his satisfaction, he pivoted and indicated her ornament. "Now, we'll hang your angel. Where do you want to put it?"

With her head tipped to one side, Garnet considered. Painted wooden ornaments, satin balls with lace trim, paper stars, and garlands of cranberries and popcorn already festooned the tree. She pointed to a bare spot on a limb over her head. "Right there, I think."

Cole hung the angel on the spot Garnet indicated, and together, they surveyed their handiwork. Garnet giggled.

He raised an eyebrow. "Care to let me in on the joke?"

"The tree looks like it was decorated by a drunken maniac, but it's charming."

"A drunken maniac, huh?" Cole gave the tree a quick once-over. "You're right, but don't tell my mother." He grinned when he swung his gaze back to her. "What do you think of our Christmas traditions so far?"

The sight of Rafe, with one hand clasped about Daisy's as together they hung the fragile angel on a limb over her head, distracted Garnet from Cole's question. If Rafe was merely amusing himself with Daisy, she'd deal with him herself. But Cole thought Rafe might be sweet on her friend...

At that moment, Della Wild Wind and Coral Logan entered the parlor. They carried trays loaded with cups of steaming spiced cider and began passing mugs to those who wanted a drink.

Coral crossed the room to where her husband sat beside the Franklin stove and offered him a cup. When

Coral offered a mug to Asa Morrison, he took the cider with a nod of thanks.

Garnet watched the by-play. What did her father think of all this holiday cheer? Normally, he shunned all Christmas festivities and sequestered himself in his office to avoid the seasonal revelry. His presence in the parlor was a small miracle.

"Garnet?" Cole's voice recalled her to his presence. "What do you think of our Christmas traditions?"

Garnet thrummed with his nearness. "I love it all. I've never decorated a Christmas tree before, or been around a family. I could get used to this."

Cole gave her a look meant for her only. "You will. You'll be a permanent part of this family and will celebrate many Christmases with us at the Slash L."

With Cole's possessive gaze devouring her, she couldn't help but catch his optimism. "Oh, I do hope so. I've never had a family. To be a part of this..." She encompassed the room in a sweeping gesture. "I always wished for a family like this."

Cole's face screwed up in mock horror. "Be careful what you wish for. When they're all telling you what you should be doing with your life and poking their noses into your personal affairs, you may change your mind."

Before Garnet could reply, Cole's mother clapped her hands. "Now that the tree is decorated, we'll sing some carols. My daughter will put her little ones to bed, but the rest of us can stay here and sing."

While Cole's sister herded her brood from the room, Della laid her empty tray on the piano's lid and seated herself on the piano stool. Her hands hovered over the keyboard.

"My mother is an accomplished pianist," Cole said in Garnet's ear.

"Who has a favorite?" Della sang out.

"Deck the Halls," Jake's wife said.

Della launched into a lively rendition of the carol, while the family joined in. As the music transitioned from one Christmas carol to another, a sense of belonging filled Garnet's heart. The family crowded the room and belted out the songs with gusto. Though some sang off key, no one seemed to mind. The kerosene lamps cast a mellow light over the room, and the tree twinkled with its dozens of ornaments. Festoons of tinsel added more glitter and gave the room a magical air.

Garnet swept a glance around the room. Busy with the fixings of one of his ever-present cigars, her father remained aloof from the festivities. Wild Wind stood alone before the medallion-back sofa, booted feet planted wide, arms crossed, and his gaze focused on his wife. Adoration for his spouse burned in his blue eyes. Jake and his wife stood behind Della. Jake's arm curled about his wife's as they peered at the sheet music. Over by the tree, Flossie leaned against her husband, and her two brothers and their wives mingled with their assorted offspring. Rafe stood at the back of the crowd, his arm about Daisy's waist.

A lump choked Garnet. The love evident here was something, in her bleak childhood, she could only have imagined. If she could grasp the moment and hold it forever, she'd be content. She shook away the specter of a loveless marriage to Albert filled with empty Christmases and refused to let it taint this magical vignette.

Cole reached for her hand and laced his fingers through hers. She didn't resist. Let her father make of their endearment what he would.

When the carol singing broke up, the parlor emptied as the family called out cheerful good nights and headed to their rooms. Rafe and Daisy slowly made their way to the stairs, his arm still curved about her waist. Cole lingered in the doorway to bid his parents a good night.

His mother tidied the sheet music on the piano rack and turned to Garnet. "I hope Cole has gotten you comfortably settled."

"Yes, he has. He put me in your old room. I hope you don't mind."

Della smiled. "Certainly not. You should be cozy there."

"I'm sure I will be. It's a lovely room." Garnet returned the older woman's smile.

While they'd talked, Wild Wind had approached his wife and draped a possessive hand over her shoulder, pulling her against him. The tender expression on his hawkish face left no doubt about how much he still adored her. Della craned her neck and tossed her husband an upward glance filled with love.

Hot tears formed behind Garnet's eyes at the ardent look the couple exchanged. She longed to be cherished as Wild Wind cherished his wife. At that moment, she felt watched, and she turned her attention to Cole. Their gazes mingled, and Cole's expression revealed his own love for her.

She *was* loved. Cole loved her. He'd shown her so in

many ways, but here in the home where he'd grown to adulthood, thriving beneath his parents' love, the reality of his love settled about her like a protective cloak. A parched corner of her heart blossomed like a flower opening to the sun.

His attention still on Garnet's face, Cole addressed his mother. "Mother, I'd like to take Garnet riding tomorrow before the snow flies and show her the ranch. She'll probably need to be outfitted with suitable riding clothes. Can you help with that?"

Della cocked her head and ran an appraising look along Garnet's form. "You're much the same size as me, at least close enough to get by. I'm sure I can rustle up something."

The prospect of a horseback ride with Cole dazzled Garnet. "Thank you. I didn't bring any riding clothes with me."

"I have plenty. We'll find something for you to wear." Della clasped Garnet's hand. "Good night, and sleep well. We'll have our talk before you leave."

Upstairs, Cole and Garnet dawdled in the darkened hallway outside her bedroom door.

"I had a lovely time tonight." Garnet leaned against the doorjamb. "I like your family. Everyone has made me feel welcome."

"I knew they would. And my mother loves you." Cole braced a hand on the wall beside Garnet's head.

"She's been so kind."

"That's my mother, the perfect hostess. But more than that, she approves of you as a wife for me."

Garnet looked up into Cole's lean face bent close to her own. Her uncertainties on that score lingered. "Truly?"

"Yes, so stop worrying." Cole leaned toward her and angled his head. His mouth took hers in a slow kiss. When he raised his head, he smiled. "I've wanted to do that all night." He straightened away from the wall. "Now, I'd best get to my own room. Sleep well." He reached around her and opened her bedroom door.

Inside her room, Garnet pressed her fingertips to her lips and smiled to herself. She so enjoyed Cole's kisses.

Her head full of dreams, she pulled the pins from her pompadour and shook out her hair so the golden red curls tumbled down her back. She pulled her nightgown from a dresser drawer and slipped the garment over her head. Across the room, between two windows that overlooked the front yard, the four-poster bed waited. She hurried to its side and climbed beneath the blankets.

A soft rap sounded on the door, and Daisy stuck her head around the portal. "I came to help you get ready for bed."

"I'm already undressed, but come in."

Daisy slipped into the room, a slender wraith clad in a red flannel robe belted over her night-rail. Her blonde braids trailed over her shoulders.

Garnet plumped the pillows behind her back and leaned against the headboard. She patted the mattress. "Daisy, come over and sit. We have time for a gossip."

Daisy crossed the room and crawled up onto the mattress. She leaned against the carved post at the foot of the bed and curled her legs beneath her, tucking her nightwear over her toes.

Garnet eyed her maid. "Are you having a good time?"

Daisy's face lit. "I'm having such a good time. Rafe's family makes me feel welcome, and his mother is nice to me."

"Yes, she's nice to me, too. I was so afraid she wouldn't like me."

"I wasn't sure if she would like me, either. She wasn't expecting me to arrive with Rafe."

"She may have been surprised, but I'm sure she likes you. She's not a snob."

Daisy twisted the tail of one tawny braid about her forefinger. "Rafe and Cole have a lot of family."

Garnet nodded her agreement. "They do. I think I have them all fixed in my head now."

A brief lull followed while Garnet debated whether she should question Daisy about her feelings for Rafe. She didn't want Daisy to get her heart broken if Rafe was merely being accommodating. Still, Rafe had spent a good deal of time with Daisy since they'd returned from the mine, and Cole suspected his brother might be sweet on Daisy, so perhaps she needn't worry. Daisy's next words eased her concern.

"Trystan seems nice, don't you think?"

Garnet cast a sharp glance at her maid. Daisy's tone had seemed too casual, and a flush colored her cheeks. "I saw Trystan helping you trim the tree. I thought he seemed nice."

Daisy's fair skin betrayed her flush. "He was very friendly tonight. And he told me he'd like to get to know me better."

If Daisy could be flattered by the young man's interest,

she wasn't in danger of getting her heart broken by Rafe. Garnet stopped worrying about her friend. "How nice for you. He does seem to be a worthy young man."

"And Rafe said he wants to take me for a drive tomorrow to show me the ranch. He said we're going to get snow, and once the snow comes, the road will be impassable for his motorcar."

Garnet laughed. "Well, aren't you the heartbreaker."

Daisy twisted her braid about her finger again and smiled a guilty smile. "Do you mind? I'm not doing much work right now."

Garnet fluttered a hand in Daisy's direction. "Enjoy yourself while you're here. Don't worry about me. If you'll just fix my hair in the mornings, I can take care of myself the rest of the time. Go break a few hearts."

Sharing a glance, the girls burst into laughter. When Garnet could speak again, she said, "Besides, now is your chance to wear all those new clothes I bought you."

Chapter 29

Garnet kept her mare close beside Cole's buckskin gelding. She and Cole had set out right after lunch. The breeze that blew off the mountains to the west and buffeted her face sliced the air with an arctic chill. Pewter-colored clouds drooped low over the prairie and promised to bring the snow Rafe had predicted.

Ecstatic at being included, Brutus loped ahead.

Garnet eyed Cole's sheepskin jacket, his leather gloves, denim jeans, and his brown cowboy hat. She indicated his clothing and tossed him a mischievous grin. "The handsome cowboy I fell in love with is back."

His gelding strode through the tawny buffalo grass. With one hand on the reins, Cole caught her grin and returned it with one of his own. His cheeks creased. "It feels good to be a cowboy again."

"You're even wearing your six-shooter."

"This may be 1911, but it's best not to ride about the range without packing iron." He raked her with a glance of his own.

"And I'm glad to see the hoyden I knew back at the mine is back. I love you when you dress for society, but I love you when you dress like this, as well." He nodded at her outfit.

Garnet looked down at her borrowed clothes. "It's a good thing that your mother and I are much the same size."

They rode in companionable silence along the utility track that connected the ranch buildings with the horse and cattle pastures and eventually, the oil fields. They reached a pasture enclosed by a railed fence that paralleled the lane. Cole pointed to the horses inside. "Those are the two-year-olds my father and his wranglers will break in the spring."

Garnet followed his pointing finger at a herd of stocky horses, wooly with their winter coats. The horses lifted their heads and trotted to the fence, ears pricked.

"What will you do with these horses once they're trained?" Curiosity to know everything about the ranch filled her.

Cole settled his free hand on his thigh as his mount walked along the track. "Most of them will be sold to other ranchers. We'll keep a few for our own use."

"Didn't you tell me that the Slash L raises Quarter Horses?"

He slid her a glance. "Back when the ranch got started a few years after the Civil War, Uncle Clint bred Morgans for the cavalry. The army was in the middle of the Indian Wars, and it needed cavalry horses. Once the Indian situation was settled, the army didn't need so many horses. Cattle ranchers began settling in Colorado and

Wyoming. They needed horses to work their cattle, so Uncle Clint began breeding Quarter Horses."

"Your uncle is a very enterprising gentleman."

"He's very forward-thinking."

A tall windmill on a skeletal metal frame thrusting up from the middle of the pasture caught Garnet's eye. A round metal tank flanked the windmill's base. "Why is that windmill there?"

Cole glanced at the structure. "The windmill pumps water into the tank for the horses. You'll find windmills all over the ranch, providing water for the cattle, the homes, even for the oil men. When we were young, Rafe and I swam in the water tanks. Swimming in the tanks was a favorite summer pastime for all of us boys who lived here." He grinned at her.

"I think every boy should grow up on a ranch." Garnet's wistful tone mourned her own bleak childhood.

"It was a great place for all us young'uns. A lot of cowhands' children have grown up here."

The track wound over knolls and between ridges. With its withered grasses, the prairie stretched to the horizon like a buff-colored sea. The tawny pasturage rippled.

"Don't you think Rafe and Daisy should be getting back soon? They've been gone since this morning." Garnet tried not to fret, but the murky look of the clouds worried her.

"Rafe packed sandwiches and tea, so they won't be back for a while. I think Rafe planned to take Daisy as far as the oil fields."

"Daisy told me that Rafe predicted you'd get snow. I hope they get back before the storm starts."

Cole lifted his head and sniffed the air, then studied

the sky with narrowed eyes. "We have a few hours before it snows. I doubt the snow will start before dark. Rafe and Daisy will be home safe and sound before then."

Garnet cast a wondering look at him. "How do you do that?"

"Do what?"

"Sniff the air and look at the clouds and predict when the snow will start."

He shrugged. "I learned it from my father." His cheeks creased in a smile. "Can't you smell the snow?"

Garnet lifted her head and tested the air. A crystalline quality scented the breeze. She frowned. "I think so. I've never thought about what snow smells like."

"My father always taught us to scent the air. Sometimes a man can smell an enemy before he can see him."

They rode until they reached a barbed wire fence that stretched along the track until the posts vanished over a knoll. White-faced Herefords grazed inside the enclosure.

Cole halted his gelding and nodded in the direction of the cattle. "That's money on the hoof. Providing the beef market holds, and we don't lose too many cattle this winter, we should see a good profit in the spring."

Garnet followed his gaze. "Do you lose many cattle in the winter?"

Cole shrugged. "A lot depends on how much snow we have, and how cold the temperatures get. Cougars and wolves get a few of the weaker cows. And a blizzard can wipe out a lot of the herd."

Garnet studied the rolling terrain again. Until she'd ridden over the Slash L's vast acreage, she'd had no idea of the immensity of Clint Logan's holdings. "I never imagine the ranch was this big."

"My uncle owns several thousand acres. The far reaches are where the oil rigs are located, but most of the property is given over to pasturage for the cattle."

"And you don't want to stay here, even though you love the Slash L. I can see that you love the ranch." Garnet wriggled her toes. Even with three pairs of socks, the cold seeped through her leather riding boots.

Cole stared into her face, his expression thoughtful beneath the brim of his cowboy hat. He settled deeper into his saddle seat and stacked his gloved hands on the horn. "My roots run deep into this soil. The ranch reaches into my very bones, but as you can see, too much family already lives and works here. As much as I love it, I have to make my own way elsewhere."

Reaching out, Garnet laid her hand on his arm. "I understand why you have to make your own mark on the world."

He covered her gloved hand with a wide palm. "I'm not content to follow in Uncle Clint's footsteps."

"You love the mine, too."

"I do." He raked her face with a considering glance. "Will you mind living at the mine after we're married? Before, I had only myself to consider. Now that I'm about to take a wife, I must start thinking of you. Perhaps I'm being selfish in taking you there."

His willingness to put her needs before his touched her heart. She turned her hand beneath his and laced their fingers. "I don't want you to give up your dream. I'll share your dream. Besides, I loved living at the mine. I felt alive, and useful."

The air crackled between them, reminding Garnet of the lightning that had accompanied the summer thunderstorms in the mountains. When he leaned toward her, she tilted toward him and met him halfway. He curled an arm about her shoulders and drew her close. His lips met hers, warm against the cold, and she poured her love into the kiss.

When he broke away, he laid his cheek against hers. "Your face is cold." His husky voice sounded in her ear.

"So is yours."

"We'd better head back. I don't want to be caught out here in the dark." He dropped a kiss on the tip of her nose. "Your nose is red, but you're beautiful anyway." With a grin, he pushed away and straightened in the saddle. He tipped his head at her. "When we get back to Denver, I'll ask your father for your hand in marriage. Now that he's seen the Slash L, he can't deny I can provide well for you."

"I doubt that will make a difference. He's made up his mind that he wants me to marry into New York society."

"Don't give up hope. Remember, we've been praying about this since the summer."

"I know, but—"

Cole placed two fingertips over her mouth, silencing her. "Shh... no more of that." He ran his knuckles across her jaw in a tender caress. "Now, let's ride."

Chapter 30

Christmas Eve dawned with a cold, gray light. Garnet grimaced when her bare feet touched the icy floor. She located her slippers beneath the bed and slipped her feet into their warmth. After she'd donned her wrapper and belted it about her waist, she drifted to the window. Sweeping aside a lacy curtain, she peered out.

Snow lay like a pristine blanket over the ranch yard and mounded up on the corral fence posts. Like an eiderdown quilt, drifts mounded against the buildings in blue-white banks.

Garnet dropped the curtain and spun from the window. Her teeth chattered as she threw on a slim, dark green skirt and frothy, long-sleeved white blouse.

When Daisy dropped by her room, Garnet couldn't help but notice her friend's glow. "You must have been dreaming about your beau. You're glowing."

A flush swept up Daisy's neck to her hairline.

Garnet grinned. "You're quite the heartbreaker."

"I'm sure I'm not breaking any hearts."

"Ha! Rafe didn't like Trystan flirting with you last night, and Trystan glowered when Rafe kept his arm about you during the carol sing."

A reluctant smile curled Daisy's lips. "I don't know what to do with the two of them."

"Enjoy their attention and be your sweet self. Now, let me look at you." Garnet circled her friend and studied her appearance with an appraising eye.

Since she'd been going about with Rafe, Daisy had acquired a glow that lent her understated looks a quiet beauty. This morning, her stylish new outfit mirrored Garnet's own. A sapphire brooch nestled in the lace at her throat, and filigree platinum earrings swung from her ears. With a fringe of short curls about her ears and forehead, she resembled a wood sprite.

"You look smashing this morning, Daisy. Rafe and Trystan will be at loggerheads over you."

"I don't want them to be at loggerheads over me."

"Why not? It might be good for Rafe to have some competition. Anyway, he has no claim on you." Garnet surveyed Daisy one more time. "Your hair needs something... I have just the thing." She hurried to the vanity across the room and rummaged in her jewelry case. "I found it!"

When she'd returned to Daisy's side, she waved a curved platinum hair comb embossed with rose blossoms beneath her friend's nose. "This belongs just above your pompadour. Stand still while I put it in." A frown crinkled her brow as she worked the comb into Daisy's tresses. "There. Now you're quite the lady."

When the girls poked their heads into the dining room,

some of the family still lingered at the table. Della Wild Wind sat with her back to them, sipping coffee from a flowered china teacup. Coral Logan sat at the hostess's end. Dirty dishes at their husbands' place settings showed that the men had already eaten and left while Cole and Rafe still dawdled over their coffee.

Garnet's father sat between Coral and Della.

When Cole spied the girls hovering in the doorway, pleasure lit his face. "Come join us for breakfast. We're just finishing up." He rose and pulled out the empty chair beside him. "Have a seat."

Garnet crossed to his side and settled herself in the chair he offered.

Rafe rose and pulled out a seat on his other side. "Daisy, here's a place for you."

Daisy rounded the table and slid into the chair.

"Good morning." Rafe bumped Daisy's shoulder with his and tipped his head in her direction. "You didn't have to get up so early. You could have slept in."

She flashed him a smile. "I'm used to getting up early."

Della beamed at them. "Ranching families get up with the sun, so you fit right in." She sipped her coffee and returned the cup to the saucer. "Maisie will bring your breakfast."

They'd just finished eating when Trystan and several of his cousins paused in the dining room doorway. The young people had bundled up for the outdoors.

Trystan leaned into the doorway. "Daisy, we've challenged the girls to a snowball fight. Won't you join us?"

Daisy's expression lit before indecision dimmed her excitement. She glanced first at Garnet and then Rafe.

Rafe gave a nod. "Go on, Daisy. You'll have fun."

Doubt clouded her eyes. "What about you?"

"Cole and I plan to spend the morning at the horse barn helping our father and Uncle Clint. Anyway, you don't need my permission." Not giving Daisy another moment to dither, he rose and pulled out her chair. "Go along. I'll see you later."

Daisy tossed him a grateful look and fled the dining room.

Rafe punched Cole lightly on the shoulder. "Well, big brother. Are you going to sit here all morning after we promised our father we'd help him?"

Cole took a last sip of his coffee and returned the cup to its saucer. A light *ting* of china against china rang in the silence. When he rose, his chair scraped back against the rug. He rounded the table and pecked his mother on the cheek. "Rafe and I will leave you ladies to your own devices. I'm sure you don't need us men underfoot."

As the brothers left, Garnet's father excused himself and disappeared.

Della gazed across the table at Garnet. "Aunt Coral and I will join the other ladies in the kitchen preparing tonight's Christmas Eve dinner. We give our cook time off during the holidays, so if we want to eat, we women do the honors. You're welcome to join us."

"I'd love to, although I must confess I don't know much about cooking. Before I lived at the mine, my kitchen experience was limited to choosing the week's menu with our chef." Garnet sent an apologetic look across the table at Cole's mother.

Della gave a throaty chuckle and shared a

commiserating glance with Garnet. "That was my life before I came West." She leaned across the table. "I'll let you in on a family secret. I can't cook, either. No one wants me in the kitchen, but they have to let me help at Christmas."

Her grin took years off her face and gave Garnet a glimpse of what she must have looked like as a younger woman.

Flossie, her sisters-in-law, and Jake's wife joined them in the kitchen. Warmed by the cookstove, the cheerful room resounded with female chatter, laughter, and good will. Scents of cinnamon, apple, and ginger spiced the air. Pies, cookies, and puddings weighed down the sideboard that stretched along one wall.

Halfway through the morning, Garnet stood at the kitchen sink, her arms in hot, soapy water up to her elbows. Her heart overflowed. This homey room held everything her heart craved. Cole's family seemed like the family she'd been denied.

His mother stopped beside her and put an arm about Garnet's shoulders. "A penny for your thoughts."

Garnet swallowed at the opportunity for shared confidences. "Christmas at the Slash L is very different from my home." She hesitated. "My mother died when I was very young, and my father never celebrated Christmas after that. He never even put up a tree."

Cole's mother tightened her arm about Garnet's shoulders. "I hope you'll consider us your family."

Garnet nodded, unable to speak around the lump in her throat.

"Cole has told his father and me that he wants to marry you, but your father has other plans."

Garnet nodded again.

"Cole loves you very much. I've never seen him so content as he is now. You're good for him."

Garnet swallowed hard. "I don't know about that, but Cole has been good for me."

"Well, we believe that the Lord has answered our prayers and that He sent you to Cole. Wild Wind and I have every confidence that the Lord will bring your father around."

Garnet sniffed. "That's what Cole tells me, but you don't know my father."

Della squeezed again. "Our Heavenly Father is more powerful than even your father."

With the baking done, Garnet hurried to her room and rummaged in her luggage. With her arms full of presents wrapped in colorful holiday paper, she tiptoed down the stairs and hurried into the parlor, where she added her gifts to the growing pile of gaily wrapped packages. Garnet stepped back to survey the tree.

The evergreen filled the corner and scented the room with its resin tang. Silver tinsel hung in glittering strands among the shiny spun-glass ornaments and swags of popcorn. Garnet sighed with pleasure. This beautiful tree, decorated with love, more than made up for all of the Christmases she'd spent treeless and alone with the servants in her New York mansion. She closed her eyes and let the season's spirit, represented by this tree, fill every lonely corner of her heart.

She'd just stepped into the foyer when the glass-fronted door swung open, and the young people tumbled inside on a waft of cold air and the scent of snow. Daisy was laughing at something Trystan had said. The cold air had pinkened her cheeks.

She needn't worry about Daisy. Daisy had been absorbed into the younger set and didn't need anyone's help socializing.

"Who wants hot chocolate?" Trystan sang out over the hubbub as his cousins shrugged out of coats and boots. "I'm sure there's a pot of chocolate warming on the stove."

Amid a chorus of agreement, the cousins trooped in the direction of the kitchen. Quiet descended once again after the kitchen door swung shut behind them.

Garnet watched them go, an ache around her heart as she pondered her own lonely teenage years.

Chapter 31

Christmas Eve ended with another Slash L tradition, a candle-lit service in the schoolhouse that doubled as a church.

The service touched Garnet's heart as the carols, accompanied by Della on the pump organ, celebrated the birth of the Christ child. The words of "O Little Town of Bethlehem" and "Silent Night" rang to the rafters as the ranch families lifted their voices in song. The beautiful message of the holy babe born that night who would be the savior of mankind seemed especially precious.

Cole gripped her hand and entwined their fingers. She cut a sideways glance at his face. They exchanged a look that reached into their hearts and exposed their new and fragile love. Her heart overflowed with an excess of emotion that Garnet didn't think she could contain. This memorable Christmas with Cole's family and the significance of the season filled her soul with joy.

After the last carol had been sung, Clint Logan read the Christmas story from Luke 2.

At the conclusion of the service, Garnet turned toward the door. Her heart jolted when she spied her father along the back wall. When had he come in? She couldn't remember the last time he'd entered a church. As far as she knew, he hadn't been inside a chapel since her mother's funeral. Had some of the love and joy that abounded in the godly Slash L families seeped into his heart? Perhaps his hard shell had cracked.

* * *

Garnet woke early on Christmas morning. Excitement shivered through her. Voices and thumps sounded downstairs. The family was already up. She couldn't wait to join them.

Shivering in the chill, she dressed in her slim, long-sleeved dress of Christmas-red velvet overlaid with lace, then drifted to the marble-topped vanity near the stove. She lifted a ruby choker in a platinum setting from her jewelry box. She fastened the clasp and stepped back to view the results in the mirror. Cole might say he liked the casual look she'd adopted for life at the camp, but he couldn't help but be impressed by her holiday finery.

She met Daisy in the hall outside their bedroom doors. "Daisy, you look so festive!"

With a grin, Daisy twirled to give Garnet the full effect of her outfit. "I feel festive. I've never had a Christmas dress as grand as this." She stroked the slim skirt's soft green velvet.

"Thank you for buying me these beautiful clothes."

Daisy's Christmas-green velvet dress mirrored Garnet's

in style. Her dangling earrings and glittering hair jewelry matched the sparkle in her eyes.

"You're socializing with the family now, so you have to dress the part. Besides, Trystan will be bowled over when he sees you."

Daisy ducked her head and hid a smile. "He does seem to like me. He asked me if I was Rafe's girl."

"And what did you tell him?"

"I let him wonder. I don't want him to think no other man is interested in me."

Garnet laughed. "You're turning into a real coquette."

"Do you think Rafe will like my dress?" Daisy couldn't hide her eagerness to gain Rafe's approval.

Garnet hugged her friend. "Of course, Rafe will like your dress. And he can't help but think you're beautiful."

When the girls joined the family in the dining room, Rafe's eyes widened when he caught sight of Daisy, and he tossed his napkin onto the table. He rose and strode to her side. When he halted before her, he took both her hands. "Merry Christmas, Daisy. You look like a Christmas present in that dress."

Daisy colored a deep pink as every eye in the room turned to her. "Thank you, Rafe. Merry Christmas to you, too."

Rafe's parents watched their son smile down at the petite blonde girl. A speculative gleam lit Della's eyes, but she remained silent and added another dollop of jam to her toast.

Without releasing Daisy's hand, Rafe towed her around the table to his place. "There's not an empty chair right now, but I was almost done. You can have mine." He seated her in his chair and scooted her closer to the table, then cleared away his dirty plate and silver. "I'll get you a clean place setting."

Silence dropped over the dining room as Rafe departed with his soiled dishes. Garnet cast a look at Daisy. Her friend stared down at the table and seemed to shrink into her chair. Daisy hated the limelight.

After a hurried breakfast, the family gathered in the parlor to open gifts. Cole ensconced Garnet in a leather wing-back chair near the door, while he propped himself against the chair's back. Rafe followed them with Daisy on his arm. He seated her in a corner of the medallion-backed sofa and settled beside her.

Trystan scowled at Rafe from across the room, and Garnet smiled to herself. Daisy's young swain seemed to be jealous.

The whirl that followed made Garnet's head spin. Amid laughter and teasing, Clint Logan distributed the gifts. Hugs and kisses abounded. The little ones romped among boxes and shiny paper.

Cole's great uncle dropped a small object, tied up with red ribbon, on his wife's palm. He seized the moment to plant a lusty kiss on her mouth. Garnet's throat tightened. What must it be like to still be loved after so many years of marriage?

As if he could see into her head and know what she was thinking, Cole touched the back of her hand. She glanced up at him. An intent expression tightened his features. A wordless promise of lifelong devotion shone in his dark eyes, gifting her with a promise more precious than any material object could have been. In that moment, she and Cole seemed to exchange silent vows of lifelong commitment.

Across the room, Wild Wind stood behind his wife's chair. One hand rested on her shoulder.

Over by the window, Daisy pulled the ribbon from a small package. Rafe watched with his head tipped toward her, a smile turning up the corners of his mouth.

"I wonder who would be giving you gifts?" Rafe teased in mock surprise, one arm draped behind her along the sofa's back. His lips twitched. "You must have been a very good girl this year to get a gift like that."

Daisy elbowed him in the ribs. "Of course, I've been a good girl. I never get lumps of coal at Christmas." Her eyes danced as she tore at the wrapping. The silver paper fell away to reveal a leather-bound book with gilt edging. Daisy flipped open the cover and read the note Rafe had inscribed on the flyleaf, then lifted a shining gaze to his face.

"Edgar Allen Poe's short stories. I love Poe! And thank you for your note." She blushed.

Rafe nudged Daisy with his shoulder and whispered something private in her ear, then raised his voice for the family's benefit. "I had a little help choosing that book. Someone told me you like to read, and that Poe is one of your favorite authors."

"I wonder who could have told you that?" Daisy tossed a smile at Garnet. "Yes, Poe is my favorite author."

Cole distracted Garnet when he bent down to murmur in her ear, "Let's get out of here."

In the hall, he said, "I have a surprise for you. Get your coat and meet me down here."

Bundled against the cold, Cole led her to the horse barn. Scents of hay, leather, and horses greeted her. The moment they stepped inside, he pulled her into his arms. He took her mouth in an ardent kiss, which was the highlight of Garnet's Christmas.

At last, he lifted his head. His warm gaze roved over her face, touching each feature with a tender reverence. "Merry Christmas, Garnet. You're love has made this Christmas the best one of my life."

Garnet tightened her arms about him. "Merry Christmas, Cole. Without doubt, this is my best Christmas."

Cole pressed Garnet's face into the curve of his shoulder. Her cheek rested against his sheepskin jacket, while one of his hands tightened about her neck. Behind them, the horses shuffled in their stalls. The sound of contented munching and soft snorts filled the silence.

"I have something for you." His roughened voice spoke above her head as he released her. Fumbling in his jacket pocket, he retrieved a small package wrapped in silver paper and dropped the parcel on her palm. "This is for you. Merry Christmas, my darling."

Garnet stared at the exquisite little package, then lifted her gaze to Cole. Her heart thudded against her ribs. "Thank you."

The next moment, she tore away the gleaming paper and dropped it to the floor. A burgundy velvet jeweler's box rested on her hand. With fingers that trembled, Garnet flipped open the lid. On a bed of white satin, a gold brooch encrusted with garnets and diamonds glittered with rich luster.

She caught her breath, then flung herself at him. He

closed his arms about her. "This brooch is beautiful, Cole. I love it."

"The garnets are for your name, and the diamonds are for how much I value our love."

"What a romantic you are." She palmed his cheek. "I'll treasure your brooch. Every time I look at it, I'll think of you."

"I hope the next item of jewelry I give you will be a diamond ring. I intend to ask for your hand in marriage when we return to Denver." He covered her hand with his own.

She leaned against the circle of his arms and smiled up at him. "Cole, that would be wonderful! I'd be honored to wear your ring." In this magical moment, anything seemed possible, even her father's permission to marry Cole.

Garnet remembered her own gift and slipped a hand into her jacket pocket. With a flourish, she offered him the wrapped token. "My gift to you."

He scooped the present from her palm and tore away the paper to reveal a silver pocket watch with an engraved lid.

With Cole's gift grasped in her fist, Garnet clasped both hands at her bosom. She rocked up on her toes. "Open the watch."

Touching her face with a curious glance, Cole pressed the watch spring with a thumb, and the lid sprang open. Ornate numerals on the watch's face indicated each hour. On the inside of the lid nestled a photo of Garnet's face. Her likeness gazed from the silver frame, on her face a dreamy smile forever frozen in time.

With a husky murmur, he gathered her to him in a one-armed embrace and buried his face against her neck. "Thank you, darling. With this watch in my vest pocket, I can keep you close to my heart even when you're not with me."

Chapter 32

Garnet woke to the sound of voices in the hallway and footsteps thudding down the stairs. From somewhere in the depths of the house, a door slammed. Groggy with sleep, she pried open her eyes to stygian darkness. *What time is it?*

She tossed back the covers and thrust her feet into her slippers, then pulled on her robe. She hurried to the door and peeked out.

Della Wild Wind stood at the top of the stairs. Her curly hair sprang in riotous disarray about her face, and her night rail peeked out from beneath a half-closed robe. One foot poised over the top step.

"What's happened?" Garnet stepped into the hall.

Cole's mother wheeled. Distress tightened her lovely features. "We think Uncle Clint has had a heart attack. Cole and Rafe have gone to the ranch office to call the doctor. My husband is with Uncle Clint now. Wild Wind has a great knowledge of tribal medicine. He should be able to help my uncle until the doctor arrives."

Garnet sped to Della's side and curled an arm about her shoulders. "I'm so sorry. Can I help?"

Della shook her head, making her curls dance. "Thank you for offering, but there's nothing you can do. I'm going to the kitchen to boil some hot water. Wild Wind will make an herbal tea for Uncle Clint." She gulped back tears. "Uncle Clint has been like a father to me. I can't bear to lose him."

Garnet patted her back. "We can pray that between your husband's remedies and the doctor, your uncle will be restored to you."

Della sniffed. "Thank you. We've all been praying, and we appreciate your prayers, too, but I must be willing to let Uncle Clint go if the Lord wills it."

Garnet had no words for that truth, so she didn't comment. She hugged Cole's mother again. "My father and I will leave this morning. You don't need us underfoot right now."

"You don't have to go. You're no trouble at all." Della's mouth wobbled when she tried to smile.

"Thank you for your offer, but we should leave. You and your Aunt Coral have been wonderful—your whole family has been wonderful—but this crisis is for family only. We'll pack and get away before lunch, if you can arrange transportation."

"My husband will make arrangements. Someone will drive you to Denver." Della turned away, and her hurried footsteps faded down the stairs.

By midmorning, all their luggage had been packed and was stacked at the foot of the front steps beside a tall, ungainly motor vehicle with huge tires and a wooden plow attached to the bumper. Cole and Rafe wrestled the last trunk into the boot.

Della, her eyes puffy and red, hugged Garnet. "Aunt Coral asked me to give you her regards, but she didn't want to leave Uncle Clint. My husband is with him, too, or he'd be here to see you off." Cole's mother gripped Garnet's shoulders and whispered in her ear, "And thank you for loving my son. His father and I gladly entrust him to your care."

Garnet hugged her back. She tried to speak around the lump that filled her throat. "I'll do my best for him." She moved on to the next person who had gathered on the porch for their leave-taking.

Flossie flung her arms about Garnet's neck. "When you get back to New York, you must visit me. Washington, DC isn't so far by train."

Garnet returned Flossie's embrace. "I'd love to visit you."

"Call me when you get back to New York, and we can plan a visit. Have a good trip." Flossie indicated the motor vehicle that waited to transport their visitors from the ranch. "That contraption will shake your bones, but it will get you to Denver."

Garnet turned away to follow her father.

Trystan gripped both of Daisy's hands. "Will you write to me? I'll write to you and will send my letters to the Grande Palace."

Daisy squeezed Trystan's hands. "Yes, if you write to me, I'll write back." She pulled her hands free and followed Garnet down the steps.

Cole and Rafe waited at the bottom of the steps.

Cole thrust out a hand to Asa Morrison. "Thank you for visiting the Slash L. I'm sorry your visit was cut short." He canted his head at the motor vehicle. "Petey will get you safely to Denver."

Asa shook Cole's proffered hand. "Thank you for inviting us to spend Christmas with your family. I'm sorry about your uncle. I hope he recovers."

"We all pray for his recovery." Cole wrenched open the front passenger door, and his business partner climbed up into the cab. When he pivoted to Garnet, Cole seared her with a look that expressed all of his pent-up hopes and longings. He pulled her into a rough embrace, despite his whole family and her father looking on. "I'll be in touch, although I can't leave the Slash L until I know what's going to happen with Uncle Clint."

Garnet tightened her arms about him. "Of course, you can't leave. We'll be waiting for you. I'll miss you."

"I love you," he murmured the words in her ear as he nestled his face in the curve of her neck. He squeezed her once more and let her go, then opened the vehicle's back door and lifted her up onto the seat.

Rafe clasped Daisy in a hug and whispered in her ear, making her smile. His hands spanned her waist, and he lifted her onto the back seat beside Garnet. With a final goodbye, he gripped her hand once more before he slammed the door and stepped back.

As the vehicle lurched into motion, Garnet leaned around Daisy and peered out the window. His family waved from the porch. When she'd arrived here, she'd never guessed how much she'd come to love these people.

Her magical Christmas had ended, and the future loomed, full of uncertainties.

Chapter 33

Garnet stretched beneath the blankets and opened her eyes. Painted cupids cavorted on the ceiling amidst garlands of plaster flowers. She was once again in her bedroom at the Grande Palace. Petey had delivered them to the hotel last night.

She shoved her unruly copper curls out of her face and pushed back the covers. When she'd donned her rose satin robe and tied the sash about her waist, she stepped into the adjoining sitting room. Her father sat at a table before the fireplace, shoveling a bite of ham into his mouth. An extra place setting occupied the opposite side of the table.

He gave her a sharp look and jabbed his fork in the direction of the empty place setting. "Sit down, girl, and eat. I ordered breakfast to be delivered here so we wouldn't have to eat in the dining room."

Garnet approached the table and dropped into the empty chair across from her father. Without bidding him a good morning, she spooned a small helping of fried potatoes onto her plate. She added a slice of ham and then ladled fresh strawberries into a crystal fruit bowl.

"Coffee?" Her father held a silver pitcher aloft over her cup.

Garnet nodded and watched as her father filled her cup with the steaming dark liquid.

When he'd set the coffee pot down on the white linen tablecloth, he turned his attention once again to his breakfast, content to eat in silence.

With a wary eye on her parent, Garnet picked up her fork and ate. *How did Clint Logan fare? And what of the rest of the Slash L family?* Yesterday morning when she'd woken in her bedroom at the ranch seemed an eon ago.

And Cole. What was he doing? She missed him already.

Asa Morrison wiped his plate clean with a bit of toast and popped the morsel into his mouth. He washed the food down with a swig of coffee, then beetled his eyebrows in a fierce frown and stabbed a stiffened finger in her direction. "I have something to say to you, girl, so listen up."

Garnet laid her fork down and turned her attention to her father. His tone, and the way he stared at her, warned her she wouldn't like what he was about to say. Her stomach knotted.

"I've been patient with you. I've let Cole Wild Wind squire you about and not said a word." Asa Morrison tapped the table in an impatient tattoo and glared at her. "You've had your little romance with him. Now it's time to behave as an adult and do your family duty. Tomorrow, we'll take the morning train to New York, where you will accept Albert's proposal of marriage."

Garnet stared across the table at her father. Her limbs trembled, and her breathing hitched. "No. I won't marry Albert."

Silence settled between them like a cold draft. Her father's eyes slitted. When he spoke, his tone froze her.

"You'll not defy me in this, Garnet. My mind is made up. You *will* marry Albert."

Garnet forgot her quivering knees and leaped to her feet. Her chair rocked back. "I don't love Albert! I want to marry for love. Cole and I love each other."

Her father made a dismissive motion. "What does love have to do with marriage? A woman of your station has a duty to her family to make an advantageous marriage. A daughter must acquiesce to her father's wisdom in matters of the heart."

"Your idea of an advantageous marriage and mine aren't the same. And besides, how is marrying Cole not marrying well? You've met his family. You've seen how they live. Cole can provide for me very well."

Asa Morrison sliced the air with a chopping motion. "Albert Davies' family is one of the oldest and most prominent families in New York. Your marriage to him will cement a dynasty."

"I have no interest in establishing a dynasty."

"Put the notion of marrying for love right out of your head. You can learn to love Albert after you've married him."

"I'll never love another man except Cole. And besides, Albert isn't a God-fearing man. I want to marry a God-fearing man."

Her father snorted. "Wherever did you get that notion?"

They glared at each other across the table. Asa Morrison slitted his eyes at his daughter and ground his teeth. Garnet forgot to breathe.

She kept her voice reasonable when instead, she wanted to scream. Garnet tried again to change her father's mind. "Albert has character defects that I can't admire, much less love. I can't marry a man whom I don't even respect." With both hands braced on the table, she attempted a coaxing tone. "Papa." She hadn't called her father "papa" since she was four years old. "Don't you remember what it felt like to be in love? I know you loved Mama."

Her father surged to his feet and loomed over her, seeming about to explode. Instead of the outburst Garnet expected, he breathed heavily through his nose and dropped into his seat. He scrubbed a hand across his face. When he spoke, his voice had lost its edge. "Garnet, you have no idea how difficult it is for a man to rear a daughter. I know nothing about girls. Without your mother..." He heaved a sigh. "You may not believe me, but I want only what's best for you. Right now, you think you love that handsome cowboy, but after a while, the novelty will wear off. You'll waste yourself in a squalid mining camp, cut off from everything familiar. You'd miss your old life in New York."

Garnet sat down and stared at her father. Was he admitting a weakness to her?

"With his Cheyenne heritage, Cole Wild Wind will never be your social equal. Albert is worthy of you. The two of you will have a marriage that will exemplify the American dream, and you'll be secure with Albert after I'm gone."

Once more, Garnet pleaded with her father. "I hate New York, and I don't care that Cole has Cheyenne blood. Please let us marry."

Asa Morrison maintained a brooding silence and fixed his daughter with a hooded stare. Though her insides shook, Garnet held her father's gaze. Her whole future rested on his next words.

He shoved away from the table and rose.

Garnet lifted her chin and waited for him to speak.

"I'm sorry, girl." Her father's gruff voice ravaged her hopes. "I can't allow it. Someday, you'll thank me for this." He reached an imploring hand to her. "Once you've had a child or two, you'll be so busy you'll have forgotten all about Cole Wild Wind. Think of your children. What advantages would they have, living in a mining camp? You want the best for your children, don't you? They should grow up in New York, where they'll have all the benefits that come with our wealth and social position."

Garnet's future crashed about her and lay in rubble at her feet. Her father had just destroyed her dreams. Tears pooled in her eyes, but she refused to let them fall. She sat in rigid silence, certain that if she moved, she'd shatter into a thousand jagged pieces.

Apparently taking her silence for consent, Asa Morrison continued, "I know I haven't been the best father to you, but I'm trying to make it up to you now. I'm doing my best for you by ensuring your future. I'll call Cole Wild Wind this morning and tell him that we've gone to New York to celebrate your engagement and wedding. After you're married, I'll return to Denver. I still have business with the brothers."

Garnet struggled to breathe. She couldn't look away from her father's face.

"You will have no further contact with Cole Wild Wind. Now, ring for Daisy. Remind her she's here to work. I don't pay her to consort with her betters. You have one day to pack."

New York City
January 1912

Chapter 34

Garnet tiptoed down the stairs, one hand on the mahogany railing. Silence shrouded the house. She hadn't encountered any of the servants in her trek downstairs. Perhaps she could reach the telephone and call Cole before anyone saw her.

She stepped off the last tread. The silk carpet runner that layered the staircase had muffled her descent, but when she placed a foot on the foyer's parquet flooring, the wood creaked. She halted and held her breath. When no one appeared, she took another step.

The spacious foyer of her father's luxurious New York townhouse pressed down on her. Although sunlight sheened the walls' large mahogany panels and spilled onto the polished floor through a pair of tall windows that flanked the wide front door, the house suffocated her. She stifled the urge to dash outside. Focused on her goal, she hurried to the marble-topped table on which rested a candlestick-style telephone.

She had just reached for the telephone when a tall

woman with an imperious bearing swept from the drawing room into the foyer and halted.

"Garnet." The woman's mouth pursed in disapproval. The moustache atop her upper lip bristled. With her back ramrod stiff, she crossed her arms below her bosom. Her black bombazine gown, buttoned to her throat, garbed the figure of a female soldier. Her graying hair had been scraped into a tight bun. Not a hair dared to slip from its pins. "Shouldn't you be upstairs for a fitting of your wedding gown? What is that lazy seamstress doing that allows you to waltz about downstairs?"

Garnet's hand dropped to her side, and she pivoted to face the gimlet gaze of the woman her father had hired to prepare her for her wedding. She couldn't move without the presence of Miss Adelaide Barker.

"I'm taking a break. Miss Sparrow is having her tea."

"Miss Sparrow can get back to work. Your wedding gown and your trousseau must be ready in two weeks. She has no time for tea."

"The poor thing's been sewing all day. She deserves a break."

"I'll tell Miss Sparrow when she can take a break. Now, my girl, get yourself back upstairs. You have no time to waste."

Garnet's gaze clashed with Miss Barker's. The older woman stared her down out of dark raisin eyes in a pudding face. Her martinet's air demanded obedience. With her head high and her shoulders squared, Garnet spun and retreated up the stairs.

In her bedroom, she leaned against the closed door, and her head drooped. In the two weeks since they'd returned to New York, her every attempt to contact Cole had been thwarted. Miss Barker monitored her every movement.

She'd been herded to the millinery shops, the fabric shops, and shops that sold shoes. Miss Barker had accompanied her on every excursion. When Garnet balked and refused to choose fabric or hats, Miss Barker had exerted her will and placed orders on Garnet's behalf. The trousseau being assembled for her was more Miss Barker's than her own.

A light rap sounded on her bedroom door. Garnet stepped away and pivoted to face the entry. "Come in."

Daisy poked her head around the portal and slid into the room, closing the door behind her before she spoke. "You weren't able to telephone Mr. Cole?"

Garnet shook her head and clenched her hands. "No. Miss Barker caught me before I could make the call. I don't know that I'll ever be able to reach Cole. What must he be thinking?"

Daisy stepped closer and patted Garnet's arm. "Mr. Cole knows you love him. He isn't fooled by your father's lie that you've decided to marry Albert Davies. He'll come for you, don't worry."

"Even if he comes to New York, he couldn't get inside this house. He'd be turned away." Garnet spun and paced across the room. "And I'm never allowed outside alone. I'm beginning to lose hope that I can avoid marrying Albert. Every day I feel the net tightening about me."

She halted before a polished mahogany vanity set between two large windows. Her image stared back at her from the mirror. Her mouth appeared tight, and her eyes seemed haunted. Whirling away from the looking glass, she tripped back to Daisy and clutched her friend's hands. "My father actually thinks he's acting in my best interests. I can't blame him for that, but he refuses to see my side. I can't allow myself to be trapped into marrying Albert. We need a plan."

"Perhaps I can help. I could mail a letter to Mr. Cole from the nearest post office."

"Do you think you can get out of the house?"

A determined expression firmed Daisy's jaw. "I can try. Miss Barker doesn't pay as much attention to me as she does to you."

"Miss Barker watches my every move and reports everything to my father. I have no money to give you to buy a stamp, and I can't get any."

"I've saved enough from my wages to buy a stamp." Daisy squeezed Garnet's hands.

Garnet glanced at Daisy's earnest face. "You're a good friend, Daisy. I don't know what I'd do without you." A sudden thought occurred. "Have you received any letters from Trystan or Rafe?"

"I haven't heard from either of them, but Rafe promised he'd telephone me." Daisy's face crumpled. "And Trystan promised to write."

"I think our mail is being monitored. Undoubtedly any letters we get from the Slash L are being intercepted. Even if Rafe called, I have no doubt he'd be told you're not interested in speaking to him."

A shadow darkened Daisy's blue eyes. "I hope Rafe wouldn't believe that."

"I'm sure he wouldn't." Garnet paced to the fireplace

and stared into the empty grate. Steam from the modern coiled heating register between the windows hissed. "Whatever we do, we must do it soon. I only have two weeks before the wedding."

"Your father sure is in a rush to get you married."

Garnet pivoted and stalked across the room to Daisy. "I think he's afraid that if he doesn't marry me off right away, I'll somehow escape his clutches. The Wild Wind brothers are two men whom my father can't control, and that worries him." She narrowed her eyes. "He hired Miss Barker to watch me because he doesn't think his sister is strong enough to control me. He thinks I could get around Aunt Belle."

Before Daisy could reply, the door burst open, and Adelaide Barker appeared in the aperture. She glowered at Daisy. "Don't you have duties elsewhere, missy? You should be pressing your mistress's gown for tonight's theatrical performance. Why are you loitering here?"

With a hunted look at Garnet, Daisy fled the room.

Adelaide Barker stalked toward Garnet.

Garnet lifted her chin and refused to flinch. When her custodian halted before her, she took the offensive. "Let me remind you that Daisy works for me, not you. You have no right to give her orders."

Miss Barker glared down at her, and her dark eyes burned. "Perhaps your father didn't make it clear that he placed you, and everything regarding you, under my authority. That makes Daisy my business."

"I can't believe that my father would give you such latitude."

A smile curled Miss Barker's thin lips. "Believe it. He's placed your welfare at my disposal."

Garnet lifted her chin a notch and studied the older woman's florid face. After a moment, she drew a breath. "You don't like me, do you, Miss Barker?"

Cold disdain crimped the older woman's features. Her dark gaze bored into Garnet's face. "No, Miss Morrison. If we must be frank, I don't like you."

"Why? What have I ever done to you? I'd never even met you before we returned to New York."

"You are a spoiled rich girl. You think you have the world at your feet." Adelaide drew herself up in a rigid stance as though she had a poker wedged along her backbone. "Do you know what it's like to be the illegitimate offspring of a rich New York socialite, yet to be excluded from his world? To be denied the luxury, the privilege, and the family that should have been mine? To be denied everything my father's legitimate children have experienced by legal right?"

Struck mute, Garnet gaped at the other woman.

Adelaide Barker swept a large hand in Garnet's direction. "Have you no idea of what it's like to be pitied for your lack of money or looks, to have men pass you by for prettier, richer women?"

Garnet swallowed and found her voice. "I'm sorry for what you've suffered. I'm sure it's most unfair, but I'm not responsible for how other people treat you. And you know nothing about me."

Like a flash, Adelaide seized Garnet's upper arm and thrust her face close. "You're part of the system that has relegated me to that unmentionable class of society where

I'm regarded with contempt." She released Garnet's arm and straightened. "Now, Miss Morrison, you will stop loitering in your room, and you *will* return to the nursery for your fitting. Miss Sparrow is waiting for you."

As she looked down her nose at the older woman, Garnet drew on every bit of training she'd received in finishing school and adopted her most imperious attitude. "Two things, Miss Barker. One, you will never again open my door and enter this chamber without first knocking and receiving permission to enter. Secondly, you will never put a hand on me again."

Garnet stepped away. With her head high, she swept past her opponent and marched to the door. A boring fitting for a hated wedding dress that she didn't want to wear awaited her.

Chapter 35

The gold velvet curtains onstage went down, signaling for the intermission. At the same time, the theater lights came up. On the main floor, people streamed from their seats to enjoy the benefits of the interval.

From her private box on the second floor, Garnet watched the activity below. Would this evening never end, and would she never be free of Albert's company?

Beside her, Albert stirred. He placed one elbow on the velvet arm of his theater chair and leaned close. "Well, my dear. We must take advantage of the intermission to show off our newly engaged status. And I must say, you're in fine looks tonight. I'll be the envy of every man here."

Garnet refused to acknowledge her companion and kept her gaze on her lap. Her hands, sheathed in her elbow-length black silk gloves, clutched a filigree ivory fan. With its square neckline and overlay of black crystal beading, her Empire-style copper satin gown draped her figure with stylish slenderness. A diamond tiara nestled in her golden-red curls piled atop her head. She couldn't bring herself to care what Albert thought of her appearance. She had no aspirations to make him the envy of other men.

He reached across her lap and picked up her left hand. His thumb stroked the diamond ring on her fourth finger, which Garnet wore outside her glove. "This ring shows the world you're mine."

Garnet pulled her hand from his. "I'm not a possession. I don't belong to you."

Albert pinched her chin between his thumb and forefinger. He forced her head toward him until she had no choice but to meet his gaze. "You most certainly do belong to me. And in two weeks, our wedding will make that a reality. Without doubt, you will then belong to me."

Garnet looked into his amber eyes, mere inches from her own. Triumph flickered there to be replaced by an expression that made her insides cringe, though she schooled her features to impassivity. When he squeezed her chin, she refused to flinch.

"You'll be my wife, and I *will* have complete control over you. Your father was too lenient. As my wife, you'll do nothing that hasn't been approved by me."

She stared back at him with defiance. "And how will you accomplish that? Will you beat me?"

Beneath his trim caramel mustache, his lips curled up in a disagreeable smile. "And if I do? Who will deny that disciplining a rebellious wife is a husband's right?"

Dread curled through Garnet's stomach. Life with Albert would be misery.

"And as your fiancé, this is my right." He dipped his head toward her.

Garnet wrenched her head from his fingers and turned her face aside. His kiss landed on her cheek instead of her mouth.

Anger flared in his eyes and mottled his cheeks. He grabbed her face once more. "Don't ever do that again." He glared down at her before he forced a kiss on her.

Garnet endured the indignity without a response. Memories of the kisses she and Cole had shared, given and received with love, made Albert's caress a travesty. Her stomach heaved.

Albert straightened and released her chin. "Now, we're going outside to mingle in the upstairs lobby."

"I don't want to mingle in the lobby. I'd prefer to stay here. Feel free to socialize without me."

Albert surged to his feet. Gripping her upper arms with vicious strength, he drew her up with him and jerked her against the fine fabric of his black dress jacket. Garnet thumped against his chest and wedged her elbows between them. Determined to stand her ground, she stared into his furious face, resolved not to be bullied.

"That you don't wish to leave this box is of no concern to me. You're going out there with me, and you *will* put a smile on your face. You *will* act the part of besotted fiancée. Flash your diamond about and let people see how much I've spent on your ring."

Garnet disdained to reply.

His low voice held a quiet threat. "Don't embarrass me in front of our peers. If you do, Garnet, I promise you'll be sorry."

* * *

Garnet halted in the middle of her room and surveyed her surroundings. Her bedroom had been her haven since childhood. One way or another, she'd soon be forced to leave this sanctuary. The thought hollowed her out inside.

Daisy tapped on the door and slipped into the room. "Did you have a good time at the theater?"

Garnet kept her gaze on her hands and shook her head. She removed Albert's engagement ring and drifted across the room to the silver jewelry box on her dresser, then dropped the ring into the box and shut the lid. Fixing her attention on her gloves, she peeled them off and tossed them onto the dresser. Shoulders slumped, she turned to face Daisy.

Her friend's anxious expression warmed her heart.

"Truthfully, the evening was a disaster." When she recalled the moment Albert had revealed his true, unvarnished nature, her stomach lurched.

"Poor miss! I don't wonder at it. Mr. Albert isn't the man Mr. Cole is."

Garnet shuddered. "Certainly not. I can't marry him! Tonight, Albert showed a vicious streak. I don't think my father realizes his true nature."

Daisy wrung her hands. "What are you going to do?"

With her fingertips pressed to her temples, Garnet closed her eyes and drew in a deep breath. Her lids swept up, and she met Daisy's stare. "I don't know. My father won't believe me if I tell him. He'll think I'm being missish and will get over it once I'm married." Her mind whirled. "Quick, Daisy. Unfasten me. I'll get out of this dress, and then we can talk. I must have a plan." She presented her back to her maid, and Daisy began the process of unfastening each tiny hook.

When Garnet was clad in a pale green chiffon nightdress and matching robe, the girls climbed onto Garnet's four poster bed. With the pillows behind her back, Garnet sat cross-legged and snuggled the blankets over her lap. At the foot of the bed, Daisy leaned against one of the carved walnut bedposts and hugged her updrawn knees.

"We have two weeks before the wedding. Whatever we do, it must be done quickly." Garnet shared a desperate glance with Daisy.

"If you write a letter to Mr. Cole tonight, I can try to slip out tomorrow and mail it."

With her fingertips pressing her temples, Garnet considered the plan. "We don't have enough time for that. I don't know for sure where Cole is now. He may still be at the Slash L with his Uncle Clint. And I don't know how often the mail is delivered to the ranch."

"Yes, I see what you mean."

Broken only by the click and hiss of the heating register, silence descended as Garnet contemplated one plan after another. The germ of an idea took root. "Daisy, I think we must run away."

Astonishment rounded Daisy's blue eyes. "Run away? Where?"

"I'm not sure. Let me think." Garnet tapped her chin with her forefinger. Perhaps she could find refuge in Washington with Flossie. "Flossie invited me to visit her, but I don't know if she's back in Washington yet. I suspect she won't leave the Slash L until her uncle's situation is resolved, one way or another." Garnet couldn't bring herself to mention the word *death* in reference to Clint Logan. He may have been up in years, but he'd still been a vital force on the ranch and much loved by his family.

"My family could hide you." Daisy's tone sounded doubtful. "My parents have an extra room upstairs now that two of my brothers are married."

Garnet gripped Daisy's hands. "That's very kind, Daisy, but I don't want to involve your family in my affairs. My father would probably think to look there, and your parents could be in big trouble for sheltering me." She leaned back against her pillows and sighed.

She was about to speak when a floorboard creaked outside her door. Her gaze flashed to Daisy's face, and she put a finger to her lips. With her other hand, she turned off the light on the lamp table beside her bed. Darkness swallowed the light.

After a moment, another creak from outside her room and soft footfalls on the carpet runner signaled that the listener had departed.

"That dragon was spying on me!" Garnet balled her hands into fists. "That does it! I won't stay here any longer."

She scrambled from her bed and crossed the shadowed room to snatch her jewelry box from the dressing table. After she'd returned to bed and cradled the box in her lap, she rummaged in its depths. "The expensive jewelry is in the safe in my father's library, but I have a few things here you could pawn."

As she rooted through the box, she recognized each piece by touch. "Here's a sapphire ring. And here's a cameo brooch." She dropped the jewelry on the coverlet. Rummaging further, she found a pair of platinum earrings. "Take these earrings. If what you get from this jewelry isn't enough, I'll pawn something else." Garnet hesitated. "I'd better give you the jewelry in the morning. I don't trust that dragon not to search your room. She'd have you arrested for stealing." Garnet up scooped the items and dropped them into the box.

"She wouldn't hesitate to have me arrested." Daisy clutched her elbows.

"I'll cause a scene at breakfast tomorrow morning. Perhaps I'll break a few dishes and throw a high-class tantrum. Something that will involve bringing a couple of maids into the breakfast room. Perhaps I'll involve the cook, as well. Anything that will distract the dragon." Garnet warmed to her plot. She couldn't wait to see the expression on Adelaide Barker's face when Garnet started smashing china on the breakfast room floor.

Daisy giggled at Garnet's daring. "While you're having your tantrum, I'll slip out through the kitchen."

"Find a pawn shop that won't be patronized by the servants of anyone we know. We don't want you to be recognized."

"I know of such a shop. It's in a part of town where society nobs or their help don't go."

"Good. After you get the money, go to the train depot. Purchase two coach tickets from New York to Chicago. When we reach Chicago, we'll buy tickets to Denver." Recalling her uncomfortable trip from Denver to Indian Pass, Garnet sighed. This journey across the continent by cheap fare would be nothing like last summer's luxurious Pullman excursion with her father.

Daisy hugged her knees. "We're going back to Denver? Won't your father have men watching the train station there?"

"He will, so we'll need disguises. Should we wear wigs? And he might not expect us to travel by coach, although nothing is certain."

"What about Mr. Cole?"

"I'll telephone the Slash L when we get to Denver. He'll come for me, I'm sure." Another silence fell while Garnet contemplated her plan. "When you're purchasing our tickets, dress very plainly and cover your hair with a large hat. Buy the tickets under assumed names. We mustn't give away any clues. And arrange for us to leave as soon as possible on a night train."

"What name shall I put on your ticket, Miss Garnet?"

"Hmm…" Garnet tipped her head to one side while she pondered an alias. Something similar to her real name might be best. "I think I'll be Ruby Morris. And what about you, Daisy?"

Daisy's eyebrows rose. "Me? I'll be plain Jane Brown."

With the choice of false names, the plan took on reality. She might escape her father and Albert, after all. A weight rolled from Garnet's shoulders. She lifted her hand in a mock toast. "Here's to us, Ruby Morris and Jane Brown. May we live in peace."

The girls doubled over in giggles. When they could talk again, Garnet moved on to the next item. "We'll need to take a few things with us."

"I'll pack us a couple of valises," Daisy said.

"We can only take with us what we can carry."

"The house is locked up when the servants go to bed."

Garnet shrugged. "I know where the keys are kept. And Daisy, we must be very careful. Once he discovers we're gone, my father will no doubt hire Pinkerton agents to look for us."

When they'd finalized their plans, Daisy crept to her own room on the third floor.

With the blankets snuggled about her chin, Garnet stared through the gloom at the embossed ceiling above her and clutched Cole's Christmas gift against her heart. Holding his brooch lent her courage. They'd been so optimistic when they'd exchanged their Christmas gifts, so sure her father could be convinced to let them marry. Little had they suspected they'd be a continent apart just days later.

She brought Cole's face into focus and recollected his fine character, his leadership, and his strength. His tenderness eased her heart soreness after her experience with Adelaide Barker's bullying and Albert's brutish behavior. If she kept her mind fixed on the life she and Cole had planned together, she had the courage to take the leap that would pit her forever against her father's control.

Garnet closed her eyes and conjured up thoughts of Cole's arms about her. She saw once again his smile and the way his eyes crinkled when he gave her the look he reserved only for her. She could almost feel his kisses and hear his voice telling her that he loved her. With a prayer for wisdom and protection, she turned her burden over to her Heavenly Father and fell asleep.

Chicago, Illinois
January 1912

Chapter 36

Garnet, with Daisy trotting at her elbow, hurried to the rail coach that waited alongside the train station's platform. Her worn satchel bumped against her knee.

Except for a few gas jets in the ceiling that spread their luminance in a weak glow, darkness shrouded the station. Loud clangs echoed in the cavernous building. The unsavory atmosphere goaded Garnet toward the rail car's dubious safety. Sensations of being watched prickled down her spine.

They reached the train and paused at the steps at the back of the one of the passenger cars. A conductor, clad in a navy-blue jacket with gold piping, inspected their tickets and motioned them aboard. Inside the coach, the girls tumbled into a worn leather seat halfway down the aisle.

Daisy rested her tapestry bag on her knees and hunched her shoulders. "We did it. We escaped." She tucked a brown curl that peeped from beneath her broad-brimmed felt hat behind her ear.

Garnet tipped her head toward her friend. "I can't

believe we got out of the house." She glanced at a tall man in a dark, knee-length belted overcoat and chocolate-colored fedora hat who sauntered down the aisle toward them. He met her gaze, and she turned her head toward the window, breaking the contact. When he'd moved past them and dropped into a seat behind them on the other side of the aisle, Garnet murmured in Daisy's ear, "I feel watched."

"I'm sure we haven't been discovered yet. Miss Barker won't suspect anything until you don't come down for breakfast," Daisy whispered after she glanced over her shoulder at the man in the dark overcoat.

"And since I told her not to enter my room without permission, we might gain a little time. She may hesitate a few minutes before she forces her way in." Garnet leaned down to stow her scuffed leather valise beneath her seat.

The girls sat in silence while other passengers—families with cranky children, men traveling singly or in groups, and even a couple of nuns in black habits—filled the seats. Despite the assurance their escape couldn't have been detected yet, a sense of urgency rode Garnet like a winged black bird. She kept her face turned from the window and her head tipped down. When the whistle shrieked and the train lurched into motion, she drew a relieved breath.

"At last. We're leaving New York."

Daisy gave a nervous giggle. "I think we're the only two ladies who aren't traveling with men, except for the nuns."

Garnet craned her neck to inspect the other passengers, then slumped against the leather seat back.

"You're right. I hope that fact won't call attention to us, but we had no other options."

"If anyone asks, we're meeting your fiancé. That should be respectable enough."

The train picked up speed. Miles passed beneath the wheels with a rhythmic clacking sound. The car swayed, and the seat vibrated from the metal track's segmentation. Silence descended over the car as tired children fell asleep in their parents' laps and adults tried to doze.

Garnet leaned her head against the seat back and closed her eyes, but she couldn't sleep. Her mind whirled. Had they covered their trail well enough? How soon would her father put Pinkerton agents on the search for her and Daisy? Would the newspaper headlines scream with the news of the missing New York heiress, or would her father manage to keep her disappearance secret?

She shivered and huddled into her sheepskin jacket. The coal stoves on either end of the railcar couldn't banish winter's chill.

When dawn filled the coach with its rosy light, Daisy stirred and lifted her head, then knuckled sleep from her eyes. "I have a crick in my neck."

Garnet rolled her shoulders. A cramp jabbed her muscles along her spine. "I'm afraid this trip won't be as comfortable as last summer when we rode first class with my father." She cast a look at her friend and couldn't suppress a chuckle.

"What's funny?" Daisy's brows drew together in a puzzled frown.

"Your wig. You have so much hair, and I can't get used

to you with that golden-brown color. Your own mother wouldn't recognize you."

"That's good. I don't want to be recognized." Daisy eyed her companion. "I don't think anyone will recognize you as a blonde. And you're not dressed as a society lady, so that changes your look."

Garnet patted her own wig, then tucked a stray wisp of blonde hair into her pompadour. "The real test will be when we arrive in Denver. My father will have Pinkertons at the train station."

Daisy shivered. "I don't want to think about it."

Garnet straightened in her seat. "The Lord can cause the agents to miss us so we can slip into the city without being noticed."

Daisy gripped Garnet's gloved hand. "He can. He'll be with us."

Children stirred and woke, and the adults shifted in their seats.

The conductor entered their car on a blast of cold air and halted halfway down the aisle. "We'll be stopping in fifteen minutes to take on more water. You'll have half an hour at the station café if you want to buy your breakfast." His voice carried above the children's chatter and the wheels' clacking. Bracing himself against the car's swaying, he slowly made his way down the aisle and halted beside Garnet and Daisy's seat. "Are you girls traveling alone?"

Garnet lifted her chin, but she tried not to act too much like an imperious society miss. "We're meeting my fiancé. He'll be waiting for us."

"Hmm... most irregular." He adjusted his cap while he pinned them with a suspicious glare.

Garnet stared him down.

With a shrug, he moved on down the aisle and left the car by the end door. The girls exchanged a glance.

When the train had slowed to a stop, Garnet and Daisy waited until the other passengers had left the car before they made their way to the diner located in one corner of the station. Garnet's breath plumed in a white cloud as they hurried into the eatery's warmth. The door shut with a clatter behind them.

"It sure feels good in here." Daisy scanned the dining room. "I don't see any empty tables. I think everyone on the train is getting breakfast."

"We can eat standing up if we can order from the counter. I'm afraid all we can afford is a muffin and coffee."

"I don't mind."

After they'd ordered, they turned away from the counter and squirmed through the throng toward a vacant corner. As they passed a small table where two men sat, one of them rose and stepped into their path. He swept off his fedora and pressed the felt hat against his chest.

"Excuse me, ladies. I see you're looking for a table." The gentleman from the train intercepted them.

Garnet halted, her attention arrested by the man's sharp gaze in a thin face. "We intend to eat standing up."

"No need for that. I just finished, and I'm sure my friend here would be willing to give up his seat for you." He rested his other hand on the man's shoulder and squeezed.

His companion put down his mug and rose. "Certainly. You ladies must have our seats."

Garnet cut a glance at Daisy. Uncertainty marked her friend's features. "We don't mind standing. We've been sitting long enough."

"What kind of gentlemen would we be if we let you ladies stand while we sit? No, we won't hear of it. Please sit." With one hand about Garnet's elbow, the man urged her to sit.

Although her nerves screamed a warning, Garnet sat, and Daisy took the chair across from her. "Thank you, gentlemen, very much. We appreciate your chivalry."

The man in the overcoat seemed inclined to hover, but Garnet dismissed him with a nod and sipped her coffee, then bit into her muffin without looking at him. She wanted no conversation with strange men.

Daisy ate her breakfast in silence. When they'd finished, the girls made a quick visit to the ladies' repairing room. While she washed her hands, Garnet examined her reflection in the spotted mirror above the round metal sink.

The unadorned brim of her dark felt hat cast a shadow across her face. Wisps of blonde hair curled at her temples, and a fat golden pompadour coiled at her nape. Her serviceable black skirt and plain cotton blouse, hidden beneath her jacket, decried any pretensions of wealth. Garnet Morrison had vanished, while Ruby Morris stood in her place. She smiled at her reflection. No one who didn't know her well should ever suspect who really hid behind her disguise.

Daisy joined her at the sink.

Garnet stepped aside. "We've been traveling for six hours. We should arrive in Chicago by early afternoon."

"We can't get to Denver soon enough to suit me." Daisy scrubbed her hands with the harsh soap supplied by the railway.

"As soon as we find a hotel room in Denver, I'll put a call through to the Slash L. Even if Cole isn't there, his mother will know where he is."

"And Rafe will probably be with him." Daisy smiled as she dried her hands on her skirt, ignoring the dirty cotton towel that hung from a rack.

"I think Rafe will be with Cole when Cole comes to get us." Garnet nudged Daisy's elbow. "You'll see Rafe again."

A wash of color tinted Daisy's fair skin. "I hope so."

"Remember what he whispered in your ear when we left the Slash L." Garnet grinned down at her friend. "He'll come."

A gust of frigid air greeted them when they stepped from the retiring room, and pellets of ice peppered their faces when the boarded the train. They dropped into their seats with a sigh.

As Garnet sat, her leather purse slid off her lap into the space between the seat and the wall. She reached down to free the handbag and tugged on the handle, a long length of faux gold chain. The bag popped free. She frowned as she laid the purse on her lap and examined the clasp that attached the chain to her handbag. The clasp seemed loose. She made a mental note to herself to hold the bag with care so as not to loosen the chain further.

The train huffed and shuddered as it prepared to pull out of the station. Just as the engine jerked into motion, the gentleman in the overcoat slid into the seat on the opposite side of the aisle. "I hope you ladies don't mind if I move a little closer." He doffed his hat. "I'm weary of my own company."

Garnet eyed him with misgiving, but she tried to reply in a civil tone. "You're free to sit wherever you can find an available seat. Don't mind us."

He seemed to ignore her cool welcome and smiled. "Conversation always relieves the tedium of travel. And one never knows whom one will meet."

"So many people travel these days, one can meet many strangers." Garnet shrugged and turned her head toward the window. Snow flurries danced outside the pane, tossed about by the wind.

"It looks like we may be in for a storm." The gentleman persisted in his attempt to draw the girls into conversation.

Garnet tossed him a glance, but she didn't reply. Warning bells at his interest rang in her head. Allowing a strange man to become too familiar would be foolhardy, even without her escape. Logic insisted there hadn't been time for a Pinkerton agent to find her, yet her nerves clanged a warning.

She angled her head toward the window, and her thoughts turned to the brooch Cole had given her. She'd sewn the precious brooch into the hem of her skirt for safekeeping. The bauble represented Cole's love for her, and she couldn't bear to lose it.

The train's motion lulled her into an uneasy slumber. When Daisy poked her arm sometime later, Garnet roused.

"Look outside." Daisy leaned around her to peer out the window.

Garnet swiveled her head toward the window and caught her breath. A swirling wall of white blotted out the landscape, and the train had slowed to a crawl.

Chapter 37

The gentleman in the overcoat propped his elbow on the back of the seat in front of him as he leaned into the aisle. "I hope you ladies aren't in a hurry to reach Chicago. We won't make it there on schedule."

Garnet turned away from the window as the urgency that rode her ratcheted up a notch. The more time they spent traveling, their chances of encountering Pinkerton agents increased. She tried to assume a nonchalant air and shrugged. "A snowstorm is one of the hazards one can expect when traveling in January."

The man gave an approving nod. "Such a sanguine attitude. I commend you for your optimism. No point in fretting, I say. We'll get there when we get there."

Daisy cocked her head at him. "Sir, do you have the time?"

He pulled a silver timepiece from his vest pocket and flipped open the lid with his thumb. "Why, the morning's almost gone. It's half-past eleven o'clock."

"Thank you, sir." Daisy settled herself against her seat back and stretched out her legs.

Garnet's rumbling stomach reminded her she'd eaten only a muffin for breakfast, and the time for the noon meal approached. She thought of the food both she and Daisy carried in their valises. They'd managed to filch a few slices of bread and a couple of apples each from the kitchen to be eaten when they couldn't purchase food. Perhaps they should dip into their rations for lunch.

"Are you ladies stopping in Chicago?" The gentleman persisted.

Garnet cast him a repressive look and declined to reply.

The conductor entered their coach with a whirl of snow. White powder dusted his coat and settled on the floor before he shut the door. He reached for the coal scuttle and loaded the stove with fuel, then made his way toward the back of the car.

A young husband with a child cuddled in his lap reached a hand toward the conductor. "Sir, can you tell me when we'll reach Chicago? Will the train become snowbound?"

The conductor halted. "When we stopped to take on water, a rotary snowplow was hooked to our engine. We should be able to keep moving and should arrive in Chicago early tomorrow morning."

Tomorrow morning! Garnet had hoped to be halfway across Kansas by then. Their chance of slipping into Denver undetected would depend on their disguises, since the delay meant her father's agents would be entrenched in the Denver railway station before she and

Daisy could arrive. She leaned her head against the seat and prayed.

After she and Daisy had nibbled on pieces of bread and an apple each, Garnet peered through the rime ice that frosted the window's exterior. Snowflakes still whirled down in a thick curtain. She sighed, then cast a curious look at her friend.

"Let's play a game. It will help us pass the time."

Daisy lifted an eyebrow. "What kind of game?"

Garnet pitched her voice low enough so their inquisitive neighbor couldn't hear. "I ask a question, and you answer. Then you ask me a question, and I answer. If one of us forfeits a reply, then that person must sing a song."

Daisy's forehead wrinkled, and she hesitated. "All right, but I hate to sing solo, so don't ask me anything I shouldn't answer."

Garnet's eyes gleamed. "That's what makes the game interesting." She flapped a hand at Daisy. "You go first. Ask me something."

Daisy's face assumed a thoughtful look. "After you and Mr. Cole are married, where will you live?"

Garnet thought of Cole's dream—the mine—and her promise to help him establish that dream. "That's easy. Cole and I will live at the mine, at least when the camp isn't snowed in."

"Now it's your turn to ask me something."

Garnet tipped her head and considered Daisy. "If you could be anything you want, what would you like to be?"

For long moments, Daisy contemplated the question before she turned a frank gaze to her friend. "Please don't be offended when I say this, but I don't want to be a lady's maid all my life. I'd like to be a nurse."

"A nurse?"

"Yes. Ever since I was a little girl and patched up my baby brother's knee when he skinned it, I've wanted to be a nurse."

Garnet eyed her friend with new respect. "I never suspected you harbored such an ambition, and I'm not offended." She wriggled, trying to ease the ache in her back. "Come to the camp with Cole and me this summer. The mine employs a doctor, and you could be his assistant. That would give you a taste of nursing, and you could decide if that's something you still want to pursue."

Daisy hesitated.

"The camp isn't as primitive as we thought." Garnet turned a sly grin on her friend. "Rafe will be there."

Color washed over Daisy's face. "I couldn't be so bold as to chase after Rafe. And we don't know if the doctor wants an assistant."

"Don't you worry about a thing. I'm sure I can work something out. After all, I'm going to marry one of the mine owners." A cold draft slithered across the back of her neck, and she shivered, wishing she and Daisy could travel in the luxury of a private compartment such as they'd enjoyed on their previous trip across the continent. "It's too bad we didn't have room to pack a blanket. I haven't been warm since we left the café this morning."

By the time the locomotive labored into the Chicago rail station, another day had dawned. Sometime during the night, the snow had stopped, though a bank of gray clouds obscured the sun.

The gentleman in the overcoat rose when the train ground to a halt and paused by the seat where Garnet and Daisy sat. "Do you ladies need assistance? I'd be pleased to offer my aid, since I noticed you're traveling alone."

Suspicion lent Garnet's voice an edge. "We thank you, sir, for your offer, but we can manage on our own."

With only a moment's hesitation, the man nodded and joined the other passengers who pressed toward the exit.

Garnet lowered her voice as she rose. "The storm slowed us down, so my father has had time to hire agents to watch the train station. He knows we must travel through Chicago, so undoubtedly, he has someone here. We'd be harder to spot if we mingle with the other passengers."

The girls gathered up their bags and eased into the aisle between a family with several children and two men. When they stepped off the train, Garnet swept the platform with a quick glance. Since she and Daisy had eaten all their food last night, nerves made her forget her empty stomach. Her skin crawled.

Amid the bustle to her right, a lone man strolled along the platform with his hands in his pockets. Over to the left, another man stood beside one of the coaches of their train. Could either of these men be searching for her and Daisy? Garnet's breathing hitched.

They followed the family toward a café at one side of the echoing building, leaving behind the trains who huffed on their tracks. A movement behind a shadowed pillar caught Garnet's attention. Without turning her head, she cut her eyes in that direction. A man with a cap pulled low over his brow and wearing a workman's dark jacket was half-concealed by the cement colonnade, though he kept a watchful gaze on the disembarking passengers. Fear turned her blood to ice.

She hustled Daisy into the diner on the heels of the family they'd been following. With a hand clamped about Daisy's elbow, she turned them toward the back of the dining room. They fell into two empty chairs at an available table and dropped their valises at their feet.

Daisy scanned the room. "I don't see the man from the train. What do you think he wanted?"

"He couldn't have been after us. I think he only wanted to pass the time with two women who weren't accompanied by a man." Garnet leaned forward and pitched her voice loud enough so Daisy could hear her above the noise in the diner. "There are at least three men out there who may be Pinkerton agents. We'll have to be very careful. Even though we don't look like ourselves, we're still two females traveling alone. That in itself will be enough to warrant their scrutiny."

"Someday we'll look back at this at a grand adventure." Daisy bit her lip as though she doubted her own words.

"Of course. When I'm married to Cole, and you're a nurse, we'll laugh at our fears."

After the girls had eaten, they gathered up their things and threaded their way through crowded tables to the door. Just outside, Garnet paused and sent a quick glance about the depot. Daisy hovered at her elbow.

"The ticket office is over there. We might as well purchase our tickets now." Garnet took a step forward. Feeling as though her real name was emblazoned across her forehead, she began a slow saunter toward the ticket office. Her insides quaked, and her hands sweated inside her gloves. Her skin crawled with the sensation of being watched.

They were halfway across the depot when a middle-aged woman who looked like she might be a teacher eased toward them from the direction of the ticket office. Garnet slowed her steps. Could a woman be a Pinkerton agent?

With only instinct to guide her, Garnet pivoted away from the woman. She gripped Daisy's arm and plunged deeper into the station, away from the tracks. Against everything that screamed for her to bolt, she quickened her step but didn't run. Daisy kept pace with her. They squirmed between groups of people entering the depot. Garnet didn't dare look back to see if the woman followed them.

A movement to her left caught her eye. The man whom she'd seen skulking behind the pillar eased through the crowd as though to intercept them. Beside her, Daisy stiffened, and they ducked around a group of school children.

Ahead of them, the depot doors opened onto the street. *The doors.* They had to reach the doors, where they could lose themselves among the crowds.

Garnet turned her head just enough to glimpse the man who seemed intent on blocking them. He'd gained ground, though someone pushing a dolly loaded with luggage blocked his path.

The girls gave a burst of speed that plunged them through the doors and onto the street.

"Run, Daisy!" Garnet whirled to the left.

The sidewalk teemed with people, and the girls darted between men and women who hurried about on business of their own. Garnet's valise banged against her side, and her breath rasped. She grabbed her hat with her free hand when it threatened to fly off her head. A quick peek over her shoulder revealed the man in the cap and dark jacket burst through the doors. He halted and scanned the crowd.

Garnet kept moving, though she slowed her pace so not to call attention to herself. Daisy. Where was Daisy? Garnet checked her pace and whirled in a frantic circle. People—men in wool overcoats and derby hats mingled with men in working clothes, women bundled against the cold—pushed and shoved about her. Panic clutched her by the throat. *Where was Daisy?*

"Miss Garnet, I'm over here."

At the sound of her name, Garnet spun toward the voice. Daisy stood at one side of the sidewalk, clutching her satchel with whitened knuckles. Garnet swooped toward her friend and grabbed her in a quick hug. "I thought I'd lost you."

"Me, too."

"That man came out of the station. I'm sure he's looking for us. Let's cross the street and go down that block." Garnet indicated a street that intersected with the one that fronted the depot.

With an eye on the motorcars, buggies, and bicycles that clogged the street, the girls darted across and fled down the sidewalk. With her nerve ends jangling, Garnet left the station behind.

Chapter 38

The newsboy who hawked his papers on the streetcorner held a newspaper toward Garnet. "Care to buy a paper, Miss? Five cents."

Garnet glanced at the paper, which had been printed in New York city the day before. *Banking Heiress Missing, Presumed Kidnapped* emblazoned the headlines. Her face, framed by a broadbrimmed hat festooned with silk flowers, stared at her from the page. Somehow, the reporters had gotten wind of her escape and had put their own twist on the news. Her stomach clenched. With her face splashed across the papers, she'd be at greater risk. The black and white photo gave no hint of her hair color. "No, thank you, sonny. I don't need a paper."

The boy narrowed his eyes at her. "Hey, lady, you look like the woman who's missing." With another close inspection of her features, he turned away. "Extra, extra! Heiress missing! Read all about it!"

The girls hurried down the sidewalk. Garnet's insides shook. If the newsboy had noticed the resemblance between herself and the newspaper photo, would her disguise continue to offer her anonymity's protection?

"I can see why your father is desperate to find you," Daisy said. "Do you think it's possible he believes you've been kidnapped?"

Garnet pondered the likelihood. "I'm not sure. With people like us, kidnapping is always a possibility, but you're missing, too. I don't think he believes kidnappers would take you as well."

A clock in the bell tower of a nearby church chimed the hour. The frigid air that nipped at her, combined with hunger, made Garnet long for a warm place to sit down and eat.

"Why don't we find a café and have lunch? Then we can decide what to do next. Somehow, we have to get past the Pinkertons to buy tickets to Denver." Garnet scanned the businesses along the sidewalk for a place to eat.

Daisy slowed her steps. "Miss Garnet, do you know where we are?"

Garnet halted and tried to find a street sign. Her mouth went dry when she realized she didn't know where they were. "We've been walking for so long, I'm all turned around."

Daisy met her gaze. "We can ask directions for the train station at a café."

"Let's find someplace to eat. Then we can figure out how to get to the depot."

A block down, they found a diner and bustled toward the door. "I'm starved." Garnet paused at the steps and reached for her purse that should have been dangling at her hip. Nothing but empty air met her groping hand. Her heart lurched into her throat. She felt for the gold chain she'd looped over her shoulder—the chain that doubled as a strap for the purse—but no chain draped her shoulder.

"Miss Garnet? What's wrong. You're as white as a sheet." Daisy's voice held a hint of anxiety.

"My purse is gone. I must have lost it when we were running from the Pinkerton agent." She recalled that the clasp that attached the chain to her purse had seemed loose. "I think the clasp may have broken."

The girls stared at each other.

"All my money was in my purse." Garnet's voice trembled. She took a deep breath and tried to quell the panic that threatened to swamp her.

A man and a woman, intent on their lunch, brushed past them and mounted the café steps.

Garnet backed away and searched once more for her purse. Nothing. Her purse wasn't tangled with her jacket, or her valise. Her purse had vanished. She met Daisy's wide-eyed stare. "We have no money."

Daisy's face drained of color.

The enormity of their situation hit Garnet like a blow to her midsection. They were two women alone in a strange city, hunted by Pinkerton agents, without money or resources. She didn't have the funds to make a phone call, or purchase a meal, or find shelter for the night. Even at midday, cold air bit through her gloves and coat. Pewter-colored clouds sagged earthward, heavy with snow.

"What are we going to do?" Daisy's voice quivered.

Garnet's mind whirled as she met Daisy's gaze. "We can go back to the train station and allow the Pinkerton agents to find us. They'd feed us, at least, and take us to a hotel where we'd be warm."

Daisy lifted her chin. Resolve strengthened her voice. "If we do that, they'll take you back to New York. You'd have to marry Albert."

"And you'd be out of a job. My father would sack you for helping me escape."

Daisy shrugged away her friend's concern. "Don't worry about me. I can get another job. Maybe I could go to nursing school, but you can't marry Albert."

Garnet closed her eyes. Her shoulders slumped. She stood on a gray sidewalk among gray buildings beneath a gray sky. Even the air looked gray. She felt gray, drained of all hope and promise.

Daisy tugged at her sleeve. "Miss Garnet, we should pray."

Garnet's eyes flashed open. Of course. How could she have forgotten to seek help from her Heavenly Father? "Yes, let's pray."

The girls bowed their heads, unmindful of the passersby, and sought the help of their Heavenly Father. When they'd finished, peace flooded Garnet's soul. "Daisy, let's go back to the station and try to find my purse. Perhaps it's lying on the sidewalk."

Daisy looked doubtful. "We'll have to take care not to be seen. And someone may already have picked it up."

"All true, but it's better than turning ourselves over to the Pinkertons. I'll ask someone at the diner for directions to the train station, and then we can look for my purse."

* * *

Garnet stepped out of the way of a troupe of school children herded along the sidewalk by two harried teachers and put down her valise. Her shoulder and arm ached from hours spent carrying the bag. It couldn't have weighed this much when they'd left home.

Her feet hurt, and her stomach rumbled.

The clamor of motor traffic and streetcars, the shriek of a train whistle, and the babble of voices jangled her nerves. With the train depot within sight, the sensation of being watched prickled along her spine.

Daisy halted beside her.

Garnet hugged her friend. Daisy hadn't complained, even though they hadn't eaten since breakfast, cold made their teeth chatter, and they hadn't found her purse. "You're a good friend, Daisy. I'm sorry I got you into this mess."

"I'd still rather be here with you than back in New York city."

Garnet scanned the area around the depot. The street bustled with commerce, with pockets of grass and trees interspersed between the buildings. Dead for the winter, trees lifted gnarled bare branches to the sky. She felt as lifeless as those trees.

What time was it? How many more hours before all businesses in the city closed their doors for the day? Where would she and Daisy be then, on the street without protection and exposed to the frigid nighttime temperatures? They seemed to be out of options, except to allow themselves to be found. Thoughts of marriage to Albert swamped her. Panic paralyzed her.

Garnet breathed deeply through her nose and

straightened her spine. They weren't beaten, not yet. Her mind scrambled to think of an escape from their dilemma. "Let's walk, Daisy. We can't stay here." She retrieved her valise and stepped out. Something hard bumped against her shin, and she halted. Cole's brooch, concealed in the hem of her skirt.

Cole's brooch. His Christmas gift to her, encrusted with diamonds and garnets. The brooch represented his love for her, and she treasured it above any other possession. The bauble was worth a year's salary for most people and could provide money enough to see her and Daisy to Denver if she pawned it. But could she part with it?

Daisy watched her, curiosity etched on her face, but she said nothing.

Garnet gnawed on her lip. Indecision rooted her to the sidewalk. Though loathe to admit the fact, pawning the brooch seemed to be their only recourse. In their wanderings that morning, she and Daisy had passed a pawn shop. After a few more moments of inner struggle, she capitulated to the inevitable "I have an idea, but I don't want to discuss it here. Let's find a place where we can talk."

With her chin in the air and her shoulders back, Garnet led the way across the street.

Chapter 39

The brick pawn shop squatted with an unassuming air between a vacant brick building and a corner mart. Metal bars marched vertically across its windows and gave the establishment the air of a local jail. Garnet halted before the door and gulped. Could she really part with Cole's brooch?

An icy-fingered breeze touched her cheek, and a swirl of snowflakes rode the current, then danced along the sidewalk. Leaden clouds scudded across the sky.

She couldn't linger outside the shop all afternoon. The money from the brooch would provide food and shelter for herself and Daisy. She had no choice, though parting with the jewelry broke her heart.

Garnet gulped. "I'd better get this over with."

Daisy didn't comment, though she trudged at Garnet's elbow. A bell above the door clanged and announced their arrival. Just inside, they halted.

Heat enveloped Garnet like a wool blanket. For the first

time since breakfast that morning, she stopped shivering. She cast a curious eye about the shop.

Hooded lights hung from the ceiling and cast a dim glow over the interior. Glass cases lined all the walls of the small space and displayed available goods.

The girls browsed the merchandise. Books, dishes, paintings, revolvers, and a chessboard with its pieces in a box were all displayed. Several pieces of jewelry rested in the display cases, but Garnet saw none that equaled the value of her brooch.

They approached a glass-topped counter along the far wall. A burly man with a walrus moustache stood with both hands braced on the counter's edge. He peered at them through round spectacles.

"May I help you ladies?" His gravelly voice grated against Garnet's ears.

The girls halted before the counter, and Garnet laid her valise on the glass surface. "Do you buy jewelry?"

The store's proprietor waved an expansive hand. "I buy all kinds of items, as you can see from my stock." He stared down at her. "What are you offering?"

Garnet opened her satchel and rummaged inside, then drew out a small object wrapped in a white silk handkerchief. The initials *GM* had been embroidered in one corner in red thread. She laid the parcel on the countertop and peeled open the handkerchief. The brooch, with its tiny diamonds and garnets encircled by a delicate gold setting, sparkled in the light. The quality of its workmanship gave evidence of the bauble's value. Garnet's heart wrenched as she stared down at her brooch, offered up for sacrifice upon the alter of necessity.

The proprietor cast her a suspicious look, then removed his spectacles. He fitted a loupe to one eye and picked up the brooch. In silence, he inspected the piece, examining the gems from all angles.

A thin-faced man wearing a ragged coat and a worn cap who had been idling at one of the counters sidled closer. He eyed the brooch with the air of a hungry fox watching a fat hen.

The shop's proprietor laid Garnet's jewelry on the countertop and gave her an intent stare. "That brooch is one of the most valuable pieces I've ever laid eyes on. It's worth more than someone like you can afford. Where did you get it?" Skepticism laced his tone.

Garnet swallowed. She hadn't expected to be questioned about her ownership. "The brooch was a gift."

"To you?"

"Yes."

The proprietor's expression turned sly, and his gaze roved over Garnet again with a hint of insolence. "Fallen on hard times, have you?"

Her face flamed at his inference. "You're wrong. I'm a respectable woman!"

"Uh huh." The shop's owner's stare touched Garnet's face, her hair, and her clothes as if speculating on her morals. "It don't matter to me if you're the spurned plaything of a wealthy lover. Business is business."

Heat surged through her, and her voice sharpened. "How much for the brooch?"

Daisy stepped back as the shabby customer eased closer.

The proprietor contemplated the bauble, then turned

his attention to the silk handkerchief with its incriminating initials that lay beside the brooch. His gaze sharpened as he lifted the hankie and examined the embroidered letters. "*GM*. Hey, aren't those the initials of the heiress who's been kidnapped? I read about it in the papers."

Garnet's pulse stuttered.

The shop owner plucked the handkerchief from the counter and thrust it beneath Garnet's nose. "Maybe you're in on the kidnapping, and this kerchief and the brooch belong to the heiress. Did you steal it? Maybe I should call the police. That heiress's rich daddy would offer a plum reward for information about his daughter."

Garnet's gaze met the greedy stare of the man behind the counter. He thought he could shake down her father for more money than he could get for the brooch, with the added bonus of publicity if he involved the police or the press. Publicity would make his shop infamous and perhaps bring in more business. She snatched Cole's brooch and her valise off the counter and wheeled, then sprinted for the door with Daisy at her heels.

The portal banged closed behind them, and they darted down the sidewalk. They ran until they reached the end of the next block. At the corner, they stopped to catch their breath. A gust of wind hurled snowflakes at them, and the afternoon's light had dimmed.

"What do we do now?" Daisy panted and pressed a hand to her side.

Garnet's chest heaved. "We'll have to find another pawn shop."

The passage of time worried her. Only a couple hours remained before businesses closed for the night. She shivered when a draught of cold air found its way beneath her coat collar.

The girls had crossed the street and begun to trudge toward a row of shops when a rush of footsteps thudded behind them. Before Garnet could turn, someone attacked her from her rear side and shoved at her with brutal force. Caught off guard, she stumbled and pitched to her knees. Her satchel skidded into the dirt, and Cole's brooch spun across the sidewalk. A male figure in a shabby coat lunged past her and scooped up the jewelry, then careened around the corner and vanished into a maze of buildings.

Garnet scrambled to her feet and stared in the direction the thief had gone.

Daisy's anxious voice recalled her to their situation. "Are you hurt?"

Garnet did a slow pivot and faced her friend. She'd just been robbed of their last option. Despair such as she'd never known washed over her. Her throbbing knees and scratched palms paled with the loss of her brooch and the freedom it offered. "I'm fine. But now I have no way to get money. I'll have to let the Pinkertons find me." Tears brimmed behind her eyes. "Cole's brooch is gone." Somehow, having the brooch stolen seemed a worse fate than having to pawn it.

"The customer in the pawn shop stole it." Daisy, a diminutive figure with a mass of pale brown hair and a worn coat, stood resolute amid the falling snow. "The man who was listening to your conversation. He nearly bumped my elbow when he tried to get a look at your brooch."

"I'll report it stolen after I've turned myself in to the Pinkertons." Garnet's shoulders rose and fell. She retrieved her valise and took a step. "We might as well head back to the depot before the snow gets worse."

Daisy shook her head. "Don't give up yet. We'll think of something."

"I have nothing left to sell. Even if we both pawned every item we have with us, we wouldn't have enough to get us to Denver. I doubt we'd get enough to rent a room for the night."

Garnet took another step, and Daisy followed.

Snow swirled about them like lace and cast a hush over the street.

Garnet ached in every bone and muscle. Her stomach cramped with hunger, and the constant trembling from the cold had exhausted her. Thirst made her tongue feel thick. Fatigue almost numbed the misery of lost dreams and a life without Cole. Only grit kept her on her feet.

They were halfway down a block when two well-dressed women exited a shop.

"Excuse us." The women nodded at them when they almost collided.

Garnet halted and stared at the shop the women had just quit. The sign above the door read, "Madame Sophia, Hair Goods and Wigs." An idea kindled a spark of hope. She clutched Daisy's arm. "I think I've found a way to save us." Excitement chased away her earlier despair and fused her with energy.

Daisy cast her a hopeful look.

"I have one asset to sell." Garnet almost laughed aloud in relief. "Hair. I have so much hair it's almost too much to deal with. But I can make money off my hair if I sell it."

"Sell your hair? Miss Garnet, not your beautiful hair!" Dismay pulled at Daisy's mouth.

"It's either my hair, or I return to New York and marry Albert. I'd rather sell my hair."

Daisy swallowed. "I see what you mean. But you won't look respectable."

"Cole will still love me without my hair." Cole might be shocked when he saw her, but he'd still love her. Garnet never doubted his devotion for one moment. "Anyway, my hair grows fast."

Daisy stared at her a moment longer, then giggled. "You may have to wear your blonde wig longer than you thought."

Filled with resolve, Garnet turned toward the wig shop and marched to the door.

Chapter 40

"What do you think? Do I look like a Coney Island chorus girl?" Garnet pirouetted in the middle of the room. Daisy's application of a heating iron had created a mass of tousled coppery curls all over her head in place of the abundant tresses that had formed her stylish pompadour.

Daisy crossed her arms and surveyed her friend with a critical eye. "You do resemble a dancer rather than a New York heiress." An impish grin turned up the corners of her mouth. "It's a good thing the pawn shop owner can't see you now, or he'd be convinced you earn your living on the stage and you're no better than you should be."

Garnet performed a bow and spread her arms in a theatrical gesture. "I'm a chorus girl and the spurned plaything of a rich man." Dropping her humorous pose, she propped one hand on her hip, elbow cocked. "I've never been more mortified in my life than when he practically accused me of being some man's mistress."

"He wasn't a gentleman, so we can't expect him to act like one." Daisy dropped into a stuffed chair and spread out her hands toward the stove. "I never want to be cold again."

"Or hungry." Garnet speared her fingers through her short hair and approached the stove. "My head feels light without my hair, but at least I received enough money to feed us and keep us in this room for a few days." She soaked up the warmth that radiated from the coal stove.

"I'm glad we decided not to go all the way to Denver. I don't think I could have borne another twenty-hour train trip." Daisy's eyelids drooped. "I'm so tired."

Garnet pivoted to warm her back. "With Pinkerton agents looking for two young women traveling alone, going back to the station to buy tickets was too chancy. And with my photo on the front page of the papers, I might as well have walked up to one of those Pinkertons and asked him to take me back to New York." Her gaze drifted about the room. An iron bedstead occupied one corner, and the chair where Daisy sat another. A pitcher and wash basin rested atop the dresser beside the door. "It was kind of Madame Sophia to recommend this boarding house."

"I'll just stay right here by the stove until Mr. Cole gets here." Daisy curled up in her chair and closed her eyes.

With a glance outside the room's windows, Garnet watched as snow hissed against the panes. She shivered. "I'm glad we're not on the street now. We would have had to give ourselves up or freeze to death. Praise God He provided us with a solution." She sighed and leveled a morose look at Daisy. "I'd hoped Cole might have been able to redeem my brooch from the pawn shop, but now we'll probably never get it back."

Daisy cracked open her eyes. "Mr. Cole can buy you another one."

"It won't be the same." Garnet crossed the room and lifted her wig off the dresser, then adjusted the hairpiece over her own curls. "I'm going downstairs to put a call through to the Slash L, and I don't want to offend Mrs. Brown's sense of respectability."

"She gave us quite the lecture." Daisy grinned at the memory. "As if two girls traveling alone would give her boarding house a bad name."

"I especially liked the part where she warned us about entertaining men in our room."

"If she should see you without your wig, she'd be convinced you're the soul of depravity." Still smiling, Daisy leaned her head against the chair's back.

Garnet crossed the small room and paused at the door. "Do you want to come with me?"

Daisy perked up. "Rafe might be there. I'll come." She untangled her legs and rose.

Downstairs in the lobby, Garnet crossed to the corner where a wooden telephone hung from the wall and turned her back to the curious clerk who lounged in his chair behind the reception desk. Daisy hovered beside her.

Garnet lifted the receiver and turned the crank, then spoke into the mouthpiece. "I'd like to place a call to the Slash L Ranch outside of Denver please." When the arrangements had been made with the operator, Garnet replaced the receiver and smiled at Daisy. "Now we wait."

When the telephone rang moments later, Garnet snatched at the receiver and breathed an expectant "Hello" into the mouthpiece, her back still toward the clerk.

"Wait one moment while I connect you with your party, please." The operator's disembodied voice sounded tinny.

Several clicks followed, and then a male voice barked into her ear. "Garnet? Is that you?"

Rafe, not Cole. Garnet swung her gaze to Daisy, who hovered at her elbow. She mouthed his name, and Daisy's eyes brightened. "Yes, it's me."

"Are you all right? What's going on?"

"We're fine. We ran away from home, and now we're in Chicago."

"Is Daisy with you?"

"Yes."

"When we're finished, put her on. I want to talk to her."

"All right. Where's Cole?"

"He left the Slash L when we read in the papers that you'd been kidnapped. He's on his way to New York. Ever since your father called with the news that he was taking you back to New York, we've been monitoring the situation. Especially when our calls wouldn't go through."

"All communication to us was blocked."

"That's what we figured. When we read in the papers that you'd disappeared and presumed to have been kidnapped, Cole headed for New York."

Garnet sagged against the wall. "New York. How will I reach him?"

"The papers are a couple days old when we get them, so Cole just left this morning. He's probably still in Denver. I know how to contact him."

Relief made Garnet weak.

"Tell me what's going on with you and Daisy." Rafe's voice, strong yet soothing, filled Garnet with assurance.

In a few brief sentences, she sketched their situation.

Rafe remained silent a few moments when she'd finished, then replied in a resolute tone. "You and Daisy stay where you are. Don't go out. I'll contact Cole, and he'll wait for me in Denver. We'll both come for you and Daisy as soon as we can get there. Now, what's the address of the boarding house where you're staying?"

Garnet relayed the information to him in a low voice. "And be careful, Rafe. My father will have Pinkerton agents watching the Denver rail station. If they should see you and Cole, it will alert them that you know where we are. And there are Pinkertons here at the Chicago station, as well."

Rafe's tone turned grim. "The sons of a Cheyenne Dog Soldier can outwit Pinkerton agents any day. Don't you worry. Now, please put Daisy on. I want to talk to her."

* * *

Garnet swung the bedroom door wide when the knock sounded.

Mrs. Brown stood in the hall outside their room, looking as though she'd just sucked on a lemon. Disapproval tightened her mouth, plowing vertical furrows atop her upper lip, and her eyes burned. Her bosom quivered. "Two gentlemen in my parlor are insisting that they see you."

Garnet's heart leaped. Cole and Rafe had arrived. "Thank you, Mrs. Brown. We'll be right down."

Mrs. Brown held her ground as though planted in the hallway. "I knew I shouldn't rent a room to two women traveling alone. I warned you about gentlemen callers. I run a respectable establishment here, and I won't have its reputation sullied by scandal."

Garnet drew herself up and swept Mrs. Brown's form with a stare. The older woman's graying hair had been scraped back into a bun, and her unadorned brown dress buttoned to her throat. Before she replied in a tone intended to soothe, an imp of mischief made Garnet wonder if a Mr. Brown really existed. "I promise we won't bring scandal down upon your boarding house. No doubt we'll be checking out after we've met the gentlemen."

Mrs. Brown's mouth crimped as though the very fact of Garnet and Daisy leaving with two men was scandal enough. She spun and marched down the stairs, with the girls trailing behind her.

Two tall, dark-haired men wearing long wool overcoats waited in the parlor. When the girls entered, Cole opened his arms, and Garnet ran into his embrace. He enclosed her in his arms, and she burrowed against him, her nose buried in his coat. Cole pressed a cheek to the top of her head, and one hand splayed between her shoulders. She breathed in his scent, and for the first time in days, she felt safe. She closed her eyes and luxuriated in the sensation.

At last, she leaned against his encircling arms and tipped up her face to his. "You don't know how glad I am to see you. There were times I thought I'd never see you again."

"Now that we're together, I can admit there were moments when I thought I couldn't prevent your marriage to Albert."

She shuddered. "Take me away from here, and let's marry before anyone can stop us."

He stroked her cheek. "I'll take you to the Slash L, but we'll do things properly. We'll telephone your father and give him the opportunity to come out and give you away at our wedding. We have to try to mend the breach with him."

Garnet didn't argue. Once she arrived at the Slash L, she'd be safe.

She sneaked a peek at Rafe and Daisy. Rafe cradled her friend in his arms, his head bent to hers, and Daisy clutched him with both hands. Cole must have been right when he guessed his brother was sweet on Daisy. Rafe appeared to be a smitten man.

Cole claimed her attention when he fingered her hair. "Since when have you been a blonde?"

"We had to travel in disguise." Thinking of her shorn hair, Garnet hesitated. "I hope you don't mind me being blonde. I may have to wear this wig for a while."

Cole narrowed his eyes and quirked a brow. "Why is that?"

She took a deep breath as she confessed her plight.

Astonishment crossed his face before he tightened his arms and kissed her nose. "Once we leave Denver, you can ditch the wig. I don't care if you had to cut your hair, and neither will anyone at the Slash L."

"Even if I look like a chorus girl?"

"Even if you look like a chorus girl. We know you're a respectable lady, no matter what you look like." He put his mouth to her ear. "Once I get you to myself, I'll kiss you good and proper. Right now, we have too many witnesses."

Garnet glanced over her shoulder. In the lobby, Mrs.

Brown and the clerk stood behind the reception desk and watched them with scandalized expressions. She grinned and buried her face in his coat again.

Rafe put Daisy from him, though he twined his fingers through hers, and tipped his face down to her. He touched her brown locks with his other hand. "I wouldn't have recognized you if I hadn't known who you were."

"That was the idea. I'm sure that's the only reason the Pinkertons at the depot didn't make more of an effort to nab us. They weren't positive who we were." Daisy smiled up at him, her face radiant.

"Let's get you girls out of here. We already have your tickets to Denver, and there's a private coach waiting for us." Rafe swept Daisy with a protective glance.

Garnet's mouth dropped open. "You reserved a whole coach just for us?"

Rafe's features were resolute. "We have a first-class Pullman car just for us, so no one else can see you. And we won't have to go through the station, so we'll bypass any agents there."

Cole released Garnet. "If you girls have any luggage, run upstairs and get it. Rafe and I must smooth the feathers of your disapproving landlady. I'm sure some extra money will compensate for her offended sensibilities."

Slash L Ranch, Colorado
January–February 1912

Chapter 41

With their hands linked, Cole guided Garnet to the camelback sofa in the parlor of the Slash L ranch house. Garnet allowed him to seat her and looked up at him with curiosity when he remained standing.

The afternoon sun reflected off the snow outside, filling the room with radiance and glancing off Cole's face with merciless clarity. He stared down at her, his expression tight, and he swallowed.

She ruffled the short tresses that twisted all over her head. After they'd arrived at the ranch, she'd abandoned the wig. No one on the Slash L had frowned at her for cutting her hair.

Cole noticed her gesture, and he shook his head at her. "You're enchanting with your hair like that. Short, curly hair makes you look like a pixie. Or a wood sprite."

Garnet dropped her hand to her lap. "You really don't mind?"

"Since selling your hair kept you from having to return to New York, how could I mind?"

"It will grow back. My hair grows fast."

They lapsed into silence, and Cole rolled his shoulders.

Garnet frowned. She'd never seen him show such unease. "Cole, what's wrong?" At that moment, she noticed the hush that enveloped the house. "Why is the house so quiet? And where are Rafe and Daisy?"

"Rafe took Daisy to the barn to introduce her to the horses. Since it appears that Daisy will be living here in the West, she must learn to ride a horse."

"Of course. And where is everyone else? The house is too quiet, especially with Flossie's children about."

Cole shrugged. "I don't know where they are, and as long as they leave us alone for half an hour, I don't care. Getting you to myself for a few minutes practically took an act of congress." He shifted his weight to his other leg and continued to loom over her.

His obvious discomfort spread to her, and Garnet fidgeted. She grasped a conversational topic like a lifeline. "I'm so relieved your Uncle Clint is recovering. I can't imagine the family without him."

"He's tough, and it looks like we'll be blessed to have him around for a while longer. Praise God for that." Cole's breath gusted out in a sigh, and he thrust his fingers through his dark, curly hair. "I thought this would be easier. It's not as if it's a surprise." He rocked back on his heels and hung his thumbs off his back pockets.

Garnet smoothed her hands across her dark skirt, one of the outfits she'd brought with her. She still had only the clothes she'd carried with her when she made her escape. Perhaps her father would ship her belongings to her if he wouldn't come himself. She took another look at Cole.

Uneasiness shafted through her when her gaze met his. "What are you trying to tell me? Has something happened?"

The Franklin stove radiated its warmth, and a wave of nervous heat enveloped her.

"Nothing's happened." Cole hovered a moment longer, then knelt before her. He withdrew a small package from his jeans pocket.

Garnet couldn't speak or breathe. Her whole attention rested on the face of the man she loved. Though the ticking of the mantel clock over the Franklin stove told her otherwise, time seemed suspended.

He placed the object in her hands and curled her fingers about it. They stared at each other. "Garnet, this is for you."

Her heart hammered in her chest, thudding with heavy beats against her ribs. She looked down at the object. A square, black leather box with white stitching about the edges rested on her palm. An embossed silver crest stamped the top. She flicked Cole a glance. "When did you get this?"

"I bought it in Denver while I waited for Rafe to join me. I figured since it seemed a sure thing we'd marry, I'd better buy you a ring."

Garnet pried open the lid with her thumb. Inside, on a bed of black satin, glittered an engagement ring in a filigree platinum setting. Smaller gems encircled a round, multi-faceted diamond. Tiny garnets mingled with the smaller diamonds and gave the icy jewels a warmer glow. Garnet caught her breath. "It's gorgeous, Cole, but it must have cost the earth."

His eyes crinkled in a smile. "When I met you, I found a rare jewel. You're a treasure and worth more to me than all the diamonds in the world. This ring is a token of the love I bear for you."

Cole's romantic words filled her heart to overflowing. She flung her arms about his neck. "Thank you for loving me. I love you, too, so much it terrifies me."

"To be honest, the idea of being a husband terrifies me."

Garnet leaned back and peered into his face, her hands on his shoulders. "I have no concerns about you being a good husband."

Cole kissed her, then plucked the ring from its box. "Here, look inside the band." He dropped the ring onto her palm.

Garnet gave him a curious look and examined the band's smooth interior. In exquisite cursive script the words "Cole and Garnet. Two hearts, one love forever" had been etched into the platinum. She read the lines aloud. "Cole, it's perfect. You're such a romantic!"

He shrugged. "It's what I felt. I couldn't say it any other way."

His sentimentality undid her. She buried her face in the curve of his shoulder. A hot tear leaked from between her lids and dripped onto his neck.

He patted her back and then put her away from him. "I didn't mean to make you cry." He swiped her tear from his neck.

"These are happy tears." Garnet sniffled and scrubbed her tears with the heels of her hands. "I'll remember your promise every time I look at my ring."

Cole took the jewelry from her and slipped the token onto the third finger of her left hand. "My diamond looks as though it belongs there."

Garnet held out her hand and examined the sparkling band. The stones' facets caught the sunlight and threw back fire. "It belongs on my hand. Just as I belong to you, and you belong to me. We belong to each other."

Cole rose and seated himself on the sofa beside her with one arm curled about her shoulders. "Do you still want to get married here at the ranch?"

She turned a determined face to him. "Yes. I'd like that very much. I don't want to be married in New York."

"Of course, it's our choice where we marry, but having our wedding here will make my mother very happy."

"I never want to go back to New York, even to get married."

Cole tipped his head toward her. "I called your father to let him know you were safe. He sounded relieved. Now you need to call him and ask him to come here for the wedding."

At his words, dread dropped like a stone in her stomach. "Now?"

"You need to make your peace with him and forgive him. I know he hasn't been the best father to you, but in his own way, he loves you." Cole swiped his thumb across her diamond. "He would have done better with a son."

Garnet turned a solemn face to him. "I think you're right. He didn't know what to do with a girl."

Leaning down, Cole palmed her cheek and threaded his fingers into her curls. His mouth found hers, and in turn, she offered him her heart's devotion. When he lifted his head, he peered into her face. His lips were a breath from hers. "If you remember, I once told you I felt sure the Lord would make a way for us to marry. Perhaps the Lord ordained our marriage to bring you and your father together."

She hadn't thought of her marriage to Cole in that light. She'd been consumed with her father's many injustices to her, his coldness, and his attempt to force her to marry Albert. Ever since her mother's death, she'd resisted his control. Perhaps her marriage to Cole would provide the vehicle for them both to forgive and to heal.

Garnet swallowed. "All right. I'll call him."

Cole ran his thumb across her lower lip. "Good girl. I'd prefer us to begin our married life together with no baggage from the past to mar our relationship with our families."

Bundled in her sheepskin jacket, she accompanied Cole to the ranch office, a small adobe building between the house and the barn. Inside, they crossed to a large oak desk on the far side of the room. A candlestick telephone rested on the desk's scarred surface. Cole seated her in the chair behind the desk and settled himself on a corner of the table, a long leg stretched out for balance.

"So, will he be at home, or at his office at the bank?"

Garnet considered what her father might be doing under the circumstances of her escape. "I think he'll be back at the office, now that he knows I'm safe."

"Very well, we'll start there." Cole snatched up the telephone and lifted the receiver to his ear.

Garnet listened while he spoke with the operator and waited for the connection to go through. She chewed her lip and clenched her hands. Her stomach roiled. What would she say? Her father would be furious. She imagined the blistering set down he'd give her.

The connection went through, and Cole handed her the phone. Garnet took the instrument with hands that trembled and put the receiver to her ear.

"Hello? Cole? Is that you?" Her father's rough voice sounded across the wire.

Garnet's tongue stuck to the roof of her mouth. She froze.

"Hello? Who is this?" Impatience tinged her father's voice.

Garnet swallowed. "It's not Cole. Papa, it's me. Garnet." The childish endearment slipped out before she realized she'd said it.

Silence from the other end.

"Papa?"

"Well, girl, you scared your father half to death." Her father's gruff voice held none of the anger she'd expected. "Especially with that business about the kidnapping."

"I'm sorry." She hesitated, unsure of what to say. "But I just couldn't marry Albert!"

A beat of silence on the other end of the line made her hold her breath, and then her father spoke.

"You made your point, although your defection is all the gossip here in New York."

Garnet didn't care about the gossip, so she made no comment on that. She took a breath and plunged on. "Will you come to the wedding? Cole and I would like very much for you to attend."

Another silence, and then her father sighed. "Are you sure this marriage is what you want?"

"Yes. Cole and I have no doubts about our marriage."

Again, silence hummed along the wire before Asa replied. "Would you mind very much if I walked you down the aisle?"

Garnet goggled at Cole as her mind scrambled to process what her father had just said.

"Garnet, did you hear me?"

She gulped and forced words past her tight throat. "Yes, yes. I'd love for you to walk me down the aisle."

"And you want to get married at that simple chapel on the ranch instead of having a grand ceremony in New York?" His voice roughened.

"Yes." Garnet couldn't imagine what it cost her father to make that concession.

"Very well. I'll leave on the next train to Denver. I'll arrange for my own transportation to the ranch." With that, he disconnected the call, and Garnet heard nothing but empty air.

Dazed, she hung up the receiver and returned the telephone to the desk.

"Well?" Cole prompted.

She turned toward him. "My father will come to the wedding, and he wants to walk me down the aisle. He didn't even try to talk me out of getting married here. I don't understand it." Her voice reflected the incredulity she felt.

Cole leaned toward her. "I think you jolted him enough to get his attention when you ran away that he's started to rethink things. You actually frightened him into realizing how much he loves you." He curled his hand about the back of her head. "The Lord is working."

Garnet's whole perception of her relationship with her father crumbled. Their conversation had initiated a tentative reconciliation, a new beginning, and another dimension to their dealings with each other. The stormy moorings that had defined their previous relationship had been cut loose, and she floated in a sea of uncertainty. She burst into tears, and Cole gathered her in his arms. He tucked her face into the crook where his neck met his shoulder.

"Things between you and your father will right themselves. It's his nature to be gruff, but underneath that thorny exterior, he loves you. Now maybe he won't be afraid to show it." Cole stroked her back. "And after we've given him a grandchild or two, he'll be a big soft teddy bear." Humor laced his voice.

Garnet tightened her arms about him and gave a watery chuckle.

Della cornered Garnet that evening after supper. "Would you care to take tea with me?"

"Certainly," Garnet said, though her heart did a flip flop.

Della led her toward the front of the house. "I've already set up the tea things in my sitting room. We can talk there without being disturbed."

Garnet followed Cole's mother to a room on the opposite side of the hall from the parlor. When they'd entered the sitting room and Della had shut the door, she motioned Garnet toward an embroidered rocking chair beside the stove. She took a chair on the opposite side. A small table on which rested a tea tray stood between them.

"Do you take cream? Sugar?" Della poured tea from a flowered china teapot into matching cups.

"Just cream, no sugar." Garnet took the cup Cole's mother offered her and leaned back in her chair. Even though Della Wild Wind had welcomed her into the family, uneasiness slithered down her spine. What had induced this *tete-a-tete*?

Della sipped with a dainty air and set down her cup. She motioned about the room. "This used to be Uncle Clint's office when the ranch first started. Once the ranch got so big it required more men to run it, he built the current office out in the yard to take foot traffic away from the house. Aunt Coral took over this room, and in recent years, it's become mine. I conduct my affairs from here."

Garnet's gaze followed Della's gesture. The room, with feminine furniture, lace curtains and knickknacks on shelves, displayed a definite woman's touch.

Della settled back in her chair. "Cole tells me your father has agreed to come out here for your wedding."

Thinking back to her conversation with her father, Garnet shrugged. "Yes. He even wants to walk me down the aisle, but it's not like him."

Della tossed her a smile. "My husband and I have been praying for your situation ever since Cole told us he loved you." She hesitated as though choosing her words with care. "Wild Wind and I faced impossible barriers to our marriage, but the Lord overcame all that, and here we are. Now the Lord is doing a work in your father's heart."

"I'm astounded, really."

Della smiled again. "So, you want to get married in our chapel?"

"Cole tells me that getting married in the chapel is a Slash L tradition. I'd love to continue that tradition."

Della stared over Garnet's shoulder as if her thoughts had taken her far away. "I got married in the chapel. Twice, actually. My first husband, Shane, and I married there, and later, Wild Wind and I had our wedding in the chapel."

Garnet scrutinized the older woman. Tamed in a French braid, her curly chocolate-colored hair with its threads of gray swung over one shoulder. Her face reflected strength of character, earned through the crucible of life's difficult trials. Exquisite bone structure would carry her beauty through old age, and her graceful carriage reflected her refined upbringing. She reminded Garnet of a delicate orchid transplanted to the harsh Western culture.

Della brought her attention back to Garnet's face. "I assume Cole has told you my story?"

Garnet met Della's gaze. "Yes. I told him your story sounded like a novel."

Cole's mother tipped her head to one side and regarded her future daughter-in-law. "I've had my share of heartache, but the Lord brought me through all that. And Wild Wind and I have had a happy marriage, despite the cultural differences." She took another sip of tea and set down the cup. "Now, we have a wedding to plan. Let's get busy."

Chapter 42

Excited chatter filled the parlor. Garnet's bridesmaids—Daisy, Flossie, and Cole's sister Lily—waited in the middle of the room for their ride to the schoolhouse, which doubled today as the chapel. Their long-sleeved, Empire-waisted gowns of amethyst velvet and lace draped their figures with elegance.

Flossie rustled to Garnet's side and pecked her on the cheek. "I'm so happy you'll be part of our family. I knew Cole loved you by the way he looked at you when he brought you here last Christmas."

"We were trying to hide how we felt." Garnet smiled at the memory. "Were we that obvious?"

Flossie chuckled. "I know my cousin well. He couldn't hide it from me." She gave Garnet a hug and turned away.

Garnet crossed the room to where Daisy stood before the Franklin stove, a petite figure in her bridesmaid's finery. She held a bouquet of ribbons and lace at her waist. Garnet halted and eyed her friend. "You look beautiful in that gown. The color becomes you, and you're glowing." She gave Daisy a closer inspection.

Beneath a wide-brimmed amethyst hat with silk roses massed on its brim, Daisy flushed. She gripped Garnet's wrist and went up on tiptoe to murmur in her ear. "Last night Rafe asked me to marry him, but it's a secret. We want to wait until after your wedding to announce it to the family."

Garnet leaned down to hug her friend, taking care not to crush their gowns. "That's splendid, Daisy, but I can't say I'm surprised. You and Rafe make a wonderful couple."

Daisy looked a little awestruck. "I'm still pinching myself to be sure I'm not dreaming."

"And to think it all started so you and Rafe could provide a foursome when Cole and I first started going out together."

"He was just being kind back then."

Garnet squeezed Daisy's arm. "Perhaps, but he couldn't resist you."

"And his parents have never discouraged Rafe from courting me. They don't care that I'm not rich." Satisfaction mingled with amazement filled Daisy's voice.

"Why should they object? Rafe's mother married a Cheyenne Dog Soldier."

"She did." A moment later, regret filled Daisy's eyes. "You don't mind that I'm not going to Paris with you and Cole?"

Garnet smiled down at her friend. "We'll manage on our own. If I need help, the hotel maids will fill in."

"Rafe doesn't want me to be gone for so long, and I

don't want to be parted from him. We'll all be together at the mining camp this summer, though."

"Cole and I will be back from our honeymoon by the beginning of May. Cole said the trail to the mine should be open by then."

"I'm going to be the camp doctor's assistant. Rafe made the arrangements. He doesn't mind if I want to be a nurse after we're married."

One of the ranch's cowboys stuck his head into the parlor door and interrupted their conversation. "Ladies, it's your turn to ride to the chapel. The motorcar is waiting."

Garnet and Daisy gripped hands and exchanged one more look. "You're a beautiful bride, Miss Garnet."

"Thank you. Now go, and I'll see you at the chapel."

When the bridesmaids had departed, Garnet did a slow pivot toward her father, who stood alone by the Franklin stove. She paced toward him and halted, still a little uncertain of how to behave in their new relationship. "Thank you for coming out here for our wedding, and especially for walking me down the aisle."

He swept her with a paternal glance and cleared his throat. "When you ran off, I began to see that if you were so desperate to escape him, perhaps Albert wasn't the best choice for you. I want to support your choice. I'm beginning to appreciate what you see in Cole Wild Wind."

"Thank you, Papa." The word still felt strange on her tongue but grew more familiar each time she used it.

He motioned toward her bridal gown. "In that dress, you look so much like your mother on our wedding day." He hesitated and then plunged on. "Thank you for being willing to wear her dress. It was the one thing of hers I couldn't get rid of."

Garnet fingered the skirt of the Victorian-style wedding dress her mother had worn on her own wedding day in 1890. In the morning light, the ivory gold satin gown with its circular train glowed with a muted patina. Pearl beading set off the ruched lace overlay on the bodice, and the wasp-style waist fell at Garnet's natural waistline. The long sleeves gathered into a puff at her shoulders. "I feel close to her in this dress. I wish I'd known her better."

Several beats of silence fell while Asa Morrison stared at his daughter. The ticking of the clock on the mantel behind the stove sounded loud in the lull. For the first time, he didn't bristle at the mention of his dead wife.

When he replied, his voice was husky. "I loved your mother very much, and her death nearly killed me. Pretending she never existed was the only way I could cope with her loss." He cleared his throat again. "And with you looking more and more like her as you grew older…"

They stared at each other, and Garnet leaned forward to peck her father's cheek. "I understand now."

Her father motioned toward her short curls beneath her lace veil. "Your new hair style may set a trend."

They shared a chuckle as the cowboy poked his head into the parlor door again. "Are you ready to leave? Everyone is waiting at the chapel."

Asa crooked an elbow for his daughter to clasp. "This is your big day. Let's go."

Clutching a bouquet of white rosebuds and satin ribbon, Garnet stepped into the chapel on her father's arm. Like a magician, her father had managed to have hothouse roses shipped in for her bridal bouquet. The scent of the roses drifted to her nose and reminded her that her wedding wasn't a dream.

The chapel had been festooned with swaths of lace and wide satin ribbon, with ribbon love knots at the ends of each row. Candles, lace, and ribbon comprised the decorations, since no flowers grew in February. At the front of the chapel, her bridal party flanked the preacher from the church Cole and Rafe attended in Denver. Her three bridesmaids stood on the left, with their amethyst gowns providing a splash of color. On the right, Rafe, Cole's half-brother Jake, and Wild Wind stood up with the groom.

As she stepped into the chapel, everyone rose and watched her float down the aisle, though Garnet had eyes only for Cole, tall and splendid in his dark suit. Each step brought her closer to him. His grave expression assured her of his serious dedication to the vows they were about to exchange. When she halted beside him, a smile chased the austere demeanor from his face, and he took her hand in his.

The preacher began the ceremony. "Dearly beloved, we're gathered here today..."

Garnet laid her purse on a nearby lamp table and stared at Cole. He loomed in the center of the parlor, a tall male figure dressed in a fine dark sack suit. His gaze riveted on her.

They'd left the Slash L right after their wedding luncheon and had arrived at the Browne Palace Hotel by late afternoon. After they'd settled into their suite, they'd enjoyed a leisurely dinner in the hotel dining room.

Now, Garnet returned Cole's look, uncertain of what to do next. She had no reason to fear him, yet apprehension filled her. More than ever before, she felt the lack of a mother. Her mother could have told her what to expect on her wedding night. Her first night with her husband seemed a terrifying mystery.

Cole drew near and reached out one hand. "Come, Garnet. It's time to begin our married life together."

She let him take her icy hand. He drew her into a loose embrace, exhibiting the gentleness he would have shown a skittish horse. With the fingers of one hand curled about her neck, he kissed her with aching tenderness, not demanding, but slow and easy, as though they had all the time in the world.

He stroked his thumb along her jaw and caressed her face with a loving gaze. "My beautiful wife." Curving one arm beneath her knees, he scooped her up and swung her toward their bedroom door. "Until we get to the mining camp and our own cabin, this will have to do." His eyes crinkled in a smile. A curling lock of dark hair hung over his brow. "All brides should be carried over the threshold of their wedding chamber."

Though the strength of his grip made her feel secure, Garnet clung to his neck as he strode with her across the room. At their bed chamber, he toed open the door with his Italian leather shoe and sidled through the aperture. Inside, he let her slide down his length. When her feet touched the carpet, he leaned over to switch on the lamp that rested on a bedside table.

Golden light bloomed and chased away the shadows. A carved armoire to her left, a mirrored vanity between two windows across the room and a four-poster bed at hand materialized with the light. Cole reached behind him to shut the door. The quiet click of the portal closing made Garnet aware that she was about to spend her first night with her husband. Her *new* husband.

Cole enfolded her again. The lamplight played over his face. Reassured by the love that shone in his dark eyes, Garnet linked her arms about his neck and waited for him to say something. The topic he brought up wasn't what she expected and distracted her from her apprehensions about their wedding night.

"Tomorrow morning, we'll take the train to New York. After we arrive there, we'll board an ocean liner for Paris."

"I've never been to Paris. I can't wait."

"I know it's not springtime, but Paris is enchanting whatever the season. And we should be there long enough to see the flowers bloom." Cole reached into his suit coat's front pocket. "I have something for you." He disentangled her arms from his neck and brought them down to her sides. With a flourish, he dropped a small package into her palms.

She stared down at the brooch that burned with glittering fire. For a moment, she couldn't speak, and then she raised her gaze to Cole's face. "My brooch!"

His mouth twitched in a smile.

"How did you find it?"

"I hired a detective with connections to Chicago's underworld to search for it. I figured the man who stole it would try to sell it. And he did. News of something like that travels fast in those circles."

Garnet flung herself at her husband and clutched him close. "Thank you, thank you. I never thought I'd see it again." She hugged him once more and went down on her heels.

He pulled her arms free and pried the brooch from her fist, then laid the jewel on the lamp table.

He stepped back, and Garnet sliced a glance at him.

"Stand still." With a smile and a peck on the lips, he freed the hat pin that secured her stylish headgear and lifted the flowered creation from her head. He tossed the hat onto the lamp table beside them and slanted her a glance. "This reminds me of the time you stowed away on the train to Indian Pass, and I brushed cinders off your borrowed hat."

The humorous memory put her further at ease, and her shoulders relaxed.

Garnet stood motionless while Cole thrust his hands into her coppery tresses and sifted her short curls, his expression intent. She kept her gaze on his face, and her pulse skittered.

"So soft," he murmured in a voice filled with reverence as his fingers clenched on her hair. Angling his head, he kissed her again. "My beautiful darling. My wife."

Garnet returned his kiss and forgot her fears.

Epilogue

Paris, May 1912

"You've been busy."

At the sound of her husband's voice, Garnet turned from the window that overlooked the sunny Paris street. Her *haute couture* frock of daffodil-yellow silk swirled about her calves. Cole paused by the sitting room door and smiled at her across the room. At the sight of his smile, intimate and tender, Garnet melted.

"I think I've finally got everything packed, except for the clothes we'll wear tomorrow." She glanced at the new luggage strewn about the sitting room floor. Cole had insisted she couldn't visit Paris and not purchase a new wardrobe.

"We won't always live at the camp. When we're in civilization, you'll need clothes, so don't worry about the money I'm spending on you," he'd said when she protested, and he'd kissed her. Now, she had several trunks full of Parisienne clothing.

Cole picked his way between trunks and suitcases to

Garnet's side. When he reached her, he took her hands in both of his. Bringing them to his lips, he kissed the back of each knuckle. His gaze held hers while his eyes warmed with a husband's desire. "Have I told you yet today that I love you, Mrs. Wild Wind?"

"I do believe you mentioned the fact at breakfast." Garnet squeezed his hands and smiled up at him.

"Not since breakfast? How remiss of me. Let me remedy my negligence." Dropping her hands, he gathered her against him and clasped his fists at the small of her back. "I love you, wife. With all my heart."

Garnet laid one palm over his heart and with her other hand brushed back the wayward curl that had flopped over his brow. "'Two hearts, one love forever.'" She quoted from memory the inscription on the inside of her engagement ring.

"One love forever." He lowered his head and kissed her with a thoroughness that left her breathless. He broke off the kiss and perused her face with a questioning gaze. "Are you happy, Garnet? Have you any regrets about our marriage?"

Uncertainty pierced her. Did he have second thoughts? Hadn't she pleased him? She returned his question with one of her own. "Do you regret marrying me? Have I disappointed you?"

"Of course not! You haven't disappointed me. I only hope I haven't disappointed you. I don't know much about women, you know. You're the first girl I ever spent much time with, aside from my sister and cousins."

Relief flooded her. Garnet's lips curled up, and with one

forefinger, she traced a line along the side of his jaw. "Well, you needn't concern yourself on that score. I think you're a model husband. You've made me very happy." She stood on tiptoe and kissed him. "I love your strength and your gentleness, your sense of duty and your thoughtfulness toward others. But most of all, I respect your love for our Lord and that you've shown me how to love Him better, as well."

Cole pulled her closer and buried his face in the side of her neck. His low voice sounded in her ear. "Thank you, wife. I'm just a man learning how to be a good husband, but you make it easy."

Garnet stroked his hair, soft and springy beneath her fingers.

Cole straightened. He traced a finger down her nose and stroked his thumb across her lower lip. "What would you like to do on our last afternoon in Paris?"

Garnet's thoughts went not to the Paris sights but to the secret she hugged close to her heart. Would this be a good time to share her news with Cole? She was still so awed by the wonder of her new knowledge that she could scarcely speak of it, yet the need to share her news with her husband burned within her.

"I don't know. Perhaps we could sit at an outdoor café and drink café au lait. But first, I have something to tell you."

Concern flashed across his face. "What is it? Is something wrong?"

"No. No, nothing is wrong." Garnet took one of his large hands and placed it across her stomach. His long fingers splayed dark against the silk fabric of her daffodil yellow day dress. "There. Right there below your hand is our child. You're going to be a father."

For a moment, Cole showed no reaction. Had he heard her?

A stupefied expression crossed his face. "What did you say?"

"Our baby is beneath your hand. We're going to have a baby."

Cole glanced down at his hand and then looked up at her. Wonder and joy, mingled with pride, filled his dark eyes. "A baby?"

Garnet nodded. "Yes, a baby."

"I'm going to be a father!"

"Yes." Garnet couldn't hide her smile.

He gave his attention once more to her stomach. His hand clenched with loving gentleness over the spot that cocooned their child. Tendons stood out beneath his tanned skin. Then, with lithe grace, he knelt before her. Wrapping both arms about her waist, he rained tender kisses over her womb.

As she looked down at her husband kneeling before her, Garnet ran her fingers through his curling hair. Love for this man, and the child growing inside her, filled her. At this moment, life couldn't be more perfect.

Cole pressed his cheek against her stomach and tipped his head up to her. "Garnet, thank you. Aside from your love, this baby is the best gift you could give me."

Acknowledgments

Many thanks to the legion of supporters who encouraged me every step of the way to Wild Heart's publication. My sons and their wives offer their support to my newsletter and other techy items.

My beta readers were invaluable to me in the early stages of this manuscript. Cindy Jantz, my lifelong friend, is a trusted sounding board and help each step of the way. Andrea Eliasson, my friend from church, is another reader who gives me honest feedback. Other friends too numerous to count offer their suggestions. Without these honest eyes on my writing efforts, Wild Heart wouldn't be here today.

I want to thank those friends who prayed me through each step of the editing process. I felt your prayers as I labored long hours to hone this manuscript into a better book that hopefully, God will use for his glory. Special thanks to Andrea Eliasson, Sally Bradley, Wendy Johanes, Jim Russell, and my Shepherd Group at church.

And a special thank you to Eden and Kara, whose editing input made Wild Heart a better book.

About the Author

Colleen Hall wrote her first story in third grade and continued writing as a hobby all during her growing-up years. Writing her Frontier Hearts Saga has allowed her to combine her love of writing with her love of history and the West. In her spare time, she enjoys spending time with her husband ad family, working Monty, her Morgan/Paint gelding, reading, and browsing antique stores. She lives in South Carolina with her husband and family, one horse, and one very indulged cat.

You can follow Colleen at colleenhallromance.com.

Also by Colleen Hall

The Frontier Hearts Saga

Her Traitor's Heart

Wounded Heart

Warrior's Heart

Wild Heart

Valiant Hear (Coming December 2023)

Made in the USA
Columbia, SC
05 May 2024

34959305R00207